RED
GLASS

ALSO BY LAURA RESAU

What the Moon Saw

DELACORTE PRESS

This is a work of fiction. Names, characters, places, and incidents either are the product of the author's imagination or are used fictitiously. Any resemblance to actual persons, living or dead, events, or locales is entirely coincidental.

 Published in the United States by Delacorte Press, an imprint of Random House Children's Books, a division of Random House, Inc., New York.
Originally published in hardcover by Delacorte Press in 2007.

Library of Congress Cataloging-in-Publication Data
Resau, Laura. Red Glass / by Laura Resau p. cm.
Summary: Sixteen-year-old Sophie has been frail and delicate since her premature birth, but discovers her true strength during a journey through Mexico, where the six-year-old orphan her family hopes to adopt was born, and to Guatemala, where her would-be boyfriend hopes to find his mother and plans to remain.
ISBN 978-0-385-73466-0 (hardcover) — ISBN 978-0-385-90464-3 (lib. bdg.)
ISBN 978-0-375-89059-8 (e-book)
[1. Self-confidence—Fiction. 2. Automobile travel—Fiction. 3. Orphans—Fiction. 4. Family life—Fiction. 5. Illegal aliens—Fiction. 6. Mexico—Fiction. 7. Guatemala—Fiction.] I. Title.
PZ7.R2978Red 2007 [Fic]—dc22 2007002408

ISBN 978-0-440-24025-9 (trade paperback)
Printed in the United States of America
10 9 8 7 6
First Trade Paperback Edition

For my mother and father, who planted the seeds years ago and have offered plenty of sunshine and water ever since

Acknowledgments

This book exists thanks to friends who have shared their stories with me—Rahima, Don Otón, and Johnny. *Muchísimas gracias* to Doña Epifania, Doña Maria Chiquita, Doña Dicio, and other friends in Oaxaca who have made this novel—and my life—richer and brighter.

Deep gratitude to the advisors and friends who have helped me along the way—Baruc, Don Fermín, the López Salazar family, Alex, María Virginia, Sergio, and Javier; and to those who took the time to answer my many research questions—Katica Terzic and Charles Griffin. Thanks to my fabulous agent, Erin Murphy, and friends from Old Town Writing Group who made sure I finished this book—Leslie, Joan, Kim, Sarah, Laura, and Carrie—and to my friends in Slow Sand Writers' Society for plenty of warm encouragement. I've been thrilled to work again with my insightful editor, Stephanie Lane, as well as the other dedicated people at Delacorte Press, whose hard work I value immensely.

My mother, Chris, has been essential to the creation of this book, reading every word of every draft many times, and offering brilliant suggestions. My father, Jim, gives me endless support, and serves as my model for hard work, wisdom, and generosity. My brother, Mike—who appeared in my life when he was two—has shown me that tender, sisterly love can spring up fast. My husband, Ian, lets me hole up in my writing room for hours on end, and when I emerge, greets me with homemade soup and heaps of love.

Rumi said, *Hear blessings dropping their blossoms around you.*

I am swimming in blossoms!

PART 1

THE DESERT

I've always loved the desert. You sit down on a sand dune. You see nothing. You hear nothing. And yet something shines, something sings in that silence . . .

"What makes the desert beautiful," the little prince said, "is that it hides a well somewhere."

Antoine de Saint-Exupéry,
—THE LITTLE PRINCE

1

Sleeping with the Chickens

Even before the boy appeared, I thought about the people crossing the desert. I imagined how scrub brush scratched their legs as they walked at night, how the sun dried out their eyes during the day, how their hearts pounded when they threw their bodies to the ground, hiding from *la migra.* I imagined them pressing their cheeks against the dust, thinking about the happy lives they would have if only they reached the end of this desert.

After I got my license the May I turned sixteen, I started driving to the desert outside of Tucson, an hour's drive from the Mexican border. I'd park the Volkswagen, then walk alone in the oven heat. I let my thoughts wander around the cacti and agave, along dried riverbeds. Within five minutes, I'd get thirsty and gulp down water from the huge bottle I carried. As long as I had water, I could forget about everything, imagine I was the only person on the planet, a stranger dropped into the desert.

One night in June, at midnight, I was in bed reading *The Little Prince,* a book I'd already read once and underlined for world lit class. I was lost in the story, right there with the pilot alone in the sand dunes when the little boy appears out of nowhere.

Right then, the phone rang. I walked into the kitchen in my nightgown, my bare feet slapping the clay tile, my mind still in the sand dunes of another planet.

I picked up the phone. "Hello?"

"Officer Douglas here, Border Patrol. I need to speak with Juan Gutiérrez."

My stomach tightened. I knocked on Mom and Juan's door. "Juan. Border Patrol's on the phone."

During the phone call, Juan listened and nodded gravely. "Yes, yes, I see. Seven dead?" His voice cracked. "I have no idea how my business card got in this kid's pocket."

I sat at the kitchen table, tracing the deep, worn scratches in the wood, trying not to stare at the tears leaking out of Juan's eyes.

Mom disappeared into the bedroom, and a few minutes later, calmly reemerged, her keys jangling. She'd already changed into a gauzy dress and turquoise necklace. She carried herself in a European-model way, her neck long, never slouching, not even in the middle of the night under the weight of bad news. Only two delicate furrows on her forehead betrayed her worry. That, and her British accent grew a bit more pronounced, as it did whenever she got emotional.

Just as Juan was hanging up the phone, Great-aunt Dika thudded into the kitchen, her eyes wide and alarmed. "What is it?" she cried. "What is it?" For Dika, being woken in the middle of the night meant bombings and attacks. She came from Bosnia and she'd materialized in our lives six months earlier. *Dee-ka* is how she said her name. Trying to understand Dika was like deciphering a code: *v*s were really *w*s, *d*s were *th*s, rolling *rrr*s were *r*s. Her words pierced the air, loud and shrill, as if she were perpetually in the middle of a big, rowdy party. Be patient with her, Sophie, Mom kept telling me, the woman barely survived a war. But I suspected she was a naturally hyper person.

Juan rubbed his face. The muscles in his arms flexed, moving the snake tattoos. "Seven Mexicans died crossing the desert." He spoke in Spanish, as he always did when he felt deeply about something. "One boy survived. They found my business card in his pocket."

On the way to the hospital in the puttering Volkswagen bus, Mom clutched the wheel and came up with possible scenarios. Juan, meanwhile, sat hunched in the passenger seat, his head in his hands.

He'd come from Mexico in the eighties, illegally, across the desert. He got residency after he married my mom nine years ago. Since then, when people crossed the desert to Tucson, Juan sometimes put them up for a night. He gave them food and water and always refused payment. His motives were good, but what he did was against the law. Mom finally put her foot down about it. Only in absolute emergencies, she said, could these people stay at our place.

Mom sped down First Avenue, her eyes flicking nervously from the rearview to the side-view mirror. I knew she was wondering if we'd get in trouble, if the Border Patrol had discovered we'd been helping immigrants. "You know, Juan," she said in Spanish, "maybe you did business with someone who knew this family. Who knows, maybe the card was passed around a lot. The boy could've found it on the street."

Dika, meanwhile, muttered in the background. "This poor boy. Poor, poor boy." She spoke her own strange version of English. Her accent moved from Slavic to Spanish to German. She was an onion, layers of language peeling off here and there, exposing bits of her sixty years of life, not much, just enough to make you wonder.

The hospital was a surreal place at one in the morning, a maze of fluorescent corridors. A man in a wrinkled orange shirt and braces met us outside the boy's room. He shook hands with each of us, and said he was with CPS, Child Protective Services.

"The kid's a foundling," the man said. "That's what the law calls them. A young child, found alone." He mumbled, trying to hide his braces. "We're pretty sure his parents died crossing the desert. He looks at least five years old, but he won't talk. When the sheriff asked him about his parents, he pointed out their bodies. Problem is, we can't ID the bodies and we don't know the kid's name."

"He's probably in shock," Mom said. "His parents dead. Three days in a desert."

"Three days in desert!" Dika cried. "That boy is hungry now!" She barreled down the bright hallway toward the vending machines.

The CPS man swung open the door and we entered the room. There was a tiny life on the bed, lost in a hospital gown spotted with hippos and giraffes. His eyes were open but lifeless. A tube was taped to the back of his hand.

Foundling. What a strange word. It made me think of the fairy tales that Juan used to tell me—didn't they start with foundlings in the wilderness who turned out to be magical?

"*Hola, amigo,*" Juan whispered.

Mom touched the boy's thin wrist. "*¿Cómo estás, mi amor?*"

No answer.

"Sure you don't know this child?" the CPS man asked.

Juan shook his head.

The man sighed. "I was hoping you might." He explained what would happen to the boy. If no relatives claimed him, he would become an American citizen, under the care of CPS.

I looked at the boy. A dark-skinned Little Prince, a lonely apparition from the desert. Around his neck hung a tangle of strings attached to square bits of leather imprinted with saints. On his cheek, a pinkish spot of skin, the color of a conch shell's spiral. Maybe a wound healing, maybe a birthmark.

"Then what would happen to the little guy?" Juan asked.

"Foster care, adoption."

Dika appeared at the doorway with a pack of Fig Newtons. "We take him!" She ripped open the plastic with her yellowed teeth, shoved a cookie in her mouth, and passed the package around the room. The man took one politely.

"We take him, Sophie. Yes?" Dika looked at me. She was always trying to make me an accomplice in her plans.

I shrugged and glanced at Mom and Juan. They were ignoring her and talking in low voices. I thought about it, the possibility of taking him. A little brother might be cute. But this boy on the hospital bed wasn't exactly cute. To tell the truth, he scared me. He was living proof of one of my worst fears: Your parents really could die and leave you alone in the world. For the first seven years of my life, it was just Mom and me. No father, no grandparents, no aunts or uncles. Early on, I figured out that if anything happened to Mom, I would be alone on this planet. Then, when Juan came along, you'd think I'd have felt safer, but my fears of a parent dying were just multiplied by two.

Dika sat her wide hips on the bed, half-smushing the boy, and pulled out a cookie. "*Aquí*, for you, *mi amor.*" You wouldn't expect a Bosnian refugee to speak nearly perfect Spanish, but Dika boasted that she spoke a dozen languages.

She half-reclined on the hospital bed and smiled proudly, watching him munch on the Fig Newton.

"That's the first he's eaten," the CPS man said.

Dika handed the boy another Fig Newton. "Of course we take him," she said again.

"Well, if no next of kin claim him, you could certainly apply to be his foster family." He gave each of us a sticky handshake. "We'll be in touch then," he mumbled, and escorted us out of the room, past a few sleepy-eyed reporters in the corridor.

I always thought of myself as a free-floating one-celled amoeba, minding my own business. The other kids at school were all parts of a larger organism. The soccer girls made up one organ—a set of coordinated, interdependent cells. They always dated the soccer guys, another organ, connected to them by veins and arteries. The speech team, student government, animal rights club—everything was part of the whole. Even the hoodlums' gold chains and graffiti tags added sparkle to the organism. Me, I was a shapeless amoeba, something that didn't belong. Not particularly noticed, definitely not appreciated, just an amoeba swimming around aimlessly.

Back in middle school I'd hung out with a group of girls. My longtime friend Jasmín was the glue holding us all together, but when she abandoned us for Catholic school, we scattered. Loneliness was tricky: a cup filled at one moment with freedom, and the next, with emptiness. Maybe the emptiness part is what made me want to connect, at least a little, with the foundling.

In the week after the hospital visit, some families who'd heard about the orphan on Latino radio stations tried to claim him, but no one could describe his distinguishing characteristic, the pink birthmark on his face. By the time the CPS man called us to ask if we wanted to be the boy's foster family, Dika had convinced us by forever moaning, "Oh, this poor, poor boy!" We said yes.

We gave the boy a futon on the living room floor next to the fish tank. Since we weren't sure how long he'd stay, we didn't get him a real bed. From my room, through the cracked door, I watched him watching the fish, his face bathed in the purple glow of the aquarium light.

In the middle of his first night with us, I woke up to pee, and he was gone.

I panicked, checked all the rooms in the house, and finally ran outside. Three-quarters of a moon shone bright in the sky. Into the yard I ran, barefoot, calling him: "*¡Niño!*" I wove around the giant agave, past the gnarled mesquite tree, ignoring the spines in my feet. There, at the end of the yard, behind the crates of old bottles, he lay, sprawled out in the moonlight, next to the wire-mesh chicken coop. His mouth hung open inches from the dirt.

I went back to the house for an old down comforter and spread it out, then moved his fragile body onto it. I settled down beside him, wrapping my body around his. My pale arms around his brown ones. "*Principito,*" I whispered. Little Prince.

He turned onto his other side, facing me now, his eyes open, a patch of dirt on his cheek just above the birthmark. How had he survived in the desert? They must have saved water for him, rationed it out, drop by drop.

"Why did you come outside?" I asked in Spanish.

Nothing.

"Will you come back inside?"

A slight shake of the head.

He had seen his parents die. I'd never seen anyone die, never even seen a dead person. I'd imagined it plenty, though.

When I was little, something as small as Mom picking me up ten minutes late threw me into a wild panic. Was she killed in a crash? Was she murdered? Worries wore down a familiar path inside me. And anything could send me running down that path.

I studied the foundling's face, inches from mine, and tried to enter his mind. What had his parents looked like when they died? What do heat exhaustion and dehydration do to a body at the end? His breath smelled faintly of milk. His body seemed both solid and ethereal, composed of soil and moonlight. Maybe he was hoping to dissolve into the night, become a shadow, a spirit, join his parents. Did he imagine his mother and father floating around in the sky? Did he hope that outside in the moonlight, they might find him so far from home?

The second night, it was Dika who slept outside with him. Maybe she, too, tried to lure him in, or maybe, knowing it was hopeless, she simply settled her giant body next to his. Dika was a murky pool of unanswered questions herself. Twenty years ago, she'd supposedly bounced around Europe with my great-uncle doing who-knew-what. They'd lived in Madrid for three years, which is where she picked up Spanish. But how she split with him and ended up back in Bosnia in the middle of a war was anyone's guess.

On the boy's third day with us, over a plate of steaming quesadillas, Dika leaned over to him and said in Spanish, "*¡Ya!* Enough! Tell us your name, *niño*!"

Without a pause, he said, "*Soy Pablo.*" But he stopped

there and ignored the onslaught of questions: What's your last name, Pablo? Your town's name? Your address?

Weeks passed without another word from him. More and more, I wanted to cup my hands around him like a shivering bird, breathe life into him, some kind of spiritual CPR. Dika and I took turns sleeping with him. On my nights, I brought a flashlight and book and read to him in English. He always stayed awake, watching my lips move. He seemed soothed by my voice, by the rhythms of words.

"First, you'll sit down a little ways away from me, over there, in the grass. I'll watch you out of the corner of my eye, and you won't say anything. Language is the source of misunderstandings. But day by day, you'll be able to sit a little closer. . . ."

After I closed the book, I lay beside him and whispered to him in English and Spanish, saying anything that came into my head. "*Principito.* Know what? Our chickens used to lay eggs. Juan says they're too depressed to lay eggs now. *Quién sabe porqué.*" Sometimes I found myself whispering things he couldn't possibly understand, silly things. "Know what? I'm an amoeba, Pablito. Floating through life. Maybe you're an amoeba, too. Maybe we're two amoebas together."

He watched me and listened and said nothing. And for some reason, I convinced myself that when he became a whole person one day—hopefully sooner than later—so would I.

2

Midnight Parties

Since I was seven, Juan has been my father. And since I met him, his shiny black braid has reached down to the small of his back, and snakes have rippled magically across his biceps. When he married Mom, she no longer had to juggle which of her friends would pick me up from school. Juan came to get me every day, always five minutes early, and we walked home together, hand in hand. Our phone stopped being disconnected and we could have our pick of food at Albertsons instead of what the food bank had in stock.

Juan is in the import business. He buys goods from Mexico—bottles of tequila, pottery, baskets, shirts—and distributes them to stores around the U.S. When you mention his name, people say, *Ah, Juan, es buena gente.* He's a good person. And he is. People trust him, and his business connections sometimes ask for personal favors. Like using our fenced-in yard for a night to let immigrants rest before the next part of their journey north.

Not long after Juan came to live with us, I woke up to strange sounds late one night. I padded into the kitchen, where a pot of beans was simmering. The back door was wide open. I peeked outside, into the darkness. Our yard was filling with people who streamed silently out of a truck. Juan shut the high wooden gate behind them, and stood whispering to a man in a cowboy hat.

At the back of our yard, a woman in a dress gazed at our muddy pond, a shallow puddle of sludge and leaves that shone in the moonlight. She knelt down as though she were praying, bowed her head, and drank, cupping the dirty water to her lips. The tip of her braid hung in the mud. Mom ran over, pulled her up, placed the hose in her hands. Then Mom turned on the spigot, and the woman drank and drank.

At the far corner of our yard, a man with a mustache was eyeing our chicken coop. He looked around to make sure no one was watching him, and didn't see me half-hidden behind the back door. But I saw him. Feeling protective of our chickens, I slipped outside and headed toward the coop. The desperate look in his eyes scared me—gave me a vague fear that he might tear a live chicken apart with his teeth and drink its blood. I hid in the shadows behind our olive tree. The man crouched down, reached his arm through the mesh, picked up an egg. He cracked it open on a rock. He held it up and let the shiny slime fall into his mouth. Then he licked the inside of the shell.

I ran back inside the warm yellow light of our house and

stood in the middle of the kitchen, my heart racing. What would taste really good if you were that hungry? I pulled out a brand-new pack of Oreos. I darted outside toward the chicken coop. He was leaning against the olive tree. I held out the package. After a stunned moment, he took it, tore it open, offered a cookie to me. I took one and twisted it apart. He placed three in his mouth at once. The rest he passed out to others who had gathered. No one else pried their cookies open and licked the icing as I did, not even the kids.

Mom appeared, her arms filled with boxes from our pantry. Instead of telling me to go back to bed, she handed me crinkly packages of crackers and peanuts. "Pass these out, Sophie. To tide them over till the beans are ready."

They politely accepted the bags from me. "*Gracias, señorita.*"

Mom returned with our best blue towels and sheets, the ones only guests could use. She looked like an angel in her long white robe that trailed behind her like streamers. She distributed glasses and went around with a pitcher, pouring water like a gracious hostess. "*¿Más agua, señora?*" She breezed through the yard, touching women's shoulders lightly, smoothing her hands over children's hair. People lined up by the hose to wash the dust off their faces and legs and arms, and Mom made sure they each had a washcloth.

It was the deepest middle of night, no car headlights, not a sound beyond the low whispers, the light clink of glasses. A party, a secret middle-of-the-night party.

The next morning when I woke up, everyone was gone, not a trace except for a stack of clean dishes on the patio table, and bright white sheets on the clothesline. They had washed their own dishes and linens, Mom told me, after I'd asked her about the people, unsure whether it had been a dream. The women had requested buckets and soap and a sponge and a dish towel, and they scrubbed the dishes and washed the sheets and towels.

"Don't tell anyone about last night, Sophie," Juan warned me at breakfast.

"No one," Mom added. "Not your friends. Not even Jasmín."

After breakfast, I looked around by the chicken coop where the man had tossed the broken eggshell. Both halves were there, in the bushes. I saved them as a kind of souvenir. At first, they reminded me that the night wasn't a dream. As I got older, they reminded me of what mattered in life.

We had about five or six midnight parties over the years. Only in emergencies, if the coyote's other plans fell through. The coyote was the man the immigrants paid to lead them across the border. For hundreds of dollars per person, he was supposed to protect them from bandits, keep them from getting lost, show them holes in the fences to crawl through, tell them to hide when *la migra*—the Border Patrol—came close. And finally, after their journey—which sometimes wasn't successful if *la migra* captured them and sent them back—the coyote had to make sure they had a ride from the U.S. side of the border to wherever they were going, like Chicago or New York or Denver. If the coyote and his helpers had a rough journey and ended up stuck with a truckload of hungry, thirsty, tired people, they called Juan.

On the night Pablo came, I couldn't help wondering: If the seven people had survived, would they have spent the night in our yard? Pablo would have been just another scared kid clinging to his mother while I handed out glasses of water and plates of food.

Mom tried to mother Pablo. That summer, she took time off her waitressing job at the café and tried to interest him in Play-Doh and dried pasta mosaics and potato stamps. Juan read him books in Spanish, and on his days off, brought him to bilingual story time at the library. I took him to the park, made brownies and Jell-O with him. But none of us could eke out even a tiny smile. He swung if we put him on a swing, licked ice cream cones when we offered them, but without joy. At story hour, he clapped and stood up and sat down as commanded, but he let out none of the laughs and squeals that came naturally to the other children.

One afternoon in July, while we were baking cupcakes, I discovered a pack of candles in the kitchen junk drawer. "Pablito. Let's put candles in our cupcakes to celebrate when I was supposed to be born. I came out two months early, you know. Which is probably why I'm messed up."

Somehow, long ago, my little kid's brain had pasted together pieces of overheard conversations: When Mom was a teenager, I started making her belly fat. And then my dad left. And then I was born too soon. And he came back to get us. But I was too skinny and ugly and sick. So he left. He left for good. So sometimes there was no money for cinnamon granola. Or sparkly heart stickers. Or the heating bill. Sometimes there was no one to pick me up from school on time. And there was no one to protect us from everything bad in the world.

I held out the bowl of batter for Pablo to lick. "You know, Pablo, today would have been my sixteenth birthday. July fifteenth. If I'd been born today, I might have turned out normal."

And then, as he was licking the batter from his finger, he said something. A complete, perfect sentence in Spanish. Very softly, with his finger still in his mouth, he said, "*Cumplo seis años en julio.*"

For a moment, I just looked, stunned, at his face smeared with chocolate batter. I tried hard to act casual so that he'd keep talking. "*Entonces,* Pablito, you're turning six this month?"

He nodded.

"*Bueno,* we'll put candles in for you and we'll have a party for you tonight, okay, *principito*?"

He nodded. "*Sí.*"

Nine months passed before he said another word.

By October, the nights were too cool to sleep outside. Pablo would drag his comforter into my room and sleep on the floor by my bed. I tried picking him up and laying him next to me, but he would always climb back down.

We enrolled him in full-day kindergarten. The teacher said he was well behaved and followed directions, but never talked. He spent recesses alone, watching the other children. He seemed to live more in the realm of spirits and shadows and night than in the daylight world of games and toys that most six-year-olds inhabited.

Sometimes, in the evenings, he slipped a book silently

into my hands. Strangely enough, his favorites were books of poetry and *The Little Prince*. It wasn't the meaning of the words that mattered to him, it was their music.

"As the little prince was falling asleep, I picked him up in my arms, and started walking again. I was moved. It was as if I was carrying a fragile treasure. It actually seemed to me that there was nothing more fragile on Earth. By the light of the moon, I gazed at that pale forehead, those closed eyes, those locks of hair trembling in the wind, and I said to myself, What I'm looking at is only a shell. What's most important is invisible. . . ."

In the early spring, he started sleeping outside again, sometimes with me, sometimes with Dika. One morning, after we woke up on the comforter, Pablo let the chickens out of their coop just like any other day, but one of them refused to budge.

"Look, Pablo. She's feeling lazy today."

He picked up the chicken and revealed a perfect white egg.

"Pablo! You made the chicken get better." I wasn't sure why I said that, but when he nodded solemnly, I wondered if maybe, somehow, it was true.

With two hands, he carried the egg inside and presented it to Mom.

"*¡Gracias, mi amor!*" She kissed the top of his head.

He smiled, just a little, not enough to see any teeth.

Mom made a big deal over the egg. She fried it the way he liked it, *estrellado,* star-shaped, broken right into the pan. She served it to him on a fancy plate with a gold-painted rim.

That night at dinner, Pablo spoke. He spoke in a burst of Spanish peppered with English. He spoke as though he were giving a school report, as though he'd been rehearsing the words in his head. "*Tenemos* chickens *en mi* town. *Mi* town *se llama* Santa María Nuquimi. *Está por las* mountains, *y tenemos* chickens *allá*. . . ."

Juan found Santa María Nuquimi on a map. It was in the state of Oaxaca, deep in southern Mexico—far from Tucson, probably a week of traveling by car. He found the phone number. It turned out there was only one phone in the village. I imagined a lonely plastic phone booth in the middle of the town square, ringing, with no one around to answer it. Pablo told me later it was inside a store where they sold lollipops and beer and strips of palm for weaving hats.

The shopkeeper picked up immediately and instructed Juan to hang up and call back in ten minutes, while she announced the call over the village loudspeaker. Pablo sat on Dika's heavy thighs, which protruded from sky blue shorts. He traced the purple rivers of veins under her skin, something that always seemed to calm him. Soon he grew restless and shifted from one leg to another. "*¿Ya? ¿Podemos llamar?*" And a minute later: "We call, yes?" Then, "*¿Ya? ¿Son diez minutos?*"

Finally, Juan dialed and we all held our breath. Juan introduced himself and explained how we ended up with Pablo. He listened and nodded for a few minutes, then passed the phone to Pablo.

Pablo talked with his uncle, mostly saying *sí* and *no* at first, and then, like a rush of water, telling him in Spanish how the chickens were laying eggs again and how many toys he had in the bathtub and how his teacher gave him a red star sticker, and how he got a strike when we went bowling last week and how we'd seen a movie about a pig who wanted his mom.

Afterward, Juan gave us the highlights: He had spoken with an uncle. Pablo's aunts and uncles and grandmother had heard about the seven dead migrants. They prayed every night that Pablo and his parents weren't part of that group. They were losing hope, as more time passed. Then they heard that one boy remained alive. They made some calls trying to get information, without success. The grandmother—who the uncle said "knows things"—assured everyone that if the boy was Pablo, he was safe and would call when he was ready. Finally, they decided to trust that if the boy was Pablo, he'd be in good hands.

In the days that followed, we called them three more times. Mom and Juan and Pablo spoke with his aunts, uncles, cousins, grandmother . . . I'd had no idea he was linked to all these people. Like the spearmint in our yard whose roots spread out, buried in the dirt. If you tried to pull out one plant, you'd end up following the root that led you, like a winding road, to another plant, and another, and another. Pablo had a whole network of hidden relatives who could take turns sleeping beside him and reading him stories.

During the fourth phone call, an aunt told Mom, "We have decided something. It would be good for Pablo to grow up in your rich country, with all the opportunities there. This is what his parents wanted for him. You see, here he will be no one. He will grow up poor. He will stop school at eighth grade to work in the fields and barely make enough to eat. We know you are good people. We hear this in his voice, in your voice. We know that you care for him well. If you want to keep Pablo," the aunt concluded, crying, "and if Pablo wants to stay with you, that is all right with us."

Mom and Juan weren't sure it was best for him to stay in Tucson, but Dika insisted it was. For once, I agreed with Dika. If Pablo left, the chickens would probably stop laying eggs, and I'd mope along with them, feeling useless. In the end, we decided that Pablo should stay at least until the end of the school year, because, after all, he was just starting to talk and raise his hand in class. That way, Mom and Juan could save up money for plane tickets and afford time off work. Then they would take Pablo to visit his relatives and he could decide where he wanted to live.

"Too big decision for little boy!" Dika clucked, shaking her head.

Over the next week, we stood in lines and waited hours in plastic seats at government buildings to get permission to travel with Pablo. The CPS man said we could take Pablo to visit his village, and if he and his closest relatives decided he could live with us, we'd have to sign adoption papers.

I wanted to stretch out my time with Pablo. We all did. Now, when Mom came home from work, exhausted from being on her feet all day at the café, instead of lying in the hammock and having a beer, she sat cross-legged on the floor with Pablo and played Chinese checkers. Juan started spending his weekends building a playhouse in the far corner of the yard, letting Pablo bring him tools and hold the wood while he sawed. As they worked, he told Pablo the folk-tales he used to tell me when I was little. Usually, the star of the story was a scraggly little orphan who went on a quest somewhere—to the moon, or the bottom of the sea, or inside a deep cave—and ended up finding a treasure and turning into a world-famous hero.

Once in a while, Pablo talked about his relatives. He mentioned how good his cousin was at catching lizards, or how fast he could run down the big hill in his village. But mostly, he seemed wrapped up in life with us and the chickens. Every morning he brought a handful of eggs to Mom. The three other hens, too, had started laying them. He was so proud of those eggs. Even though I liked fruit and cereal for breakfast, I forced myself to get used to a daily star-shaped egg instead.

3

Dika's Boyfriend

Back when Pablo first arrived, Dika decided he should learn to swim—or at least that was her excuse for sneaking into the pool at the apartment complex down the street. So, except for the cold months—November, December, and January—we spent every afternoon at the pool. Dika's daily schedule was: collect broken pieces of colored glass at sunrise, work at the Salvation Army in the morning, and once Pablo and I got home from school, lounge at the pool. She wore a bright blue sarong over her turquoise bikini. She placed her bag by the lounge chair, slipped off her sarong seductively, and settled in the chair. There she lay, her legs like two whales, one bent coquettishly. She would examine her body and check her tan lines, pleased. If anyone else was there, she'd show off the tan lines to them, too.

"My friends in Germany should to see me now! There it is snowy and cold and gray. Look at this sky, so much blue."

Germany is where she had asylum after she left Bosnia and the war.

She spread baby oil on her legs, arm, stomach. It took forever, this process—there was so much flesh to cover, and she went over every area twice, three times if a man was there. She wore a blue headband that pushed back her orangish hair, which showed the gray roots. Then her eyes closed and a smile spread over her face. A woman of leisure. The only thing that set her apart from a lady of questionable taste on a resort vacation was the series of three thick, shiny scars on her left inner arm.

A relic from the war prison camp, Mom told me. All Dika had said about the camp was that she ate raw onions for three straight months, and that her only possession was a small shard of red glass that she'd salvaged from her bombed-out house. At the camp, she kept it hidden in a pocket, and planned on one day piercing the heart of a guard. She never did, as far as I knew.

When Mom first announced that her Bosnian war refugee great-aunt was coming to live with us, I'd pictured a skeletal woman in a shawl, deep half-moon shadows beneath haunted eyes. But Dika came with mounds of flesh and cheap jewelry, a wardrobe of tight turquoise shirts, white capri pants, peroxided hair. She inserted herself into our lives loudly. I wasn't completely convinced she was even our relative.

I went to the pool with her, dragging my feet. I had nothing better to do. I hardly ever saw my only real friend, Jasmín, anymore. Jasmín was the reason I spoke Spanish. Her parents were Mexican, old friends of Juan. We'd hung out together since elementary school, and she'd stayed friends with me out of habit. Then, in ninth grade, when Jasmín got a scholarship to a private school and started working as a camp counselor in the summers, she might as well have moved to a different planet. She'd drifted away and found replacements for me, but I hadn't found anyone who came close to replacing her.

At the pool, I mostly sat in the shade reading and watching Pablo splash around, worrying my skin would break out in a sun rash. Mom blamed my mysterious rashes on the fact that I had been a premature baby. I did feel sometimes that I wasn't fully formed. Like that Native American story where white people weren't fully baked in the ovens so their clay never reached the proper brown color. My body was more underbaked than most, and all the Tucson sun did for it was make it pink and bumpy.

My spirit felt underbaked too. Most people seemed to have a hard outer shell that protected them from mean people, insults, bad memories. I was not one of those people. I wore long sleeves and long skirts, and not just because of the sun. Mom's friend from Saudi Arabia veiled and draped herself in black, only a slit for her eyes. She told me that her body was sacred and shouldn't be exposed for all eyes to see. I liked the idea of living behind so much fabric. It would be a comfortable feeling.

I usually wore a big T-shirt at the pool, taking it off only to dip myself in the water a few times. And this, only after spreading myself with so much sunscreen I left an embarrassing layer of grease on the water.

"Look at this!" Dika would say when we got in the water.

She left a slick film of oil, too. "My poor, poor boyfriend! He must to clean up all this grease!"

"We shouldn't even be here, Dika. It's illegal."

"My boyfriend invites us! He is boss of the pool!"

He wasn't exactly the boss of the pool. He was the maintenance man.

One afternoon, a few months after Pablo arrived, we'd been cooling off in the water while Pablo did flips between us. We were arguing, as always, about whether we should be using the pool. The maintenance man, meanwhile, slowly picked out leaves here and there.

Dika reasoned, "Ah, Sophie! No one uses this pool! We are only ones! Whoever made this pool will be too happy that some people uses it. And that poor pool man. He doesn't have job if no people uses it!"

The pool man was a short, stocky man—from Mexico, I assumed. Brown skin, a polite smile. We saw him fixing things sometimes, leaving an apartment with a case of tools. Dika watched him closely whenever he was around. She made a show of applying baby oil to her legs, rubbing it on the folds of flesh hanging over the bikini; made a point to check the tan line of her giant bosom as he raked the water's surface with his pole net.

This day he was hovering by the pool, waiting for us to get out of the water so he could clean it, yet pretending he wasn't waiting so we wouldn't feel rushed. I got out and dried off. "Let's go, Pablo. Come on, Dika!"

"Always you are rushing, Sophie, rush rush!" She lumbered up the pool steps and then her foot slipped. I think it really was an accident, because I saw the shock in her eyes, and how her chin jarred as she fell, but within seconds she'd recovered and decided to milk it for all it was worth.

"Ohhh! Ahhh! *Mein Gott!* My leg!" And she sat on the step, clutching her thigh, massaging it.

The pool man rushed over and crouched down beside her. She looked at him with designed bashfulness. She actually fluttered her eyelashes.

"You are okay, miss?" he asked in a thick Spanish accent.

I could see her mind at work. *Miss.* He must have noticed she had no wedding ring. Or else he just thought she was very young. Or else he was deliberately complimenting her.

He helped her up, walked her over to her chair as she pressed her body against his, coating his shirt with oil and water. He crouched by her chair and she bent her leg. "Look at it!" she moaned. "You think it will be okay? You see bruise?"

He looked at it and swallowed hard. "Is good, I think, very good."

I saw the corners of her lips curve up.

An hour later they were still talking in a mix of Spanish and English. "Children! I must to let my leg rest more before I walk home. Mr. Lorenzo helps me! You go!"

And that is how Dika snagged the boyfriend whose son would change my life.

4

Jewel Errands

School ended in June, but since Juan was swamped at work and Mom couldn't find a waitress to sub for her, they postponed the Mexico trip. That was fine by me. I'd already made a three-page list of things to do with Pablo over the summer.

Then, one sweltering evening, out of the blue, Dika announced over dinner, "We have plan. We drive to Mexico together. Me, Mr. Lorenzo, his son, Sophie, Pablo. We stay in Pablo's village for one week. They go to Guatemala and they find the jewels. Pablo can to see his poor family. Mr. Lorenzo and his son return to Pablo's home, they pick us up, and we return to Tucson. Good for everybody, no?"

"What jewels?" Juan asked. "What are you talking about?"

"Find the jewels," she said, impatient. "You know, the things they have to do, like the errands."

"Jewel errands?" Juan raised his eyebrows at me.

"Don't look at me," I said. "This is news to me, too." My pulse quickened, but no, this wouldn't really happen, it was too far-fetched.

"You've only known this Mr. Lorenzo guy for a few months, Dika."

"That is how long I *date* him. But really, we know him more. No, Sophie? We watch him every day. For one year! Watch him work." Dika punctuated her words with her fork. "Every day. He works hard."

"Hmmm." Mom looked skeptical.

"But you know me, you know I am good judge of the people," Dika insisted. "He works hard, Sophie, no?"

I shrugged.

"What do you think, Sophie?" Mom asked me.

It sounded like a bad idea. I wanted to keep postponing Pablo's trip until the idea of it faded from everyone's memory. Anyway, a road trip was way too dangerous. After all, didn't car crashes kill more people than all natural disasters combined? And I'd never traveled anywhere without Mom and Juan, never been brave enough to. Once, on a family vacation, we were in the car and suddenly a panic gripped me, a panic so strong I felt as though I were suffocating. I made us turn back. That panic would pop up at other times, too.

The worst thing was, I couldn't shake the feeling that there was always a dark, sinister shape lurking just underneath the surface. And that worry spawned another one: What if, after a big wave of fear knocked you over, you could never, in your whole life, stand up again? What if you could never feel pure happiness? I imagined my fears piled up inside me like broken pens, leaking ink and turning my innards black.

Dika's idea was terrible, too, because it meant weeks trapped with her and her boyfriend, and the son. Who was the son, anyway? How old was he? I pictured a short, stout twelve-year-old, a miniature Mr. Lorenzo.

While I was making this show of thinking about it, Pablo piped up. He hardly ever talked, so it was easy to forget he could understand us.

"I like the pool man." His voice came out small and thin, and in English at that. His eyes were lit up, more animated than ever before. "I really really like the pool man," Pablo added, louder this time.

A warm, liquidy feeling spread out from my chest.

"You really want to do this, Pablito?" I asked hesitantly.

"Yes!"

I took a deep breath. "I'll think about it."

Mom stared at me. "Okay," she said. "Let's think about it."

"The pool man is cool," Pablo said, rearranging his mouth into what almost passed for a smile.

After dinner I lay in the hammock and watched the layers of leaves quiver above me. Could I do this? Mom and Juan wouldn't let them go without me. Maybe not even with me.

The idea of traveling outside Tucson made my pulse race. Here, at least, I could control things. I could change the dish sponge every week to avoid bacteria buildup and check the radon detector's battery daily. But traveling was like standing in an open field during a storm, danger shooting from all directions like lightning bolts. I suspected Mexico would be my worst nightmares wrapped into one deadly package: exotic germs, ruthless criminals, poisonous creatures. And no turning back.

It wasn't just Mexico, or traveling, or Mom dying; all kinds of possibilities made my breath quicken and my throat start closing up. Life-threatening illnesses might creep up on me, like cancer or AIDS—not to mention hepatitis, typhoid, malaria, and leprosy. Then there were the everyday risks of getting trapped in an elevator or poisoned by a disgruntled fast-food worker. And of course, with every car ride, a giant truck could smash me, or a driver with road rage could beat me to a pulp. Then there was a whole slew of natural disasters like a building crushing me in an earthquake or a flash flood drowning me. And the more insidious dangers—molds and toxic gases and deadly chemicals seeping into our house through the ground.

I pushed myself in the hammock with my foot, rocking back and forth. Beams of sunlight sifted through the leaves, illuminating a patch of my left thigh, my right ankle, the center of my chest. Above me, the layers of green shifted, like all the layers of myself. Layers I'd forgotten about, or maybe never knew existed. I saw my trail stretching before me. Up ahead, it branched into two. One route led through a forest of thickening fears to a small, closed-in life, and the other led . . . somewhere else.

Suddenly I had the feeling that everything depended on whether I went to Mexico.

. . .

Later that night, after Pablo and Dika had gone to sleep, Juan and Mom and I sat at the kitchen table under the wobbly ceiling fan.

Juan tilted his head at me, looking baffled. "You really think this is a good idea, Sophie? You think you can do this?"

"I think Pablo needs to see his family, and we need those adoption papers signed, and, well—I think it makes sense." I tried to sound confident.

Mom raised her eyebrows. Wispy pieces of blond hair floated around her face. "His village sounds pretty remote—you won't be able to snap your fingers and be home."

"I know. I can do it." As I said this my heart was pounding. Was I crazy to think I could go?

Mom and Juan looked at me doubtfully.

"I can do it," I said again, biting my lip.

"And, Sophie," Juan said. "Remember, Pablo might decide to stay there."

My stomach contracted. "No, he won't."

Mom looked at Juan. "We can't force him to be happy here. It's been nearly a year and he's still all melancholy, still wants to sleep out there with the chickens. Sure, he's better than at first, but have you ever seen him laugh?"

I thought about it. "I guess not."

"Okay, Sophie," she said. "Go down there with them. Spend a week or so in his village. See how he feels."

The full impact hit me in bed that night: If Pablo decided to stay in his village, and Dika went off and married Mr. Lorenzo, I'd be an only child again, just me, Juan, and Mom. It gave me a thirsty feeling, but I couldn't figure out what I was thirsty for.

. . .

We planned to leave at sunrise—who knows why, but Dika had some idea that all long trips must start at sunrise. "We must to leave when the sun raises. We must!" I wasn't clear whether this was a superstitious thing or a practical consideration.

I slept outside with Pablo the night before our departure. When the sky started growing lighter, I heard people loading our Volkswagen bus, but I just wanted to lie there. I'd hardly slept from nervousness. Pablo was sound asleep, eyebrows wrinkled, intent on some dream. The rooster crowed and I covered my ears.

"We should get up," I whispered to Pablo, nudging him. *"Ya, levántate, principito."*

He opened his eyes, groggy.

"Buenos días," he said. Not to me, to someone else.

I propped myself on my elbows and squinted into the sun. A guy my age, in mirrored sunglasses, towered over me. He wore a long black leather coat, about five gold chains around his neck, glaring white tennis shoes, and a baseball cap pulled low. Reflected in the lenses were convex images of me in my dirty white nightgown with chicken feathers in my hair.

He knelt down and extended his hand. "I'm Ángel. Lorenzo's son."

5

My Feet Are Nice

His voice seemed artificially deep, as if he were trying to sound manly. He held out his hand.

I wiped the dirt off mine and shook his.

"I know you already. Sophie."

He stood back up. I looked at him more closely. I recognized the sunglasses, the way he stood, his legs firm, but his body swaying slightly, confident as a tall tree. He held, under his arm, a small wooden box, about the size of a Kleenex box. It was made of dark, rich wood, carved and polished to a bright sheen.

Now I could place him. He'd been in my woodworking class two years earlier. I was the only girl in the class, which I rebelliously took as an elective instead of Computer Skills. Most of the guys in the class skipped it regularly. Ángel came to class about once a week.

The main thing I remembered about him was this: At

the end of the semester we all displayed our pieces around the dusty worktables. Mine was a crooked little end table. One guy made a gun case, another a toolbox, another a stool. But Ángel had made a giant mahogany armoire, taller than himself, carved intricately with flowers and birds, the curves smooth, the wood brilliant. I'd assumed he'd bought it, or stolen it, or gotten it from his house and lied about making it himself.

But Mr. Mutton, the teacher, had reached an understanding with him. It turned out he had let Ángel build it in his neighbor's wood shop, where he worked after school. When he asked Ángel to tell us how he made it, Ángel went through the process step by step, running his hands over the wood as though he knew it well, like a pet's fur, or a girlfriend's hair.

"You're the one who made that gigantic armoire, right?" I asked.

"Yeah."

"I'm surprised you recognized me."

"You kidding?"

What did that mean? Outside of class, he was one of the guys who hung around huge pickup trucks, red or black and shiny, with *ranchera* music blaring. He was definitely not an amoeba. He was part of an organ. And the other cells of the organ: girls in halter tops and tight pants and thick eyeliner perched on the hood. Intimidatingly sexy girls. Whenever I'd pass them I'd pull my hat down over my eyes. It hadn't occurred to me that he might have noticed me.

"You must be Pablo," he said, turning to Pablo. "Hey, my man. Wassup?" They bumped fists.

He switched to Spanish. "You guys always sleep with the chickens?"

I felt my face warm.

Pablo nodded, serious.

"Not always," I said.

After Ángel left to help load the van, I noticed that the plastic pearl buttons on my nightgown were low enough that you could see a shadow of cleavage. I wondered if he'd been looking there. Who knew—all I'd seen from his sunglasses was the reflection of my face.

While everyone finished loading the van, I took a quick shower, scrubbing the dust off my legs and feet. After I stepped out, I stood there, dripping, in front of the full-length mirror. Repeating a mantra I had read in a magazine article, I whispered to my reflection: *My feet are nice, my ears are nice, my elbows are nice.* Actually, I was supposed to say *beautiful,* not *nice,* but I didn't want to push my luck. *My arms are nice, my knees are nice, my ankles are nice.*

Outside, they were all waiting for me in the red Volkswagen bus. Dika in the passenger seat, Mr. Lorenzo at the wheel, Pablo and Ángel in back. I stuffed my duffel bag of clothes toward the way back, and kept with me, in the backseat, a pillowcase full of books—chocolate-stained, jam-spotted books that I'd read and reread. Pablo's favorite poetry, a few novels, and my dog-eared *Little Prince.* A whole week in the van to get there, a week in Pablo's village, and a week to get back. I knew I'd be too embarrassed to talk much to Ángel. I'd just try to get absorbed in my books.

"We are ready!" Dika declared. In her hand, she cupped

the shard of red glass, about the size of her palm. Her version of a security blanket. She always said it was for her headaches, that when she held it up to the sun, the red light eased the pounding. "Better than the aspirin!" she insisted.

Saying goodbye to Mom and Juan was harder than I'd thought. A lump came to my throat when I hugged them. Mom whispered, "You're in charge, Sophie." And Juan: "If you have any problems, call us."

What kinds of problems? Corrupt cops who demanded giant bribes? Armed drug traffickers roaming around the border? Poisonous snakes and scorpions? Amoebas and diarrhea from unsanitary food preparation?

Okay, Sophie, deep breath. I'd gone over this a million times in my head. The cops and drug runners we'd just avoid. Go the speed limit, not give them a reason to pull us over. I wouldn't walk anywhere where snakes and scorpions could be lurking, and I'd shake out my shoes and clothes before putting them on. And the food—I'd squeeze lime juice, a natural disinfectant, over everything. For days and nights, I'd been coming up with possible things that could go wrong and making backup plans.

"Everything'll be fine," I told Mom and Juan.

"You sure you want to do this, Sophie?" Mom asked.

I looked at the four people in the van. Dika and Mr. Lorenzo were examining the map, their heads close. Ángel was making faces at Pablo, bug faces with his sunglasses. Pablo looked different, and it took me a moment to figure out how. He had a smile, a smile that showed his teeth, a smile that made his eyes scrunch up. He was making a little high-pitched chipmunk sound. Pablo was laughing.

. . .

"Cool box," Pablo said to Ángel as we exited onto the highway.

"Thanks." Ángel held the box on his lap like a baby. He brushed his fingertips over the carvings of leaves and trees that covered it. I noticed an old-fashioned silver keyhole. I wondered if it belonged to the skeleton key that was nearly hidden in gold chains and saints and Virgins at his neck.

"You make it?" I asked.

He nodded and didn't offer any more information. Maybe it was drugs. What if it was drugs and we got caught and sent to a Mexican prison? I didn't know anything about this guy and his father. They could be drug dealers.

I did some deep breathing and tried to act casual. "So, what are you guys doing in Guatemala?"

"Digging up my mother's jewels." Ángel said this as if it were the most normal thing in the world.

Somehow I'd assumed that the buried jewels thing had been a misunderstanding on Dika's part. Maybe they weren't drug dealers. Maybe they were just crazy. Of course, Dika attracted crazy people. My stomach tightened, and again, that familiar feeling came, the beginnings of panic—next my heart would race and my breath quicken and my throat dry up. *Relax, Sophie. We've only been gone five minutes. We can turn back.*

"Digging up her jewels?" I asked.

"My mom buried them. We're digging them up." He enunciated his words, as though that were my problem.

He leaned over between the front seats and stuck a tape into the stereo. Salsa music blared, loud and sudden. He sat back down and looked out the window and I couldn't tell if he was awake or asleep because of those sunglasses hiding his eyes.

A little while later, while Dika and I sat in the van and Mr. Lorenzo and Ángel and Pablo peed by the roadside, I asked her, "What's the deal with the buried jewels?"

"Mr. Lorenzo's wife buries them long time ago."

"I know. But why?"

"In war, when soldiers come, they take everything. You must to bury anything to save it. You must to hide your childrens, also."

"Where's Ángel's mother? Is she dead?"

Dika shrugged. "They say us when they want to say us, no?"

PART 2

CROSSING THE BORDER

When I was a little boy I lived in an old house, and there was a legend that a treasure was buried in it somewhere. . . . It cast a spell over that whole house. My house hid a secret in the depths of its heart. . . .

"Yes," I said to the little prince, "whether it's a house or the stars or the desert, what makes them beautiful is invisible."

—THE LITTLE PRINCE

6

Silent Fireworks

Our trip had a sound track, like a film or a music video. Ángel played his shoe box full of tapes: *cumbia,* salsa, merengue—a background to the scenery out the window and the antics in the van. I liked the music. When it was on, I couldn't stay wrapped in my separate world. The pulsing beats pulled me, like gravity, into the planet of the van. Surrounded by the music, I felt like someone else, riding into unknown territory, some adventurous woman in a movie.

Early that first morning, we passed through Nogales, the border town, which was already packed with people selling things, cars bumper to bumper, horns honking, music blaring from all directions. After we got through, we stopped to register the van with the police and pay fees. I stayed in the van reading, while Pablo ran around the parking lot and Ángel and Dika and Mr. Lorenzo talked to the officials at a booth. They were a strange sight—Dika, looking large and pink and nearly naked in her white tennis shorts and sapphire tank top, next to Mr. Lorenzo in his quilted flannel shirt, which he seemed to wear all the time, and Ángel in his sunglasses and baseball cap and chains.

By the time we started driving again, the sun was high overhead, burning my skin through the window. For lunch we ate food that Dika and I had prepared before the trip—ham sandwiches, apples, chips, and for dessert, fruitcake. She adored fruitcake. The bright green and red bits of candied fruit thrilled her. She brought nine tins along, and when Mom had accused her of going overboard, she shrieked, "But five of them are gifts!"

Outside the window, the dry, brown earth met an endless stretch of hazy sky. Patches of green were few and far between. Every couple of miles we passed a cluster of cement-block houses, in various stages of construction, some painted pink or blue in a failed effort to cheer things up. The signs also tried to make things seem less hellish: JESUS'S JUNKYARD, GOD'S GAS STATION. Once in a while we passed smoldering trash fires at the roadside, and giant lots of rusted cars and machine parts.

It turned out that Ángel did like to talk, as long as it wasn't about his mother's buried jewels. He told story after story about all the crazy things he'd seen and done. He had a way of making his stories sad and funny and exciting all at once. He talked about the dog he'd had in Guatemala who was so smart he could say words in Mayan. About how, when he was a little kid, he fell backward into a giant pot of chicken soup over the fire and burned his butt and had to sleep on his stomach for a week. Pablo giggled at his stories, tentatively, trying out this laughing thing.

Late that afternoon, Pablo rummaged through my pillowcase, then quietly dropped into my lap a book of poetry by Pablo Neruda—his favorite, mainly, I suspected, because they had the same name. At first I said no, too embarrassed to read in front of Ángel. But Pablo pleaded. So I agreed to read a few stanzas, about slicing a lemon, and how the lemon was really a cup of miracles, a universe of gold. Out of the corner of my eye, I saw Ángel staring. I wondered if behind the sunglasses he was watching my lips move as intently as Pablo was.

"More!" Pablo said, once I finished.

I shook my head, glancing at Ángel. He took off his seat belt and wedged himself on his knees between the front and back seats, and said, "We beg you!"

Pablo giggled, and I flipped a few pages to a poem about a diver who floats up from his underwater "pit of solitude" and gets reborn. As Ángel and Pablo listened intently, I forgot about being an amoeba and became part of the little cluster of cells in this van.

When the sun dropped low and the light grew gentle, we stopped in a dusty small town for dinner. RESTAURANT FANNY, the sign read. We sat at a little table covered with a torn plastic tablecloth with a red flower design. After our food came, the owner, Fanny, came over and apologized about the flies buzzing around us. Before I knew what was happening, she was enthusiastically spraying bug repellent over our tacos. Naturally, my fear-of-being-poisoned fear was activated.

"Stop!" My voice sounded shrill. I tried to steady it. I tried to think of a legitimate excuse. "I'm allergic to that."

She gave me a strange look and a halfhearted "Sorry, *señorita,*" and moved to another table.

"Oh, Sophie," Dika said. "You have allergy to everything! In U.S.A., everyone have allergy. In my country, no. We are strong."

And she went on and on about how Americans were allergy wusses. As she talked I could almost feel my throat closing up. There were no windows in the restaurant, so the toxic odor of bug spray lingered. I squeezed lime all over my food, drenching it, although I figured maybe the bug spray had killed some germs on contact, too.

"How much lime you are going to put on that?" Dika asked, her eyes wide.

I ignored her.

Ángel came to my defense. "Lime's good for you. Lots of vitamin C, right, lime-girl?"

Dika laughed, a snort that blew Pepsi out her mouth. "Lime-girl!"

But Mr. Lorenzo nodded, serious. "In my country, we use the limes like medicine, for the sore throat and the cough and the cold. For anything."

I appreciated that Mr. Lorenzo stood up for me. He was quiet and shy and didn't talk much, just gave Dika soft-eyed looks every so often.

"Lime-girl" is what Ángel started calling me, and I didn't mind it. I'd never had a nickname before. If someone gave you a nickname, it meant you were part of an organism.

Later in the van that night: "Hey, lime-girl, turn up the music. Lime-girl, pass me some cookies. Lime-girl, look—an armadillo."

Dika burst out laughing every time he said lime-girl. Her shrieks and laughter were another part of the sound track. When Mr. Lorenzo passed another car, for the brief moments we were in the lane of oncoming traffic, she gripped the door handle, threw one hand over her mouth, widened her eyes. *"Mein Gott! Mein Gott!"* she squealed until we were safely back in our own lane. Who knew why she shifted to German.

Mr. Lorenzo put his hand on her thigh for a moment. "Calm down. Is okay, miss." Calling a sixty-year-old "miss" seemed ridiculous, but she ate it up. She looked out the window and smiled with such clear-eyed pleasure it was hard to stay irritated with her.

The first night we stopped outside a little coastal town called San Carlos, so close to the ocean you could smell the salty, fishy breezes. Dika wanted to spend the night right on the beach so that she could work on her tan the next morning, but I reminded her we'd promised Mom and Juan we'd go straight to Pablo's village, with no delays, no distractions, no sidetracking. Dika shook her head. "Oh, you must to have more fun in the life, Sophie!"

At the roadside next to a cluster of low, spiky cacti, we raised the van's pop-top to sleep—me and Dika on the bottom bunk, Mr. Lorenzo and Ángel above us, and Pablo on a sleeping bag on the backseat. My body was squeezed to about a foot of the bed, while Dika's body spread out like rising dough, pushing me to the edge. Lying there, trying to sleep, I worried that the upper bunk would collapse onto us.

After Dika started snoring, and some loud asthmatic breathing came from the upper bunk, there was movement above and then, a pressure on my thigh.

"Oops, sorry, lime-girl." Ángel moved his foot and dropped down from the upper bunk. "Didn't mean to step on you." He didn't have his sunglasses on, or a shirt, just the gold chains that glinted light from somewhere. Until that moment I'd never caught a glimpse of his eyes, always the mirrored glasses reflecting my own face. There were tiny laugh wrinkles at the corners of his eyes. They seemed raw, vulnerable.

As he opened the van door, a little trail of sparks flew in his wake. Maybe static from his clothes and the sleeping bag. While he was outside, I felt a warm spot where his foot had touched the sheet over my thigh. When he came back through the van, he left another small trail of sparks, silent miniature fireworks.

The next morning, Ángel asked me questions, as though he was really interested in me. *What is your favorite thing to do, Sophie? What are your dreams? Do you like morning or night best? What are you reading? What's it about?*

Then he asked if he could braid my hair.

"You know how to braid hair?" This surprised me.

"My mother taught me when I was little. I used to braid her hair."

Ángel braiding my hair sent tingles from my scalp down

to every cell in my body. And then a wave of warmth that made me want to melt back into him. He smoothed my hair and parted it down the middle.

I hadn't worn my hair in two braids for ages. His fingers sectioned off the chunk of hair into three parts, gently pulling it taut, and working his way down with quick careful fingers. He wrapped a rubber band around the first braid and moved on to the second. I wished he would slow down to make it last longer.

"You know what your hair's like?" he said. "That silky part of the corn, when you peel back the husk."

I swallowed hard, afraid to break the spell.

After he wrapped the rubber band on the second braid, he ran his hand down its length, and said, "It's not even. Let me do this one again."

"Your niece is very pretty," Mr. Lorenzo said to Dika that afternoon. "Like her great-aunt."

"Oh, Mr. Lorenzo!" Dika slapped his shoulder. "Like her mother!"

Sometimes when old people look at me, they say that I am on the road to looking like my mother. I attribute it to cataracts.

"But she doesn't have boyfriend!" Dika lamented. Her eyes flicked at me in the mirror. She winked. She was playing matchmaker. I looked out the window, past the rolling hills to the Sierra Madre mountains, and hoped Dika would drop it before Ángel woke up.

"No boyfriend?" Mr. Lorenzo said dramatically.

I glanced at Ángel, and luckily, his breathing was still

steady, his lips slightly parted, his head leaning against the other window.

"No boyfriend!" Dika repeated. I prayed she would stop here.

Boys do not look at you, Dika had told me bluntly one day at the pool, *and this is your fault.* I tried to ignore her, hoped the college guys dunking each other hadn't heard her. That night I'd asked Mom if she thought it was my fault. She was more delicate. *Sophie,* she told me, *you send the message that your body and your mind and your soul—none of it is anyone's business.* Juan offered another opinion. He said that guys my age can't look at true beauty in the face—it scares them, blinds them like the sun. They feel more comfortable with mediocre girls, he said, mediocre prettiness, mediocre minds.

I liked Juan's explanation best. But really, Dika was right. It was my fault. Boys scared me, like nearly everything else in the world.

That evening, Ángel was driving, and I was next to him. It was dusk, and the mountains were dark silhouettes against the purple sky. The others were asleep in the backseat. A bizarre family—Dika in her blue-and-white-striped tube top, her tanned freckled arms around skinny little Pablo. On the other side, stout Mr. Lorenzo in his flannel shirt. Dika's and Mr. Lorenzo's heads leaned against each other, touching, forming a strange upside-down triangle.

Here on our little van planet, everything felt comfortable, as if I was exactly where I was supposed to be. Ángel wore his sunglasses, despite the growing darkness. "Why do you always wear those shades?" I asked.

" 'Cause your skin's so white it glares."

"Thanks." I reached out and punched his arm, jokingly, the first time I'd ever touched a guy that way. I put my feet on the dashboard, pressed them against the windshield, leaving imprints of my toes, the soles of my feet.

"Why *are* you so white, lime-girl? Why isn't your skin dark like your dad's?"

"Juan's not my real dad. My real dad left days after I was born."

"What an *idiota.*"

"It wasn't his fault. I stunk. I cried too much. I was skinny and ugly. So he left."

"Fathers don't leave 'cause of an ugly baby."

"You've never seen my baby pictures."

"And your mom's so hot," he said. "Why would anyone leave her?"

I rolled my eyes and looked out the window.

"Why does your mom think he left?"

I reclined the seat and stared at the torn fabric of the ceiling. "My dad was in trouble with the law, dealing acid. He jumped bail and left the state, but my mom wouldn't go with him. She had her prenatal visits and I was a high-risk pregnancy. She ended up having an emergency delivery, and he came back to see her. He wanted her to come with him. But I had to be in an incubator for a while, so she said she was staying. And he left."

"So it wasn't that you were ugly," Ángel said.

"According to Mom, no," I admitted. "I get the feeling she thinks my dad was a loser. But I've seen pictures. I was four pounds and scrawny and cried all the time. I was ugly, really ugly, red and wrinkled and skinny like a little alien."

"Lots of ugly babies turn out pretty. He probably knew that."

I shrugged. "It's too late to change. It's an idea I've had for so long it's ingrained in me. My curse." My voice was shaking, so I closed my mouth.

"Your curse?"

"Forget it. It's complicated."

After a while, Ángel said, "Hey, I never told you the real reason I wear shades all the time."

I was grateful he changed the subject. "Okay, why do you wear shades all the time?"

"Your beauty would blind me without them."

My stomach leaped. I made a sound, which I intended to be a sarcastic snort, but it ended up sounding like a strangled laugh that got stuck coming out.

Ángel had a way of drawing Pablo out of his shell. His sunglasses and gold chains clearly left Pablo in awe. Yet he was willing to play silly games and be goofy with Pablo, which I'd never tried. I'd first seen Pablo as a traumatized boy, something terribly fragile, and it was hard to shake that image. Another thing that surprised me was how much Pablo loved Ángel's stories of barely surviving deadly adventures, a topic I'd never brought up for fear of unearthing bad memories.

I liked listening to Ángel's stories too. That way he could

talk and talk, and I didn't have to worry about saying anything stupid.

Later that night, Ángel and I got into the backseat with Pablo, and Mr. Lorenzo drove along the nearly deserted Route 15 with Dika beside him. The headlights shone lonely in front of us, and we were cozy in the backseat, Pablo leaning against me, eyes fixed on Ángel, mouth half open. The *cumbia* song "Siguiendo la Luna"—"Following the Moon"—was playing, and ahead, the moon was rising, full and huge and orange near the horizon. Once in a while, once in a long while, everything lines up perfectly and you think, Wow, this is life and I am living it. This is what I was thinking when Ángel said, suddenly, "I'm used to dying."

"What?" I said.

"I've almost died four times. Every time a woman saves me."

7

Escaping Death

"The first time," Ángel said, "I was picking coffee beans. I was about four years old. To get to the finca our family had to walk for hours. It belonged to a rich family. They paid us to pick the coffee and gave us a room to stay in for a few weeks. The plants were on steep mountainsides, with loose rocks, really sharp. We each had ropes tied around our waists in case we fell. The year before, a girl fell and died. Fell into the river, hit her head, and drowned. We had to be careful. That's why we had the ropes. And we each carried a basket. So there I am, filling the basket. It's half full of berries when I slip.

"I wait for the rope to stop me. But I'm so little it slides right off. I keep falling. Rolling down the mountain. Rocks banging me, coffee plants grabbing at me. While I fall I think things. I wonder how it will to feel to fall straight down through the air. How will it feel when I smack the water? How will it feel to breathe in the river?

"Suddenly I'm lying still by a pile of giant rocks. I remember seeing candles lit there on a stone altar. I remember feeling the moss soft beneath me. No more bright sunshine, just cool shadows. I'm in heaven, I decide. And in the tallest candle flame there's a dancing woman in white—*la Virgen,* I think at first. But then she turns into my mother, then my great-grandmother who died, and my great-aunt who died. She's made of light. Glowing. Then she grows and grows until she's so big she has one foot on either side of the mountain.

"Next thing I know, my mother—my real mother, in the flesh—is kneeling over me, her hands holding my face, her lips all over my head. She presses her head to my chest and hears my heartbeat. Moves her cheek near my mouth, feels my breath. She rips off her shirt and tears it to pieces. One strip around my arm, another around my leg, another around my forehead. The white strips turn red with my blood. I feel a little embarrassed that I see her breasts. She's come first, and then the others come. I don't know how she's made it down here so fast. My father gets there and covers her with his shirt. Carries me along a path back to the hut.

"Later I ask my mother, 'How did you find me before the others?' She says, '*Hijo,* I saw a light over that spot where you were, a light that grew bigger and bigger.' You know, for a while after that I asked myself: Why was my mother glowing along with my great-grandmother and great-aunt, when she wasn't dead?"

. . .

We camped again the second night. The next morning, on the road again, Ángel leaned over to check on his carved box, which he kept under the seat and checked at least once an hour. I wanted to ask more about the box. Would he clam up if I mentioned it? I mustered up the breeziest voice I could. "Um, Ángel, so there's probably something important inside that box, huh?"

He nodded, but said nothing.

Pablo started in. "Is animal? Is lizard? Is chicken?" and on and on until Ángel cracked a smile. Then Mr. Lorenzo and Dika joined in. "Hair gel? Drugs? Gold? Dirty magazines?" Ángel laughed, but he didn't let Pablo shake the box, no matter how much he pleaded.

I loved listening to this silly banter with Pablo, because he seemed, for once, like a normal little boy. This was what we'd been trying to get him to do for the whole past year. Normal little boy stuff, stuff that could be even obnoxious at times. Mom and Juan would be amazed when we got back.

For the rest of the day, Pablo occasionally piped up with "*¡Yo sé! ¡Yo sé!* Is million dollar! . . . Is million million dollar!"

That afternoon, Pablo dozed while the road climbed uphill, through rugged mountains spotted with giant agave plants that were taller than me, their wavy leaves like jellyfish tentacles. Wet green leaves and tropical flowers filled the valley, looking mysterious through patches of fog. Ángel whispered to me, "Will Pablo come back to Tucson for vacations ever?"

"He'll decide to live with us." My voice sounded defensive. "I'm sure of it. And he'll go to his village on vacations."

"What if he wants to stay with his relatives?"

"Well, then he can. But look at him. He's like a normal American kid now."

"But this is his land," Ángel said. "His *tierra*."

"You left your *tierra* to come to the U.S."

"I didn't want to."

He had papers, I knew, papers that made him and Mr. Lorenzo legal in the U.S. Dika had told me they were legal residents, just like her, since they were all three refugees, fleeing violence in their countries. Dika had gotten her visa before she came, but Ángel and his father came to Tucson first, illegally, crossing the desert. At their court hearing, they had to prove they would be killed if they went back to Guatemala. When I asked Dika how you prove something like that, she said, *They say us when they want to say us.*

"But, Ángel, you live in Tucson now, and you're there to stay, right?"

He didn't answer.

"Ángel, you're at least finishing high school and going to college in the U.S., right?"

He shrugged. "I already made my schedule for next semester. How could I miss calculus?"

Later, at a gas station, while Ángel was filling up the tank, I asked Mr. Lorenzo if they were going to stay in Tucson. Dika pricked up her ears. "Of course they stay in Tucson!" she said.

"Of course," Mr. Lorenzo said, patting Dika's hand. He switched to Spanish. "We have jobs and Ángel has school.

And there is too much violence still in our town. Even now that there is no war, there are still weapons, and still anger. No, we will stay in Tucson. There is nothing for us in our town."

"Except for your wife's jewels," I said.

"Yes. Except for her jewels."

"Life is a long, long car ride," I said to Ángel that evening as we wound up a mountain, past shacks selling fruit and sodas and beer. We sat in the backseat with Pablo, who was wedged between us, asleep.

"Headed where?"

"I don't know. Death?"

"What do you know about death?" Ángel looked serious.

"I don't know." I laughed. I'd meant the comment as something lighthearted. "I'm still in the car ride part." I didn't say anything about all the times I'd convinced myself I was on the verge of death.

"What do you know about life, then?"

"Not much. Waiting."

"For what?"

"School to end, school to start, to go to college, get a job." To be in love, I thought. To have sex. To stop being scared.

Ángel peered out the window into the growing darkness, where the roadside dropped off steeply, a nearly vertical fall to the valley below. I couldn't look. It made me dizzy and nervous to think that with one slip, our van could tumble over the cliff and smash at the bottom. All of us dead within seconds.

"When I think of life," Ángel said, "I think of us all hanging by these ropes, feeling we're safe. But really, we could slip out any time. None of our ropes are safe—that's what I realized. That coffee-picking season, my bruises and scrapes healed up, and I went back to the coffee fields. This time my father tied the rope so tight it burned. I should have been scared, but I wasn't. I loved it more then. I loved the way the berries tasted in my mouth, kind of sweet and slimy. I loved the sound of people singing and joking around while we picked."

"I wouldn't have done that," I said. "I wouldn't want to even look at the mountainside again."

"Maybe. Or maybe not. Maybe life would taste sweeter."

Ángel said he was born in the Mayan village where his mother grew up. A midwife delivered him at home, and after she cleaned and swaddled him, she told his parents, "Your son will travel far and do great things." I wished someone had said that about me. A gem of knowledge to carry around in my pocket, to hold on to when panic welled up. I would step into elevators bravely, without a thought of the doors failing to open and being stuck inside for a week without food or water and dying alone. I would look people in the eye and move with confidence. That was how Ángel walked and talked. He had this clear stone inside him, so solid, this prediction that he would be great.

If Ángel had a gem at his center, what I had inside was a sharp, rusted piece of metal, like the rotting tailpipe on the ancient, beat-up car Mom had when I was little. Whenever it broke down, she had to find someone to give us a ride to get my allergy shots, which was hard when our phone was disconnected. Mom just bumbled around the neighborhood smiling, knocking on doors, asking for a ride, saying it would all work out, thanking everyone in her charming British accent. "Cheers! You're brilliant!" Meanwhile I worried so much that my stomach ached and then she'd have to take off work and lose that day's wages. And then my stomach ached even more, as though that shard of metal were digging itself farther and farther inside me.

The third night we slept in the van again, on the side of a dirt road just off Route 15. At some point in the night, Pablo crawled into bed between me and Dika. His head nuzzled into my neck. Light streamed through the window. Moonlight, it must have been, although I couldn't see the actual moon from my angle. His small hands were tucked up under his chin. Was he anxious about going back to his village? I stroked his hair. It was fine, so fine, so soft. I buried my nose in it.

"*Mi abuelita te puede curar*, Sophie." Pablo's voice was thin and small, like a newly planted seedling.

I opened my eyes and looked at him.

"What? Your grandmother can cure me?"

"*Sí.*" He looked at me. His eyes looked very old for a six-year-old's, enough to make you believe in reincarnation. He could have been a wise old monk in a past life.

I spoke to him in Spanish. "*¿De veras?* Really? Cure me of what? My allergies?" My fears? My curse?

He nodded. "*Todo.*"

He wound a strand of my hair around his finger, rubbed it against his cheek.

"That would be nice, *principito.*"

Someone shifted in the bunk over us.

Maybe Ángel was awake too. I pictured him curled around his locked box, smoothing the wood the way a child smoothes the satin edge of a blanket. I considered giving him a sign—clearing my throat, coughing, lightly whistling—but then I flushed at the thought, forced myself to close my eyes, and made my breathing match Pablo's. Eventually I slept.

8

Picnic with a Cop

The next afternoon, on the fourth day, a huge storm left the sky streaked with orange and yellow, the clouds glowing like gates to heaven. Ángel was driving, speeding along, winding around hills, past a huge lake and cornfields. It was probably hard to resist speeding, since there were no cars or houses or people on this stretch, and we had only one day of driving left. Suddenly red and blue flashing lights appeared behind us.

Cops. My stomach jumped. Juan had said cops here were corrupt; they would threaten to arrest you, take your license, demand hundreds of dollars to get it back. *Never get into a car with a cop,* he'd said. *You don't know where they might take you, what they might do.* Mom had told us a dozen times, *Don't speed, promise me you won't speed.*

I remembered Ángel's box. Chances were whatever he

had inside was either valuable or illegal. Either way, we'd be in trouble if the cop found it. I leaned over between the front seats to check if it was hidden. But Ángel was already moving his feet against the bottom edge of his seat, making sure the box was safely stashed. He looked terrified.

I imagined us rotting in a dungeon cell with only amoeba-infested water to drink and no limes to squeeze over unsanitarily prepared morsels of food. My head felt hot and prickly.

This is it. I'm going to die. This time, I'm really going to die. Either I'll die in prison or I'll just pass out right now and never regain consciousness and we're probably hours from a hospital and even if we made it to a hospital it would probably be unhygienic. Oh, God, this is it.

Dika patted Ángel's knee. "Don't worry, Ángel, it is okay."

In the side mirrors we watched the cop swagger toward us, one slow step at a time. He looked around, over the fields, as he walked, and saw what we saw: that this place was deserted except for a few falling-down shacks in the distance. Finally his head appeared at the driver's side window. He was a young cop with baby-smooth skin, not much older than me and Ángel. Before he could say anything, Dika leaned across Ángel, smushing her giant bosom in his lap, and began talking loudly in Spanish.

"Oh, *m'hijo,* you're just in time for our picnic. We're having roasted chicken and tortillas and fruitcake. Come join us! Watch the beautiful sky with us and share our food."

Before he could answer, she flung open the side door, climbed down clutching a bag of food, and spread a blanket in a dusty clearing next to the road. "Son, go turn off those lights and come have a picnic. You must be hungry."

He obeyed. Maybe he had a bossy mother who'd trained him well. Or maybe he was bored. "You are too kind, *señora,*" he said when he returned. He stood by the blanket, grinning.

Meanwhile, the rest of us climbed out of the van, keeping our mouths shut. Mr. Lorenzo was dripping with sweat. Ángel left the box under the seat. Outside, he positioned himself so that he could keep a close eye on the van. I clutched Pablo's hand and whispered, "It'll be okay, *principito,*" more to calm myself than Pablo, who was just watching everything curiously.

"Sit down," Dika commanded. "Sophie, Ángel, sit down and eat. Pablito, you like the drumsticks best, don't you? Now what about you, son, what's your name?"

"Jorge."

"Jorge, what would you like? A thigh?" She slapped her thigh. "A breast?" She gave a bawdy laugh.

I flushed.

Embarrassed, he said, "Anything is fine, *señora.*"

Dika dug her fingers into the chicken and tore out a chunk of breast meat. She arranged it in a tortilla, sliced open an avocado, scooped out green flesh with her slimy chicken hands. Then she cut up a tomato, threw a few slices in, and handed the taco to the cop. "And here's salsa, *mi amor.* Use as much as you like."

She made tacos for the rest of us and handed them out.

My panic subsided, and my hands stopped shaking enough to drench my chicken with lime.

"Would you squeeze some of that on mine, please, *señorita*?" the cop asked me.

I leaned over and squeezed some on his chicken.

"You like lime, eh?"

I nodded and smiled, embarrassed. I waited for Ángel to make a lime-girl comment.

But he kept his eyes cast down, on his food. Once in a while, he glanced at the van, where his box sat hidden in the shadows under the seat.

"Look at that sky, Jorge!" Dika said. "What a good job you have, driving around all the time. What a beautiful land you live in!"

Jorge relaxed after a warm Corona. He grew talkative and told us about his childhood. He'd grown up in the town where we'd bought the chicken. He felt it was a good omen that we'd stopped at Pollo Crispy because his parents owned the place. Plus, he was hungry since he'd skipped lunch—he was covering the shift of a sick cop. Our picnic invitation was a miracle, he said. He reclined on his elbows, working on his second beer. He stared at me. I felt conscious of the way I was chewing the chicken.

"What's your name?" he asked.

"Sophie," I said. He didn't ask anyone else's name.

"Look, Sophie, do you see the form of *la Virgen* in the sky? Do you see it?"

"Sort of," I said. I had no idea what he was talking about. "Oh, there it is," I lied. I didn't want to disappoint him. When you're used to guys ignoring you, and suddenly someone—an older guy, in a uniform at that—is flirting with you, it's hard not to go along.

"I see it! I see it!" Dika shouted. "There she is, in that cloud!"

"I should thank her for giving me the opportunity to meet you." He used the singular, informal form of *you.* To meet me, just me.

"What color are your eyes, Sophie?"

I shrugged. "Gray?"

"They're blue!" Dika said. "Blue!" She wanted to get in the conversation. "Here, have some fruitcake!"

"I can see the light coming through the sides," he whispered. "Like glass marbles."

I blushed. Jasmín might have called him a slimeball, but she was used to guys hitting on her. She had that luxury. Out of the corner of my eye I saw Dika smile mischievously. Her plan was working out even better than expected.

I snuck a look at Ángel. His sunglasses hid his eyes, so it was hard to read his face. His fingers, though, were nervous, rubbing the pendants around his neck, bringing them up to his lips. Mr. Lorenzo was sweating like crazy, mopping his forehead with a faded red handkerchief. The thick flannel shirt wasn't helping.

"Let me see," Pablo said, coming closer to me, examining my eyes from all angles.

The cop ruffled Pablo's hair and drained the last few drops of his second beer. "I have to go now. But on your way back, you're welcome to stay at my house. Do you have a pen, Sophie?"

I went to the van and pulled out a pen and paper from the glove compartment, conscious of his eyes on my back as I walked, as I bent over to reach inside the window. He came over to the van and stood next to me, so close his flowery cologne made my nose itch.

"Here." I handed him the pen and paper.

He wrote his name and number in curly script, then folded the paper carefully and handed it to me. He stepped even closer and looked pointedly into my eyes. "Call me."

I gave a smile as if we shared a secret, the kind of smile I'd seen girls give to guys in the hallway, saying goodbye before the bell rang and the next class started. Kind of tilting my head down but my eyes up. The soppy way he looked back at me made it clear that the last thing on his mind was throwing us in jail.

He shook hands with everyone. Ángel and Mr. Lorenzo kept their eyes down and forced polite smiles.

And then the cop drove off in a cloud of dust.

"Well," said Dika, stuffing a piece of fruitcake into her mouth. "No ticket."

"Impresionante," Mr. Lorenzo said. He smiled and wiped off the last remnants of sweat with his handkerchief. *"Muy impresionante, señoritas."*

I laughed. It *was* impressive. And kind of fun. There was something I could learn from Dika. Just when you're sure you'll end up in an unhygienic dungeon, you figure out how to turn the situation on its head. For a moment I caught a glimpse of how life could be if the sharks turned out to be dolphins. If fear went out like the tide and confidence rushed in to fill its place. If I believed that my bony elbows actually *were* nice, that maybe there *was* a shiny stone of greatness buried somewhere inside me.

Back in the van, Ángel picked up his box and ran his hands over it, as if relieved it hadn't grown legs and run away. He let out a long breath and slouched down in the front seat. "Saved again by a woman. Two women."

That evening we all wanted showers, except for Pablo, who didn't have his bath toys, so what fun would it be? In the next town, we stopped at a motel—a low building with peeling blue paint and bars on the windows. When we opened the door, shiny cockroaches skittered across the tiles and disappeared into holes in the walls. The beds were metal, painted to look like wood grain, and covered in fuzzy mud-colored blankets with beige peacock designs. Across from the beds stood a wardrobe of lacquered plywood that looked as if it could collapse at any moment.

I volunteered to shower first while Dika and Mr. Lorenzo walked to a corner grocery store to stock up on bottled water and salty peanuts. Ángel and Pablo played outside in the parking lot with a tiny, superbouncy rubber ball. The shower was tiled with cracked green porcelain and had only one faucet, for cold water. A foul odor rose from the drain—probably a dead rat or a heap of cockroaches, I guessed. Luckily I had flip-flops to wear in the shower to avoid picking up fungus.

I stepped under the shower spray, my lips pressed together tightly to keep out amoebas. At first, the shock of water was so cold it made me shudder and almost jump right out. But my urge to be clean won. With frigid fingers, I rubbed soap over my pale, purple-tinged skin and shampooed and conditioned as fast as I could. After a few minutes of pain, my body got used to the cold, until it actually felt kind of refreshing, like a snow cone on a hot day.

I brushed my teeth with bottled water, then wondered if I should leave the toothbrush sitting out so that the bristles could dry, which would reduce the germs on one hand, but on the other hand, cockroaches might crawl over it. Then there was always the risk that Dika would pick up my toothbrush and use it on her own tartared teeth. She seemed to feel that sharing toothbrushes was as harmless as sharing hairbrushes, so I always put mine out of sight. I shook it out as best I could and then hid it in my toiletry bag.

Pablo's laughs and shouts floated in through the window. A few days ago, he barely smiled, but now, he couldn't contain his joy over a simple game of bouncy ball. I got dressed and called to him. "Time for your shower!" He ran inside, flushed and breathless from chasing the ball. I pulled the blue T-shirt over his head, revealing his bony shoulders, little barrel chest, slight potbelly. He climbed out of his pants and stood naked on his knobby-kneed stick legs. I made him wear my flip-flops, which were two times the size of his feet.

"*Gracias,* Sophie!" he said, still wound up.

"See, you get to wear grown-up flip-flops in a grown-up shower now," I said.

He stepped under the dribbling water and squeaked, "Cooooooooooooollllldddd!" He shivered and smiled and chattered his teeth, animated as a zany cartoon character.

Goose bumps sprang up, and he looked like a little brownish blue package of skin and bones. What if his grandmother thought he was too skinny? That we hadn't fed him well enough? What if she wouldn't let him come back with us?

"Sophie?" Pablo said. His lips were the color of blueberries.

"Yeah, *principito*?"

He spoke in Spanish. "Why's the water so cold?"

I answered in English. I didn't want him forgetting all the English he'd learned. "Maybe 'cause we're in a poorer country," I said. "It costs money to heat up water."

"Sophie?"

"Yeah?"

"Why are there peacocks on the blankets?"

"Probably the blanket-maker guy thought they looked nice. Maybe he always wanted a pet peacock."

"Sophie?"

With the kids I babysat, the question game drove me crazy and I just zoned out and mumbled, "I don't know." But with Pablo, it was a rare treat. "Yeah, Pablito?"

"Will my grandma know who I am?"

"What?" I stopped lathering the suds and stared. "Of course."

"But I'm big now, and I used to be little."

"Grandmas don't forget what their grandkids look like. Ever." I rubbed the shampoo into his hair.

There was a knock at the door. It was Ángel, wanting to come in and wash his hands. "Hey, little man," he said to Pablo. "You look purple."

"Ángel?"

"¿Sí, señor?"

"I'm not a *señor.*"

"Sure you are. A little *señor.*"

"Ángel. You think my grandma will know who I am?"

"Of course. But, if I fix your hair like this . . ." He reached over and smoothed Pablo's hair straight up into a foamy mohawk. "Now she won't recognize you. She'll think you're a rock star. She'll be real happy a rock star's visiting her."

Pablo giggled. I wanted to hug him right then and it wouldn't have mattered if I got soap and cold water all over my clothes. I rinsed him off, and then Ángel wrapped him up in a clean towel and carried him to the bed. "See? You're like a burrito now."

We dressed him in his pajamas, and then he wanted to be a burrito again, so we wound the peacock blanket around him. "Sophie?" he asked.

"Yeah?"

"Can you read to me and Ángel?"

Ángel smiled. "Pleeeeeease?"

I picked out a few poems from my e. e. cummings book. He was a poet who didn't like to use capitals or correct punctuation, and he tossed around parentheses like dashes of cinnamon and nutmeg. His poems didn't make much sense the first time I read them, but then later I'd notice some of the lines flitting through my head, pieces of dreams. I figured that even if my brain didn't get the poem, some other part of me was soaking it up.

here is the deepest secret nobody knows
(here is the root of the root and the bud of the bud
and the sky of the sky of a tree called life;which grows
higher than soul can hope or mind can hide)
and this is the wonder that's keeping the stars apart

i carry your heart(i carry it in my heart)

Pablo looked thoughtful, wrapped in the peacock blanket. He turned his head and said, "Ángel?"

"*¿Sí, señor?*"

"What's in your box?"

"It's—" He stopped and laughed. "You're sneaky. You almost had me." He grinned at me. "Not telling."

Pablo looked at me, as though I could convince Ángel somehow. I shrugged. Pablo motioned to me to come closer. I bent over, moved my face close to his. "Sophie," he whispered loudly in my ear. "You think his mom's heart's in the box?"

At first I wrinkled up my nose, thinking of a real human heart, blood and vessels and muscle, slimy blue and red, pumping blood from nowhere to nowhere. Then I realized it was a twist on the poem. *i carry your heart in my heart.*

I glanced at Ángel. Any trace of a smile had drained from his face. He got off the bed, took the box from his backpack, and wrapped it in two plastic bags. Then he carried it into the bathroom with him and closed the door. Soon the patter of shower spray started.

"Maybe you're right, *principito,*" I said. "Maybe that's what's in his box."

PART 3

INTO THE UNKNOWN

And I realized I couldn't bear the thought of never hearing that laugh again. For me it was like a spring of fresh water in the desert.

"Little fellow, I want to hear you laugh again."

—The Little Prince

9

Sparkles in the Virgin's Hair

The fifth day, we snaked through the mountains and passed through woods and huge fields where cows and goats grazed. Gradually, the cement houses grew closer together, and the air thickened with smog, and we officially entered Mexico City, dense with people and cars and buildings, everything tinted gray. Clouds of black exhaust oozed through our open windows and made me cough so much I was sure an asthma attack would kill me. I insisted we roll up the windows, which meant we were all sweating like pigs. Mr. Lorenzo drove carefully, hunched over the wheel, wiping his forehead as taxis cut us off and horns blared.

Once we left the city, relieved, we rolled down the windows and let in the dry air, the smells of trash burning at the roadside. We wound around low hills of scrub brush and cacti until late that afternoon, when we saw the sign for Huajuapan, the town closest to Pablo's village.

"Ha-WHAT-pan?" Dika cried. She squinted at the map, holding it at arm's length. She refused to wear reading glasses. She said they made her feel like an old lady when in her heart she felt sixteen.

"Wa-HWA-pan," Pablo said.

Dika ordered us to say it ten times so that we would remember what town we were in. At first I rolled my eyes and ignored her, but after the fourth *wa-HWA-pan,* Pablo collapsed into a fit of uncontrollable giggles and I couldn't resist joining in. Ángel didn't participate. He'd been unusually quiet since the motel.

At the gas station on the outskirts of Huajuapan, two men told us the road to Santa María Nuquimi, Pablo's village, was closed because of mudslides. This was a common occurrence in the mountains in rainy season, they assured us, and in a couple of days the road would be clear. They suggested we stay in Huajuapan, since we'd arrived smack in the middle of the yearly weeklong festival for *El Señor de los Corazones,* the dark-skinned Jesus, patron saint of the city. Pablo's relatives weren't expecting us for two more days, and it would be only a two-hour drive to his village, so we decided to stay.

It seemed like a pleasant town, not too big, not too polluted, with neat rows of low, pastel-painted stores and houses. Women in checked aprons and long braids were selling pyramids of mangoes on the sidewalk. On every street corner, neighbors and shopkeepers were chatting, some leaning on brooms or mops. We splurged on a hotel on the main street with a courtyard bursting with flowers and fruit trees, and a pet parrot. All this lush color felt like a drink of cool water.

We waited in the courtyard with our bags while Mr. Lorenzo paid and got the keys. Dika and Pablo made a beeline to the parrot and offered it bits of banana leaves. It turned its nose up at the leaves, but seemed somewhat interested in the squawking noises Dika made.

A line of ants toting pieces of neon pink flower petals crossed the concrete patio, meandered around the legs of white plastic chairs and tables, and disappeared into bushes at the base of a lime tree. Ángel had to have a dozen lime-girl jokes going through his head right now, but he kept his mouth closed, his lips pressed firm. Something was going on with him, and I couldn't figure out what.

Two girls about Pablo's age were making a show of wiping down the tables, but mainly whispering and giggling and staring at us. One of the girls took a breath and asked me in Spanish, as if on a dare, "Why is your hair yellow? Do you dye it?"

"No," I said. To deflect attention from my hair, I added, "But my great-aunt does," and nodded toward Dika.

"Ha!" Dika grabbed my arm and pulled me close. She whispered theatrically, "Why you tell my beauty secrets? Eh?"

"It's not exactly a secret. Look at your roots."

"Shhh! What if my boyfriend hears you say this?"

I laughed.

"Hmph!" Dika said. "Those girls, they think you are funny with your yellow hair."

"Funny?" I said. Why could I joke around with Dika

about *her* hair, but the second my hair's turn came, my stomach knotted up and I thought, Yes, I am ugly. "What's funny about it?" I asked, hurt. "Am I ugly, Pablo?"

Ángel looked at me and opened his mouth to say something, then shut it again.

Pablo said, "You're the most prettiest girl on the world."

"Thank you, little brother." I'd never called him "brother" before.

He slipped his hand in mine. "I want tacos for dinner."

I squeezed his small hand. "Then tacos you'll have, *principito*."

After we dumped our bags in the rooms, we looked for a place to eat tacos. It was dusk, and lights were starting to turn on. We found a tiny restaurant that looked welcoming. COMEDOR HERMELINDA—Hermelinda's Eatery—was neatly stenciled in red paint over the entrance, which was essentially a garage door. One whole wall of the restaurant was open to the street, the way most of the other restaurants here seemed to be. The TV in the corner blared a comedy show with slapstick skits that the customers loved. A few bare lightbulbs dangled from the ceiling and cast a stark light that somehow felt cozy because of all the people talking and laughing. Imagine if your neighbor stuck some tables and a TV in his garage and squeezed everyone on the street in there for an impromptu party.

"Ahhh! Look!" Dika cried. "Only places for three people at this table!"

"Pablo and I can sit at this other table," I said.

"Oh, no! Pablo sits here with Mr. Lorenzo and me! I must to help him select the food."

Dika was playing matchmaker again, which was fine with me, since I was obviously bumbling my way through whatever this thing with Ángel was. It seemed as if he'd crawled into his box and locked himself up with whatever was in there.

I sat down at a table and he sat across from me, setting his box down between us. Ángel ordered three tacos and a Corona with lime. I ordered the same, glancing at Dika and Mr. Lorenzo to see if they'd noticed the beer part, but they didn't seem to care. Corona was Mom and Juan's beer of choice. Sometimes during their parties, I'd sneak a bottle and lie on the hammock and watch people laughing and talking as though they were on-screen, on a TV show with sets and lights, while I was hidden backstage.

The waitress set down our Coronas, and after the first sip, I didn't think I'd be able to finish it. The beer was warm and flat, maybe due to limited fridge space, or maybe the people here liked it that way.

Ángel wasn't talking, so I looked around the room, feeling awkward. An altar to the Virgin of Juquila—Oaxaca's special Virgin, Pablo had told us—hung on the wall above our heads. Multicolored Christmas lights surrounded her, gold tassels dripped from her shiny gown, glitter sparkled in her hair, and her crown shot out gold rays with stars perched on the ends. It made me think of the lady who had saved Ángel when he fell down the ravine. Even if I didn't have any magical ladies looking out for me, I appreciated that he did, that *someone* in this world did, that maybe there was hope for me yet. I wondered what his magical lady thought of me, whether she was rooting for me.

Ángel put his extra lime slices on my plate, a small, silent present. I watched his hands and remembered how they felt braiding my hair. Heat gathered in the center of my body and spread out. I wanted him to braid my hair again. When he'd braided it, for the first time it hadn't felt dry and thick and frizzy. It felt worshiped and full of sparkles and stars, like the Virgin's hair.

We ate without talking much at first, just a few comments about the mysterious spice in the beans, ginger or cloves, something you'd normally find in Christmas cookies. Alone, without Pablo, I couldn't think of anything to say. This was like a date. Almost. A date with a bleached-orange-haired chaperone at the next table over who periodically sent us disapproving glances. Once she called over, "You childrens have good conversation, no?"

Dessert came free with the meal. They called it *gelatina*, which sounded classier than what it really was—red Jell-O in a clear plastic cup. I looked at it closely to make sure there were no flies or roaches in there. Little ripples and bubbles were caught inside like a frozen lake. Some light bounced off the surface and some light sank in, and for a second I saw a whole world inside the cup of Jell-O. Maybe that was what Dika saw in her red glass, a distant world of light and joy.

"Hey, lime-girl. You gonna put lime on that *gelatina*?" Ángel said. " 'Cause I have another extra one." He gave me a weak smile, as though he was making a big effort. I heard that if you smile even if you don't feel like it, you might trick yourself into being happy.

"No thanks." I dug my spoon in and slurped it up and felt it dissolve on my tongue. Then I took a deep breath and said, "You're quiet."

"So are you."

"But I'm always quiet," I said.

"Are you?"

"Come on, Ángel. What's wrong?"

He tapped his fingers on the wooden box. "Just a lot on my mind."

"Like what?"

I figured he would say something about his mom or the jewels or the box, but instead he said, "Someone like you wouldn't be friends with me in Tucson."

I stuck my spoon into the Jell-O and let it stand there, alert like a dog's tail. "What does that mean—someone like me?" I was truly curious. What would someone like me be like? I'd wondered, of course, how other people saw me. Maybe it would be like when you hear your voice on an answering machine and it doesn't sound anything like how you think you sound. I hoped so. Mostly I figured other people didn't notice me. Other times I thought they noticed me enough to see that my clothes didn't fit right and my hairstyle hadn't changed since I was five, and that I never knew exactly how much to swing my arms when I walked.

Out of the corner of my eye, I saw Dika throw her head back and guffaw. I wondered if she would be surprised at how other people saw her. Probably she wouldn't care. Probably she looked at her reflection in the windows by the pool and saw a curvy sixteen-year-old in a sexy bikini. And who knew, maybe Mr. Lorenzo saw her that way too. Maybe he saw her draped in Christmas lights and gold tassels and glitter.

"Sophie, in wood shop, you never talked to me. You never even learned my name."

I looked into the lenses of his sunglasses, trying to figure out if he was joking. His mouth looked serious, no hint of a smile. "But, Ángel—"

"You only talk to me now 'cause you're stuck with me," he said.

"I didn't think you cared if I knew your name." It had never occurred to me to talk to him. He'd seemed too different, with his long black coat and the heap of gold chains around his neck. If I'd tried to talk to him, I figured that instead of really hearing me, he'd just be noticing how I never got slang right. In English class, we read a book with a passage I underlined that said when it comes to explaining to other people what's deepest and truest and most important to us, each person is trapped in her own tower and everyone speaks a different language, and the only words we share are things like "It's going to rain. Bring an umbrella." How can you express your heart's deepest feelings with words like that?

At the table next to us, Dika and Mr. Lorenzo were holding hands. Her cup of Jell-O was empty. He was feeding her spoonfuls of his own Jell-O and she was giggling and licking the spoon, then licking her lips seductively. Pablo was oblivious. He bounced up and down in his seat yelling "My turn! My turn!" until Mr. Lorenzo gave him a spoonful. If any people were from different towers, it was those three. But they'd found a way to connect. You could almost see little waves of warmth floating between them.

I looked at Ángel. "I'm not stuck with you. You're the one who's stuck with me. You're the cool one, even Pablo can see that. I'm just—" I was going to say "an amoeba," but then he'd think I was hopelessly weird.

"You really don't know, do you?" he said.

"What?"

He smiled. "You have *chispa*, even though you try to hide it."

I have a spark? I flushed. I didn't know what to say.

A shadow passed over his face. "I wish . . ." He didn't finish, just swallowed his last spoonful of Jell-O, looked at his box, and breathed out. The kind of sigh that said it was too late for whatever his wish was.

10

The White Dress

The next day we went to the single tourist attraction in town: ancient ruins of a Mixtec city, complete with temples to climb on. It was a hot, cloudless day, and I'd forgotten my hat. We'd left in the cool green morning before the sun was strong. But within an hour, by the time we reached the top of the hill, the sun was shining relentlessly overhead. I'd forgotten my sunscreen, and my face was already burning. Normally I would have hidden in a little patch of shade, swept up in a panic over skin cancer—all it takes is one bad burn, they say—but Ángel said my cheeks looked pink and nice. "Taste the berries and forget about falling off the cliff," he told me.

We watched Pablo jump from stone to stone, run along walls, up and down steps, breathless, sweating, laughing. A wild thing. All the pent-up energy from a year of sullenness suddenly let loose. Dika and Mr. Lorenzo sat under a gnarled tree looking at the sea of rooftops in the valley, pointing and speculating on our hotel's location.

Ángel and I wove around spiky shrubs toward the temple, and sat on a stone step. There were no shadows here in the center of the ruins. Everything was exposed.

"I don't feel empty anymore," he said. "Like I did last night."

"Good."

He set down the wooden box on his lap and absently ran his fingers over it. "You know, I never feel completely empty," he said. "My mother's always with me." Then he tilted his face to the sun and said, "This place reminds me of dying of thirst. You know what it's like to be dying of thirst?"

Pablo used to stare at the aquarium for hours at night, hypnotized by the sound of gurgling water. I said, "I imagine, sometimes, how Pablo felt."

He nodded. "The third time I almost died was when my dad and I crossed the desert to come to the U.S. The coyote suddenly took off. He left us there. Some people went one way, some another. Me and my dad went off one way, what we thought was north. We ran out of food and water—the coyote had told us it would only take a few hours to cross. But twenty-four hours had passed when he abandoned us. Then another day passed. All I thought about was my mother. I thought of her when my guts were empty, all tied in knots. My tongue was dry and felt huge in my mouth. My lips were cracked and bleeding and when I tried to speak only creaks came out. I thought of my mother and the towels she would put on my head when I had a fever, green scraps of towels that felt cool and wet.

"We passed a little pond. It was dark and murky, with things hidden underneath, hairy plants, green slime. My dad said, 'Don't drink it, *hijo*.' But he couldn't resist. He ran and scooped water into his mouth. 'Don't drink it,' he said. Water was running down his chin, down the front of his shirt. But I drank it anyway. It stank but we didn't care. A minute later, our stomachs were cramping like fists squeezing everything out of us. Vomit poured out of our mouths and we shook, and the whole time I thought of her, watching me, the way she watched me sleep when I was sick. The way the beads on her necklaces clinked together when she leaned over me."

He ran his hands over the box. It made me think of a Buddha's belly, worn smooth from so much praying and rubbing.

We sipped our water bottles, and after a while, I said, "That was the third time you almost died?"

He nodded.

"What about the second?"

"I never talk about the second."

That night, Dika moaned, "*Mein Gott!* My legs fall out if I make one step more!"

Mr. Lorenzo said, "Oh, I need rest too. I am very sleepy."

"So you children go to eat without us," Dika said, eyeing Mr. Lorenzo and smiling, not very subtly.

I felt tired too, my face warm and pink from the sun, not

too burned, just a glowing feeling. I changed into a green fitted shirt, a present from Mom that I'd never worn outside my house before. The shirt had seemed too daring a leap from my usual shapeless amoeba clothes. Tonight I felt bold for some reason. Maybe because I hadn't gotten a sun rash after all. Or because the slimy cop had liked my eyes and asked what color they were. Or because Ángel had said I had *chispa*—spark—even though I wasn't exactly sure what that meant.

Pablo and Ángel and I went off to find some dinner. It was dusk, and yellow streetlamps lit up the zocalo—the main square. The zocalo was full of huge bushes trimmed into shapes of horses bucking and dinosaurs stretching their necks and long wavy snakes. It gave me an Alice in Wonderland feeling.

Around us, people were strolling arm in arm, not worried about getting anywhere, just happy making slow circles around the zocalo. Vendors in palm hats pushed carts selling ice cream and popcorn. Boys offered shoe shines and three tiny packs of *chicles* for one peso. A woman in a red and white woven tunic knelt on a blanket with jewelry displayed in neat rows. A nearby streetlamp bathed her face in light, making her dangly earrings sparkle and the ribbon in her braids shine. The jewelry on her blanket was made of smooth discs of what looked like polished wood, the color of chocolate flecked with caramel. The discs were coconut, the woman told me. "Only ten pesos! *Lléveselo, güerita.*" Take it, white girl.

So I did. I chose a necklace and a bracelet that made me think of beaches lined with palm trees and jungles

Ángel bought Pablo a purple wooden turtle. We decided we'd use chewed-up gum to stick it to the dashboard so that its head would wiggle around as if it were rocking out to the music. For himself, Ángel picked out a gold Virgin of Juquila pendant. The patron Virgin of Oaxaca. *"Muy milagrosa, esta Virgen,"* the woman assured us. Very miraculous, this Virgin.

And then, as we walked away, she called out, "Wait, *güera*!"

I turned.

She held up a white dress. A breeze caught it and filled the skirt and made it float there, a little cloud. "This is perfect for you," she said.

It was fitted cotton with a flared skirt and low neck. White embroidered flowers circled the neck, and more flowers ringed the hem. Usually buying clothes was a long, stressful event that made nervous sweat trickle down my sides. I would try on something while Mom waited, then we'd walk around the mall and I'd think about it while my stomach wrung itself out, then I'd try it on again, and then, back home, I'd try it on once more and feel sick. The problem was, if it made me look like the same old Sophie—lost inside droopy fabric—then I got a little queasy, as though I were looking at slightly moldy three-week-old leftovers in the fridge. But if it made me look how I *wished* I looked, then I'd think, Who am I trying to fool?

The woman held up the dress, and pressed it against my body with her palm. "Perfect, *güera*!" Her face lit up.

I looked at Pablo, who was sprawled on the ground, playing with his purple turtle. "What do you think, *principito*?"

He glanced up at me, his mouth still half open in concentration. "Wow," he said.

Ángel agreed. "Wow." He whistled softly through his teeth. "Buy it, and let's go eat."

I bought the dress, just like a confident, normal person. I wondered: If I act like this enough, will I actually turn into a normal, confident person? Maybe it would happen someday without me realizing it, the way day can turn into night, and after you notice it's dark, you can't exactly pinpoint the moment it changed.

We turned down a side street and passed a cozy-looking place to eat, just a few tables and a grill outside someone's house. Over a square metal fire pit, a giant pot of something steamed. It smelled like chocolate and cinnamon. A little girl stirred the pot with a long spoon, and then ladled white foamy liquid into a paper cup. "*¡Atole!*" Pablo cried, sniffing the air like a puppy. "And *picaditas*!" He bounced up and down and pointed to a grill sizzling with meat and small, thick tortillas sprinkled with guacamole and salsa and crumbly white cheese. Behind the girl, a stout woman in a checked apron smiled at us through the smoke.

"Let's eat here!" Pablo said.

He picked out a table covered with a plastic cloth, the color of a tropical ocean on postcards. We sat down on wooden chairs. Ángel set his box on the table and tapped his finger on the plastic. "This here, this is the color of your eyes, Sophie. Right, Pablo?"

Pablo studied my eyes, then the tablecloth, then my eyes, and finally nodded, serious.

"See," Ángel said, "I would never have to ask what color your eyes are, Sophie."

I didn't know what to say, but at that moment the girl came to our table to take our order. Ángel and I got Coronas with lime and three *picaditas* apiece, and Pablo got two *picaditas* and some *atole*.

While we were waiting, Pablo said, in Spanish, in his most angelic voice, "*Por favorcito*, can I touch your box?"

Ángel made a show as if he were thinking about it, and finally nodded. Pablo brushed his hands along the edge and poked his pinkie finger into the keyhole.

"Can I hold it?"

Ángel moved his head close. "You can shake it."

Pablo picked it up as though it were made of glass.

"But only three times," Ángel said. "And gently."

Pablo held it next to his ear and shook it once. No rattle, no clink, just the soft whisper of something hitting the side. Paper, maybe. He shook it twice more, then laid it back on the table and looked at it, thinking hard.

"Can I open it?" he asked.

Ángel shook his head. "Only I open it. And I won't open it till Guatemala."

"After you come back from Guatemala can we see what's inside?" I asked.

He didn't say anything.

Our food came, and Pablo pounced on it. As we ate, a few curious people stopped by our table, full of questions. "What are you doing all the way down here? Are you from *el Norte*? Do you speak English? How long will you stay? What do you think of our pueblo? I have a brother working in Chicago, a sister in L.A., a son-in-law in Washington," and on and on and on. We got an invitation to two weddings and a fifteen-year-old's birthday party, all of which we declined since we'd be leaving for Pablo's village the next day. Ángel had a second beer, and then I did too, and then Pablo licked the last bits of grease off his fingers and slumped asleep in his seat. The streets grew emptier, and we were the only customers left. We sat in the smoke, talking.

I realized, all of a sudden, that I hadn't squeezed any lime on my *picaditas*, but my stomach felt fine.

After our second beers were done, everyone else had left, and the stout woman and her daughter started to clean up. Ángel picked up Pablo and laid him over his shoulder. "Will you carry my box, Sophie?" he asked, and I felt honored, even though he kept glancing over to make sure I had a good grip. The plastic bag containing my dress was securely looped over my wrist.

On our way back to the hotel, the streets were almost deserted. I felt light as a leaf. The world moved around me like a series of photos: Ángel's arm muscles; Ángel's hand on Pablo's hair; streetlamp reflections in Ángel's sunglasses; the glow on his cheeks; fantastical animal bushes in the background. I tilted my head back and looked at the sky. "Did you know you can buy your own star?"

"Really?"

"I saw an ad once. It's thirty-four ninety-five per star. And you can name it after yourself. You get a certificate and a star chart and everything."

"I'd pick that one," he said, pointing with his chin. "Right over the tip of that church steeple."

"I'd pick the one next to it," I said. "Just to the right."

I looked at Ángel's face, and then, in one swift, impulsive movement, pushed his sunglasses up on his head. He couldn't stop me because his arms were holding Pablo. His face looked naked.

"Ángel, tell me the truth," I said. "Are you staying in Guatemala for good?"

He kept looking at the sky, but I could still see his eyes, how they crinkled around the edges, as if the moonlight were too bright for him.

"I think so, Sophie. I think so."

The sky looked huge, and I thought of how our stars were so tiny and giant at the same time. I felt very melodramatic, like Dika, and inside my head, I asked how one particular star—which until last week used to be like any other star—could suddenly matter so much.

Back in the courtyard, the lights were off in Dika's and my room. "She must be asleep," I whispered to Ángel. I opened the metal door slowly so that it wouldn't clank too much, and Ángel followed me in to put down Pablo. Once our eyes adjusted to the dark, we saw the room was empty. Ángel pulled back the blanket and laid Pablo on the sheets. He unlaced Pablo's shoes and pulled them off gently, then tucked the covers around his neck.

"Where's Dika?" Ángel asked in a low voice. Our heads were close, and I breathed in his skin, which still smelled like sunshine and sweat and dusty stone from earlier today.

"Maybe they went out for food." I wondered if he noticed the warmth of my breath.

"Or maybe . . ." He walked out the door into the courtyard and I followed. The light was on in Mr. Lorenzo's room. The windows were open, the thin curtain over the window blowing in slow motion in the breeze. We glimpsed, through the window, Mr. Lorenzo and Dika, sitting close on the bed. It was as though they were lit up onstage and we were hidden in the wings. They appeared to be getting dressed, leaning over to slip on shoes. Mr. Lorenzo's chest was bare. It looked more solid and compact than I would have expected. Dika wore a cropped spaghetti-strap tank top that exposed thick beige bra straps at her shoulders and rolls of tanned fat hanging over the waist of her white capri pants. Of course, I'd seen her in a bikini, and usually looked away, but now my eyes felt glued to this scene.

Mr. Lorenzo took Dika's neatly folded shawl from a chair and wrapped it around her shoulders. They stared at each other. They looked like creatures from two different species. A sea lion and a basset hound. A hippo and a chipmunk.

Ángel said, "We shouldn't be looking at this."

But I was transfixed. Now Dika was holding out her arm, showing Mr. Lorenzo the inside of her elbow. I knew what they were looking at. Three parallel scars across the inside of her arm.

"Scars from the prison camp," I said.

Ángel was watching them intently now, too.

Mr. Lorenzo moved his thick fingers across the scars,

then pulled Dika's inner arm up to his face and brushed his lips against them. He seemed to be kissing each scar. And then, he turned so that his back was facing her. She moved her face close, then far from it, the same way she squinted at maps. She brushed her fingers, weighted with cheap rhinestone rings, slowly over his shoulders, down the curve of his backbone.

"His scars," Ángel said. "What the soldiers did to him."

"What did they do?" I asked.

He shook his head, said nothing.

Dika put the flannel shirt on Mr. Lorenzo and buttoned it up, starting from the hem.

Ángel shivered. "They tortured him. Burned him with cigarettes. Cut him with knives." His voice cracked. "Look, they're coming out. Pretend we didn't see. Pretend we're talking about something else."

"Like what?"

"Like our stars."

But they barely noticed us as they walked through the courtyard to Dika's room. She gave us a little beauty queen wave and a soft smile. Mr. Lorenzo nodded at us and returned to his room.

Ángel and I stayed outside for a while, talking about distant celestial things. It seemed easier to talk about things hundreds of light-years away.

"I wonder if our stars have planets," he said.

"I wonder if there's life on our planets," I said.

"If there ever was life."

"If there ever will be."

I must have fallen asleep on the plastic patio chair,

because sometime during the night, Ángel woke me up and led me into my room. I sat down on the bed, groggy, and took off my sandals, watching Ángel tiptoe out of the room and shut the door behind him. A few sparks lingered like a comet's tail, then disappeared.

11

Explosions

I woke before dawn the next morning, first jarred by the sound of a firecracker, and then, a moment later, by Dika screaming. She was out of bed, holding Pablo, then leaning over me, grabbing me, pulling my arm, sobbing and ranting in another language.

I struggled to make my mind work, my mouth move.

Another explosion of fireworks.

Dika ran to the doorframe of the bathroom. She crouched down, one hand clutched in a fist in her lap, the other shaking, its fingertips digging into Pablo's arms. "Sophie!" Her voice was high, frantic, and she gestured for me to come.

"Dika, it's okay. It's just—" I stood up to turn on the light, to try to snap her out of this.

With the light on, I saw it. Blood dripping down her

bare arm, turning Pablo's white T-shirt red. I knelt beside her and pried open her fist, which was soaked with blood.

Inside her hand was the piece of red glass. She had been squeezing it tightly, the way a baby clutches a finger. So tightly it gashed open her palm. Her eyes were wide, two terrifying circles.

I put my arm around her shoulders. Her whole body shook.

"Dika, you're okay," I said. "I'm here. It's okay."

And then our eyes connected and it was as though she'd come back into her body. Her expression now was pure confusion. "The bombs? The guns? What happens, Sophie?"

"It was just fireworks, Dika."

Mr. Lorenzo was at the door, banging on the metal. "Dika! Dika!"

I opened the door with bloody hands. He ran to her and sank beside her on the floor and held her. He rocked her and held her bloody hand and spoke to her in Spanish, murmuring like a father to a child. *"Chchch, tranquila, tranquila."*

In the bathroom I wet a washcloth and wiped the blood off her hands. I examined her palm. There were three jagged cuts, but they looked shallow, with the blood slowly oozing. I wrapped a clean towel around her hand. Meanwhile, Mr. Lorenzo was holding her, pressing her face to his flannel shirt, murmuring and stroking her shoulder.

She'd loosened her grip on Pablo enough that he squirmed away. He had tears too, silently flowing. I sat with him on the bed and rocked him the way Mr. Lorenzo was rocking Dika and whispered to him in Spanish.

"Just fireworks, *principito,*" I said. "For the town fair. They just scared Dika, that's all. Just fireworks." Once Pablo stopped crying, I took off his white shirt, wiped Dika's blood away, and put a clean blue sweatshirt over his head.

Ángel appeared in the doorway in loose basketball shorts and a T-shirt and his black leather coat that skimmed his ankles like a robe. "Dad? Sophie?"

I led Pablo to the door, and on the way out, took Ángel's hand. "Let's go, Ángel." We went out into the cool air of the courtyard. I was wearing my white nightgown, the same one Ángel had seen me in that morning when I'd had chicken feathers in my hair.

"It's okay," I whispered to him, trying to convince myself as much as him. "She's upset. Not badly hurt. Your dad will take care of her."

"What happened?"

"They bombed her house in the war. She must have thought the fireworks were bombs."

Once, she'd showed me a picture of what her house used to look like. It was old and big, three stories high, with stained glass windows. The backyard was shaded with trees and bushes, and in the sunny spots, flowers and grapevines. In the picture, she was sitting at a picnic table full of people laughing and raising their glasses in a toast. "One day, we eat and drink together," she had said. "Next day, they steal things, kill families, burn houses. Everything kaput."

"Her house is gone now, Ángel." Goose bumps sprang up on my arms. It was barely dawn, half-light, before things completely took on their daytime shapes, their clear boundaries, when hidden layers lay exposed.

Ángel said, "She's an amazing lady, isn't she? To be able to leave everything behind and start a new life."

"You and your dad did," I said. I remembered what he'd said the night before about his father's scars.

"I don't know." He looked at the ground, at a line of ants. "Maybe my dad did."

Pablo squatted by the ants, following their path around the patio, to the base of a flowering tree.

"Why did the soldiers hurt your dad?" I asked. "What happened to your mom?"

He shook his head.

"Tell me, Ángel."

"Sophie, you don't want to know these things."

I looked down at spots of Dika's dried blood on my knuckles. For once, I wasn't worried about AIDS or hepatitis B or C. Fretting about germs multiplying on a toothbrush seemed ridiculous compared to what Dika or Mr. Lorenzo had been through.

"I do want to know, Ángel."

He took off his coat and put it around my shoulders. "Here. You're cold."

The leather was lined with a soft fabric that held a hint of his smell. Pablo slipped inside the coat and leaned his head against my waist.

Ángel had left his sunglasses in his room. Through the dim blue air I could see his eyes. They were shinier than most people's eyes, and I couldn't tell if it was because of held-back tears or if they were naturally that way.

. . .

After we'd been sitting together in silence, I noticed the sound of trucks idling outside on the street, and voices. There was more commotion than you'd expect for six a.m. We peered outside the iron gate.

Dozens of people knelt, all the way up and down the street, pouring buckets of colored powder over stencils on the pavement. Very carefully, they sifted patterns through cardboard cutouts. Then they lifted the stencils to reveal perfect flowers and moons and stars and Virgins and crosses and hearts and birds. They worked intently and quickly. Back in Tucson, one of Mom's artist friends had a painting of women in a tower, hard at work weaving the world into existence. Now, waking up before dawn, I had the feeling we'd caught them in the act.

A girl my age, covered with green and purple powder, spotted us watching and nodded. "*Buenos días.*"

"*Buenos días, señorita,*" Ángel said. "Excuse me. What is it you're doing?"

"Decorating the streets with colored sawdust."

"Why?"

"For the parade!"

Pablo wanted to watch, so we dragged two plastic lawn chairs from the patio to the sidewall and watched the pictures take form and color as the air grew warmer and the light changed from purple to lemony white. Pablo fell asleep in my lap and when his weight made my leg numb, I moved him to Ángel's lap. Ángel closed his eyes and pressed his nose to Pablo's hair and breathed in the little-boy smell. I smiled at the sight, as if we were married and

Pablo was our son. Imagining this made my chest tingly at first, and then achy.

Another firework sounded, and I jumped and hoped Mr. Lorenzo was holding Dika tight.

"You think they'll get married, Ángel?" I asked.

"My dad's crazy about Dika." He opened his mouth to say something else, and then closed it.

"What?"

"Nothing. Just—" He paused. "I want her to be happy."

I nodded. A few weeks ago, I would have asked why on earth anyone would marry Dika without a gun at their heads. But now I wondered if her zaniness was a veneer for something tender and real. It reminded me of our door-frames, which used to be painted in a seventies palette of pea green and rust orange and dead-leaf brown—until Juan scraped the paint off. Underneath was solid maple that he sanded and polished until it was so pretty and smooth I couldn't resist running my hand over it whenever I walked through.

In the weeks before our trip, Mr. Lorenzo would sometimes walk with Dika to the Salvation Army. That was her glass-collecting time. One day, out of curiosity, I followed them.

All business, Dika tromped down the streets carrying a plastic grocery bag. Mr. Lorenzo walked beside her in his flannel shirt. When Dika spotted a good piece, she bent down like an aging geologist and held it to the light, examining it, and offering it to Mr. Lorenzo. He admired the glass too, and sometimes ventured to pick up a piece himself. Once he found a red piece and spent about five straight minutes looking through it, tilting it this way and that, his eye only millimeters from the glass. Then he put down the glass and looked at her. I studied her too, and saw a large sixty-year-old body with tanned cellulite and orangish blond hair with an inch of gray-black roots showing. But the look on Mr. Lorenzo's face said he saw something else, a goddess, saturated with colored light.

We watched the artists' slow progress down the street. Right in front of our hotel they'd made a dove inside a circle of flowers. Now, farther down the street, they were making a picture of the Virgin of Guadalupe in her starry cape on a sliver of moon.

The sun was peeking behind a building now, illuminating the walls across the street, each painted different colors. Deep red, mustard yellow, lavender, candy pink. Next to the rainbows of sawdust paintings, so many colors were almost dizzying.

After Dika's house was bombed, she stayed for a little while in the rubble—minutes or hours or days, I couldn't tell, because she was crying as she spoke, and it didn't seem right to ask questions. She shuffled and sorted through the debris, picking out pieces of green crystal wineglasses, sharp bits of vases, amber and violet, crushed wings of a blue glass angel. Some of the glass was smooth, melted in the heat of the explosions, some jagged. Finally, she picked out one shard of red glass, and put it in her pocket.

When I asked Dika why they bombed her house and why they put her in prison, she said, "No reason. No reason. Only the hate." Juan explained what he'd gathered from the asylum paperwork and what he'd read about the war.

Serbian soldiers had rounded up Bosnian Muslims to kill or imprison. Dika didn't practice the religion, but that didn't matter. The Serbian soldiers bombed her house, found Dika in the ruins, and sent her to a prisoners' work camp. After her release, she got political asylum in Germany and worked in a factory there until her visa expired. That's when she called us. Until then, I'd never known she existed.

The day of Dika's phone call—the year before Pablo came—was my fifteenth birthday, in May, just before rainy season, when my allergies were worse than ever and I had to sit on my hands to keep from scratching my red, goopy eyes. We were celebrating, Mom and Juan and me. We sat at the kitchen table, drinking champagne beneath the fan that blew around hot, dry evening air. Mom always found excuses to pop open a bottle of champagne and celebrate life.

The phone call came just after I'd opened my presents—a book of e. e. cummings poetry and a moonstone ring—just as we were about to cut the cake that said *¡Feliz Cumpleaños, Sophie!* I was holding the knife, in the middle of a sneezing fit, getting my inner elbow snotty, when the phone rang.

Mom answered. She listened a few moments and looked confused. "I'm sorry. *Who* is this?" she asked in a few languages before she ended up back with English.

After she hung up, my sneezing fit had stopped, and the cake was cut and put on plates, the blackberry sherbet melting into pools beside it. Mom said, "Looks like my great-aunt will be coming to live with us."

"Who?" Juan and I asked at the same time. Mom hadn't

had any contact with her family since she'd run away over fifteen years earlier.

"I don't know, really. I think she said her name was Rika—or Dika—or Mika or something."

Juan and I looked at each other and then at Mom.

"She's Bosnian." Mom drew out her words, looked out the window, squinting, as if there were a faraway TV screen. "She says she married one of my great uncles in England—met him on a business trip he took to Yugoslavia. They got divorced a few years later. I think I remember her. I think one time she had Christmas supper with us, when I was about your age, Sophie. And we drank bottles of spiced wine and ate loads of cinnamon biscuits together." She bit her thumbnail and stared at the melting purple sherbet. "But that could have been someone else."

At first, Mom figured she had only a vague, slippery memory of Dika because of the champagne, but the next day, she felt just as foggy. Over breakfast, she shrugged and said, "Well, whoever she is, relative or not, she's been through a lot and she needs help." Over the next few days, Mom wrote letters to INS and filled out forms to say she'd sponsor this Bosnian lady. We searched Mom's single worn childhood photo album for a picture of Dika, but found nothing that jogged Mom's memory. In the middle of getting the spare room ready, she suddenly said, "Hey! I think when we were drinking that spiced wine, she told me about her travels. My mum and dad were big worriers, hardly ever left our town. So this lady was refreshing. A free spirit. I think I wanted to be like her, fun and adventurous. . . ." Her voice faded out, lost its confidence. "I think."

Mom couldn't call any of her relatives in England to check up on her alleged great-aunt's story. She had run away from England when she was eighteen with an American guy she met there, a vagrant backpacker who her mother despised. Mom traveled with him to Nepal and Morocco and India, and while they were passing through Tucson on the way to Mexico, she found out she was pregnant with me. They decided to stay in Tucson, at least through the pregnancy. But then my father got busted for dealing acid and took off. Mom decided to raise me alone.

When Dika arrived in the late summer, once the visa papers were in order, all she brought were three bags: one of clothes, one of toiletries, and one of glass, each in its own canvas duffel bag. Bags of newly collected glass filled her closet. Piles of glass were heaped on her dresser, which she'd moved to the center of the room, where it got the most sun. Sometimes I caught glimpses of her in there, sitting in the worn armchair, watching the glass, occasionally holding a piece up to the light, close to her eye. In the prison camp, gazing into her red glass helped her make it through each day. And still, her favorite piece, it seemed, the one closest to her heart, was that original red shard.

What it came down to was this: if she hadn't forced her way into my life, I wouldn't be here now, sitting in the fresh morning air by a street of strange artwork, with Pablo sleeping beside me, and Ángel secretly playing with wisps of my hair and sneaking glances at the top of my nightgown in the shadow between my breasts.

. . .

At midday the sun was blazing and people lined the streets, crowds of people, some carrying umbrellas for shade. There were old women wearing checked aprons and shawls folded on their heads; old men in woven palm hats and stained white button-down shirts and goatskin sandals; little kids in Disney T-shirts holding each other's hands; guys my age with baggy jeans and baseball caps; girls with tight skirts and halter tops. We had no umbrellas, so we pressed ourselves against the wall and waited for the parade and breathed in smells of roasting corn and sizzling meat. In front of us, a sawdust picture of a big white flower spanned the street, and farther on, a swirling medley of animals—foxes, deer, rabbits—filled an intersection.

Earlier, over scrambled eggs and refried beans in the courtyard, Dika had insisted on coming with us to see the parade, even though every few minutes more fireworks exploded. Mr. Lorenzo held her hand the entire time, and with every boom, I saw him squeeze it while her eyes tensed up and beads of sweat broke out above her lip. After each explosion, she wiped her forehead with a handkerchief and said, "Ha! That was not so bad!" and I breathed out in relief.

I held Pablo's hand, and when no one was looking, Ángel would slip his hand into mine for a moment, or I would let my arm graze his, or he would touch me with the excuse of pointing out something and let his hand linger a few beats. The crowd was pushing us into each other and we let it happen. I loved the shade created just for a moment between his arm and mine, his face and my neck, my hair and his hand. And in this space, I could almost forget that he was leaving for good.

The parade came into view, first a big truck with the *moreno* Jesus on it—the dark-skinned Jesus on the cross—*El Señor de los Corazones,* the patron saint of Huajuapan. He had black flowing hair and a red velvet skirt trimmed with golden tassels and covered with *milagros,* silver prayer charms, pinned to the fabric. His skin was deep brown, darker than Pablo's or Ángel's. Women walked behind him, carrying umbrellas for shade, singing a hypnotic song about the Virgin and the Father and the Son, a mournful tune that I knew would be stuck in my head for days.

Then I realized something that gave me chills: The parade was destroying the artwork. But of course it would get destroyed. What had I been thinking? That the people would just push their way through crowds along the sidewalk instead? That the pictures would magically stay there forever?

I turned to Ángel. "They worked so hard on that! It's so beautiful!"

He nodded.

The truck carrying Jesus inched toward us, followed by the women's wobbly, high-pitched song. I tried to soak in the flower and fox and rabbit and deer before the wheels plowed through. After the women passed, children in uniforms marched by, playing earsplitting trumpets and drums. Then people from the sidewalks joined the parade, and children wove around their parents, screaming and laughing and kicking up the sawdust.

My heartbeat quickened; my skin grew prickly, my head dizzy.

At that moment, Pablo slipped his hand out of mine and

disappeared into the crowd. "Pablo!" My voice didn't carry far with all the noise and music. And then I saw him, in the street with the other children, stomping on the colored sawdust, destroying every last trace of the pictures.

"I can't believe they're doing this!"

Ángel spoke calmly. "But I think that's the point, Sophie."

"What?" I felt faint. I took a gulp from my water bottle and tried to keep my eyes glued on Pablo. "To make something incredibly beautiful, and then, before you even get to enjoy it, mess it up?"

He gave me a puzzled look. "What about the memory? You'll have that."

I glared at my reflection in his glasses. "Memory isn't something real. Something you can touch."

"But the memory changes you, right? It makes you a different person."

I looked at him, hard, then grabbed his sunglasses and looked at him even harder. His eyes looked very fragile underneath, very uncertain. My hands shook and my head felt as if it were swarming with insects, and all the people and noises faded and Ángel and I were the only ones there.

"Forget it, Ángel." My words shot out like little bullets. "Go to Guatemala and stay there and forget everything." I threw his glasses on the ground and pushed my way through the crowd, past the ruined sawdust pictures.

At least Pablo won't stay here, I thought; at least he'll come back with us. I scanned the crowd in the street and saw him, jumping up and down on a sawdust flower. In the book, when the Little Prince was about to go back to his star, he told his pilot friend to look at the stars and know that he would be on one of them, laughing. So for the pilot, it would be as though all the stars were laughing. I wondered if one day I'd see a guy in sunglasses with skin nearly the color of the *moreno* Jesus, and instead of crying I'd smile at the memory. Or if one day Dika could think of her house and garden before it was kaput and smile, or if Mr. Lorenzo could think of his wife before whatever happened happened and smile. If we could ever wade through all that sorrow to find a little shard of happiness.

I ran alongside Pablo and cupped my hands around my mouth and yelled, "Let's go, Pablo!" He waved at me, but he didn't come. His sweaty hand had slipped out of mine so easily.

And then, suddenly, Ángel's hand was on my hip and he was turning me around and pressing me to him and whispering, out of breath, "Lime-girl." I felt my breasts against his chest, and I breathed in his soap, the detergent of his T-shirt, the sunshine on his neck. In the middle of all those people, next to the destroyed Virgin on the sliver of moon, with only a few tiny stars left on her cape, I could see why someone would want a moment of complete happiness, even if it wouldn't last. I pressed my lips against his neck and hung on.

The rest of the day passed quickly—a whirlwind of dancers spinning in swirling skirts, mayonnaise-coated corn on the cob, bags of cut-up fruit sprinkled with chile, live band music blasting through giant speakers. We went to bed early, and the next morning, on the way out of town, Mr. Lorenzo and Ángel bought their bus tickets to Tapachula, the border crossing point. Juan and Mom didn't want them driving the van to Guatemala, so the deal was they had to take the bus. They planned to go there next Monday, after a week in Pablo's village, while we stayed on with Pablo's family.

From the bus station, we headed into the mountains, winding up steep, narrow roads. Mr. Lorenzo drove and Dika squealed. "Ohhh!" she cried at every curve. When the rain started, she squeezed her eyes shut, clutching his arm.

For a while, we all laughed at Pablo's purple turtle jiggling on the dashboard. Then that got old, and we looked out the windows. Pablo watched the trees and rock formations, which must have been familiar. He traced raindrops with his fingertip and his head fell against my shoulder.

Ángel pushed open the window, stuck his hand out a moment, and brought it in, dripping wet. He rubbed it on his forehead like a baptismal rite. "Want to know how we got out of the desert?"

Pablo and Dika yelled, "Yes!"

I shrugged. Part of me thought, Why does it matter?

"We ended up wandering in circles, and finally ended up back at the border." He gave an ironic smile. "We crossed back over to Mexico."

Dika shook her head. "You boys! Well, you must to tell us how you cross finally."

Ángel continued. "We decided the Arizona border was too tough. So we took a bus to Chihuahua, near Texas, and we found a coyote. Around ten at night, he takes about fifteen of us on flimsy rafts across the Rio Grande. Man, did that river stink. Then he leads us through scrub brush, and whenever he calls '*¡Suelo!*' we hit the ground like soldiers. We press our faces in the dirt and close our eyes so the *migra* can't see them reflecting the spotlight. Someone must have left their eyes open, or made noise or moved, because we hear the *migra* running toward us, shouting. My dad takes my hand and says, 'Run!'

"Now we're separated from the group. We walk until morning, just me and my dad, following the north star. Once daylight hits, we worry. Our bodies remember how thirsty and hot we were last time. We take little sips of water from our bottles. By night, the water is almost gone, and we've eaten our tamales and fruit. Then we spot train tracks. At that moment, I feel a few fat raindrops. I tilt back my head and open my mouth to them. 'Let's jump on a train, son,' my dad says. We walk along the tracks until we hear a rumble, and then we hide behind some bushes while the first car passes. It's going pretty slow. There are people hanging on to the train, other migrants like us. My father carries me alongside the tracks and then lifts me up. I grab the ladder at the end of a car and hang on. My father runs and leaps up after me.

"Now it's raining harder and the temperature's dropping. I have to hold on with all my might. My hands keep sliding off, and my whole body's shaking and shivering, and it's all I can do to hang on."

Ángel acted it out so convincingly, trembling and convulsing and straining his face, that I could feel the train's vibration, the sting of rain, the cold wind.

I glanced at Mr. Lorenzo. His knuckles were white on the steering wheel, his lips pressed together. Dika had arranged the visor mirror so that she could watch Ángel. For once, she was quiet.

Ángel's hands clutched the seat in front of him so hard the veins stood out. He unclenched them, slowly slid them off. "And when I feel my hands slipping, the woman appears, and she turns into my mother with my mother's hands, warm and rough with calluses, and pressing mine onto the bars."

He put his hand over mine and I felt heat, almost fiery heat, so hot it nearly burned me. I read somewhere that Tibetan monks can raise the temperature of their fingertips sixteen degrees just by meditation.

"The whole night was like this," he said. "The whole night."

After a long silence, Pablo said, "*Mi mamá también.* My mom was with me, too."

I pulled him closer to me. "What do you mean, *principito*?"

He spoke in Spanish in one long rush of words. "She went up to the sky and she had on a white dress and she floated over my head until the police helped me and at night she made me warm, too, and it was just like your mom, Ángel."

Ángel smoothed his hand over Pablo's hair. For a long time, no one said anything. When Pablo's eyelids fluttered closed, and his breathing grew deep and rhythmic, Ángel said softly, "Just like my mom, Pablito. Only the difference is that I never saw her body. There's a chance she's still alive."

His words hung in the van like something you could snatch and stuff back into his mouth.

Dika spun around and stared at Ángel, then at Mr. Lorenzo. I could see a thousand thoughts racing through her mind, but she swallowed her words. Her chest heaved as though she were lifting something heavy, and Mr. Lorenzo put his hand over hers and then she looked out the window with glassy eyes.

Mr. Lorenzo took a deep breath and looked at Ángel in the rearview mirror. "*Hijo*—"

Ángel cut him off. "I know, I know, you think she's dead. But if there's any chance she's alive, no matter how small . . . I have to know the truth. I've been waiting since I was Pablo's age, waiting to find the truth."

PART 4

INSIDE THE WHALE

One runs the risk of weeping a little if one lets oneself create a bond with another.

—The Little Prince

12

Heeheeheeheehee

When we approached the village, Pablo's eyes flickered open. Maybe his sleeping body sensed the curves of a familiar road. We passed rolling mountains spotted with low trees and cacti and cornfields; a river snaking through a valley, a ribbon of dense green; scattered outcrops of rock; sudden cliffs; dried gulches; the sky, huge and dusty blue, only a few far-off clouds.

Pablo pointed out landmarks, his Spanish fast and eager. "*¡Mira!* Those trees there, that's where my mom said the forest *duendes* live."

"*Duendes*?" I asked.

"Like little people. Spirit people. No one can cut the trees there. If they do, the *duendes* will make them crazy. And below that cliff, that's where the *bandolera* lives."

"Who's that?"

"A *señora* who steals bad kids. She has turkey claws for

feet. And *la llorona* lives in that river—she cries and cries because she misses her children. '*Mis hijooooooooooooos* . . . ,' she calls. '*Mis hijoooooooooooooos* . . .' And her children miss her, too, but they can't find her because she's dead."

I glanced around to see if anyone reacted to the dead mother part. No one did, as if there was a silent agreement to say no more about Ángel's mother. To let it slip out the window into the breeze.

The village itself seemed deserted. It even smelled deserted, like old, dried wood, sunbaked stones of crumbling houses, lingering woodsmoke. A few children eyed our van curiously and ran inside to their mothers, who showed up at the doorway and watched us go by. We swerved out of the way of a woman leading a burro packed with firewood, past shacks of chipping pink and blue cement, a church with fresh white and red paint, an empty basketball court. Beyond the buildings, fields of young corn and beans made a patchwork over the hills.

"*¡Mi escuela!*" Pablo cried, pointing at a one-story building painted with white kids playing in a field of flowers. "I remember my first day at school. I didn't want to let go of my mom's hand and then she left and I cried and cried."

We went around a curve and Pablo shouted, "Stop!" and pointed out the window to something on the roadside at the edge of a cornfield. It looked like a heap of filthy clothes. At closer look, it was a very, very old woman, lying on her back on the ground.

"*Mein Gott!*" Dika cried. "This lady, she is dead?"

Mr. Lorenzo screeched the van to a stop and we all

jumped out and ran to the body. I tried to remember CPR from health class. Was it two breaths, then ten pushes on the chest? Or the other way around?

Pablo looked thrilled. "Ñola!" He crouched down, put his hands over her eyes, and said, "*¡Adivina!*" Guess!

"Pablito?" she creaked.

And he took his hands away and grinned. She laughed, an ancient, toothless laugh—"*heeheeheeheehee*"—and ran her hands over his face and then over her own face and then spoke to him in a language I didn't recognize.

"Is she okay?" I asked him.

He answered in Spanish. "Oh, she always does this. She's Ñola. My great-great-grandmother. And sometimes she feels like lying down and so she lies down, but now she doesn't do it in the middle of the road anymore because my mom made her promise to go to the side of the road."

I would like to be able to lie down whenever I felt like it, I thought. When life seemed too hard, to just drop out for a little while.

Mr. Lorenzo helped her up and she looked at each of us, one by one. Ángel held out his hand to her and she laughed, as though it was a big novelty, and touched her hand to his. She turned to me last and stared hard. Her lips curled over her gums matter-of-factly. Age spots speckled her face, a shade darker than the brown. Her skin was wrinkled, like a berry dried in a hundred years of sun. She wore layers of mismatched clothes—a pink dress, blue-checked apron, red cardigan, black shawl over her head, plastic beads and fake pearls and gold chains—saints and Virgins and crosses dangling. Cataracts clouded her eyes, but that made her look at me all the more intensely. She touched my hand with her rough one. *"Heeheeheeheehee!"*

I wondered how it would feel to be so old but not in a nursing home, just given free rein to wander. "*Buenas tardes, señora.* I'm Sophie and this is Ángel."

She nodded and laughed. *"Heeheeheehee!"*

"Ñola is a hundred years old," Pablo said proudly. "She only speaks Mixteco. That's what the old people speak."

Ángel and I put our hands at Ñola's back, and began walking.

Pablo pointed down the road, to a cluster of small houses around a patch of dried grass and dirt. They were shacks, really, some of wood and bamboo, some adobe, some cement. We walked, impossibly slowly, while Dika and Mr. Lorenzo drove the fifty yards.

In front of the houses, as though posed for a picture, was a horde of women and children. Two round young women in aprons, with shoulder-length hair, big cheeks, giant smiles. An older round woman in an apron, her long braids streaked with gray. Three barefoot children, around Pablo's age, staring open-mouthed.

I slipped my hand into Pablo's, possessively, but he pulled away and made a beeline for the older woman, his arms outstretched. *"¡Abuelita!"*

My stomach sank.

She picked him up, actually lifted him in the air. *"¡María Santísima Purísima, m'hijito!"* Her voice was deep and confident and came straight from her soul. With her hands, she made little crosses over his head, his neck, his chest, hugged him, kissed both his cheeks, again and again. She was crying now, and he was laughing and hugging her tight. "*Ay, niño*, how big you are! How big!" After a while she let him go, and the younger women fawned over him. "*Ay, m'hijo*, how handsome! How big!"

And that was when I noticed Ángel next to the van, holding his box like a baby cradled in his arm. A tear slipped out beneath the sunglasses. I was almost sure of it. Then he wiped his cheek and it was gone.

I walked over to him, my arms swinging self-consciously, my hands noticeably empty.

Ángel spoke in a raw voice. "If Pablo stayed in Tucson, he'd forget all this stuff, these people, the stories his mom told him, everything. And years later, if he came back here, maybe it would all come flooding back. And then how would he feel?"

"But we can give him a better life in Tucson. Education and medical care, and—"

"Notice how he started talking about his mom? I think she seems more real to him here. Everything here reminds him of her."

"Yeah," I admitted. "You know, I secretly hoped his relatives didn't love him very much. That they already had enough other kids around that giving one away wouldn't matter. That's terrible, isn't it?"

"It's not terrible. You love him."

We moved closer to the group. The younger women turned shy suddenly, and shook our hands softly, barely touching.

Ceremoniously, the older woman said, "We thank you

for caring for our boy. You have fed him well and given him much love, much *cariño*."

Did this mean they wanted him back now?

"Welcome to our humble home. It is not much, not what you are accustomed to in your country, but it is all we have and now it is your house too. You are welcome here, our house is your house. . . ." The other women piped in and repeated the speech like a song refrain.

Pablo, meanwhile, had run over to two more children who had been hanging back behind a wooden shack. They were touching his shirt, his tennis shoes, his shorts, even his socks with a kind of awed reverence. He led the kids to the van and dug around for the books of stickers we'd brought as gifts, and they ran around sticking stickers everywhere. I wished he'd kept his hand in mine. Holding on to his hand gave me a purpose.

The women ushered us into the cool, dark house and sat us on wooden chairs and served warm Coke in small glasses. Bits of shriveled corncobs and straw poked out from the brown adobe walls. The floor was packed dirt, and the room empty of furniture except for the chairs, a homemade wooden table, and some crates piled in the corner.

The woman Pablo had run to first, the one he called Abuelita, was his grandmother, the mother of his father. She was younger than I'd expected, her face firm and glowing. She had a heavy bosom that ran into her large belly, the buttons of her dress stretched to near bursting. She wore knee-highs pulled to the top of her calves, and when she sat down, I caught a glimpse of her round, dimpled knees. She adjusted a shawl around her shoulders. She was the leader, and spoke in a rich, warm voice. I liked her. She was a good person. *Buena gente.*

"Thank you for taking care of our Pablito," she said. "Thank you, you are a gift from God. He looks healthy, happy. You have cared for him well."

Dika said in Spanish, "Pablo is a good boy. A very good boy." And she held forth a red tin of fruitcake. "For you."

I didn't say anything about his sleeping with the chickens, or how he'd gone for days without talking or how his first laugh had been less than two weeks ago. All I could get past the lump in my throat was, "We love him. Even our chickens adore him."

The first day, Dika and I helped the grandmother and aunts strip kernels off dried corncobs. We sat on small wooden chairs and woven mats in the open area between the bedroom shack and the kitchen, slowly filling buckets. The women constantly warned me, "*¡Despacio, güera, despacio!*" Careful, white girl! They insisted if I pushed myself too much I'd get blisters because my hands weren't used to work.

We took a break at midday, and Abuelita—she told me to call her Grandma once she found out I'd never met my own grandmothers—handed me and Dika each a boiled sweet potato that she'd dug up earlier that day. She peeled hers with bare fingers just after she'd plucked it from the boiling water. Her finger skin was thick as leather gloves, so tough she didn't get burned. But my potato stung my fingertips. I dropped it on my lap and waited for it to cool while my mouth watered. Abuelita laughed a belly laugh and took my hands in hers. "*¡Manos tiernas!*" she announced, and held my tender hands out for her daughters to see.

Abuelita peeled my potato and handed it to me. I didn't worry about germs because I was so hungry and the potato smelled so sweet and good.

"*Sí, señora,*" Dika said. "We must make Sophie strong! This girl has so many allergies and rashes and sunburn, always one thing or another with her."

"*Muy delicada.*" Abuelita nodded.

"*¡Muy pero muy delicada!*" Dika agreed.

Suddenly, I felt tired of being Sophie *la Delicada,* tired of making circles inside a fishbowl, watching life through cloudy glass. Would I ever be Sophie *la Fuerte,* the strong one, a salmon swimming up waterfalls, leaping over dams? Or better yet, one of those butterflies that goes from Canada, through winds and storms, all the way to Mexico, with its velvety wings intact.

After the potatoes, we went back to the corn, and as Dika and the grandmother and aunts talked, the burlap sacks of corncobs grew emptier and the buckets of kernels grew fuller. I plunged my hands deep into the buckets, felt the kernels in my hands, hard and smooth as little pearls. Their colors filled me up, purple and orange and red and yellow, like the insides of a seashell.

Later, Abuelita boiled the kernels with water and crushed limestone until the skins came off, and then we headed to the *molino*—the grinding machine—down the road. We took turns carrying the two heavy buckets. The metal handle dug into my hand and my arm felt as if it might fall off. Be tough, I told myself, be *fuerte,* and shifted the bucket to my other hand.

We walked down the dirt road, past some other shacks where women were washing clothes. They waved and called out *buenos días* and looked curiously at me and Dika, a strange sight in the village. A few women ventured closer with bewildered smiles and questions.

"*¿Quienes son?*" they asked Abuelita, gesturing to us with their chins. Who are they?

She smiled big. "My dear sister and my darling niece."

The women looked at one another, confused. They offered hesitant smiles.

Abuelita said briskly that we had to be going. "*Vámonos,* Sister, come on, Niece." We continued on our way, lugging the buckets, and when we rounded the corner, Dika and Abuelita and the aunts burst out laughing. "*¡Ay!* Did you see her face when I called you Sister?" They threw their arms around each other and doubled over, gasping and howling and wiping tears from their faces.

They kept snickering down the muddy path to the village center, which was a big, square patch of weeds with a cathedral on one side, a cement-block building for the mayor's office on the opposite side, a small store with a phone booth on the third side, and the *molino* in a tiny adobe house to close the square. At the *molino,* we dumped the boiled corn into the grinder, and moments later, a giant mound of dough plopped out. When the owner of the *molino* asked about me and Dika, Abuelita gave her the same story, and this time, she and Dika laughed even harder.

Next we stopped at the phone booth, where Dika and I took turns talking to Mom and Juan. Neither of us mentioned the police encounter or the fireworks scare or the fact that Ángel's mom might still be alive. Dika seemed to have forgotten about all that anyway. Drunk on her burgeoning friendship with Abuelita, she gushed about how wonderful life was here, how we might stay an extra week.

When I talked to Mom, she tried to sound casual, but I heard the caution between her words. "So, how have you been feeling, Sophie?"

She was really asking if I'd freaked out yet. "Good, Mom."

"Really?" she asked, trying to hide her surprise. "But have you—have you been worrying or—"

"No," I said, my voice strong. "I'm good."

And then she asked a few questions about food and the weather and put Juan on the phone and he asked about the food and weather, and we all took turns talking about the food and weather.

Later, at home, Abuelita and the aunts ground the corn dough on the stone metate, then patted out little balls and patted them out into flat circles. The tortillas cooked on a clay plate over the fire, and everyone but me turned them with their fingers. The aunts didn't want me to flip the tortillas because of my *manos tiernas*. But finally I burst out, "How will my hands get tough if I never try?" So they let me, and sure enough, my fingertips got burned, but I bit my tongue and blinked back the tears and told myself that pain was a step to strength.

. . .

Meanwhile, that first day, Pablo played with his cousins near the river while Ángel and Mr. Lorenzo worked with Pablo's uncles in the cornfields. In the afternoon, they came back from the fields smelling of sunshine and sweat and soil. After a late lunch, the men played basketball while Pablo and I watched. It wasn't until nighttime, after chamomile tea and sugary pastries, that I got a chance to be alone with Ángel, in the hour before bed.

We followed the same routine every day, for nearly a week. The days blended together; some afternoons it rained—quick thunderstorms—but mostly it was clear-skied and gentle. I liked losing track, feeling that we were in a timeless place.

Sometimes, during the day, music blared from speakers in the village center. *Cumbia* and merengue and salsa, the same three albums, played over and over again. Some songs I liked and found myself singing along with. *Me pongo a trabajar, me pongo a trabajar,* I put myself to work. And everyone in the village *was* hard at work. All the women were making tortillas; you could tell by the woodsmoke rising from chimneys throughout the valley. I liked knowing that the men in the fields were hearing the same songs, Ángel especially.

My favorite song was "Siguiendo la Luna," "Following the Moon," which we'd heard in the van. That song transported me back in time, into the van, inside that cozy space, with the song playing and Ángel mouthing the words, watching the moon through the window. Strange how you can get nostalgic about something that happened only a week earlier.

Abuelita didn't like the music blaring. She liked peace and quiet and nature sounds. That way she could protect her animals better. When the music wasn't playing, she could somehow hear when a hawk was about to dive to capture a chicken, and then she'd run outside whooping to scare the hawk: *"Wooooosh! Wooooosh!"*

She was protective of Pablo, too. She warned him not to play in the stream and to watch out for snakes. She gave him garlic to protect him from poisonous spiders and scorpions and tied a string around his wrist with a big seed called *ojo de venado*—deer's eye—to ward off evil eye in case anyone in town was envious of his fancy tennis shoes with red lights that lit up when he walked. And once in a while she asked me to check on him, because he'd been a city boy for a year and he wasn't accustomed yet to country life. I would find Pablo and his cousins chasing lizards and playing hide-and-seek, yelling and laughing and breathless from running. When I called them back for meals, they were always rosy-cheeked, covered in dirt, loaded down with treasures they'd found in the *monte* and spouting off stories of animal encounters. Since we'd arrived, he hadn't asked me once to read to him.

Meanwhile, Ñola moved along the edges of life like a ghost. I would look up from working, and there she would be, hovering in the shadow of a tree, or emerging from a tangle of squash vines. She spent most of her day lying in a comfortable place and then, for an unknown reason—maybe a change in the breeze or the angle of the sun—she moved, so slowly, until she found another spot that made her smile, and then she settled down, sometimes with her eyes closed, sometimes open. Sometimes the spot that made her smile was in the middle of the path to the outhouse.

"Oh! *¡Perdón!*" I said the first time I nearly stepped on her.

Her eyelids fluttered open and she laughed. "*Heehee-heehee . . .*"

She didn't use the outhouse herself. On her way from one lying-down-place to another, she'd just crouch down and bunch her skirt around her knees for half a minute and then get up and keep walking. The first few times, I thought she was looking at a special flower or a little animal, and I strained to see, until I realized that she was peeing under her skirt. How would it feel to have such an utter lack of self-consciousness, such a complete at-home-ness in the world?

Whenever I saw Ángel, I wanted to talk to him, but the men seemed to have their own territory, and the women had theirs. Men hardly ever entered the kitchen—as though a force field might zap them. They even ate separately. My job was to bring them their food after they came in from the fields. At first this made me indignant—why did the women have to serve? But then I played it up, and acted like an eager waitress putting down their food.

"Anything else I can get you, *señor*?" My voice was sweet and sticky with sarcasm. "*¿Más agua*? Tortillas?" The husbands took it seriously, but Ángel smiled. He had a small dimple in his left cheek that only showed up when he was trying to hold in a laugh.

In the evenings, I watched him play basketball with the guys. They were all either little boys or older men, no other teenagers, no one even in their twenties. It felt weird, like *The Twilight Zone,* to live in a place with no one between ages twelve and thirty. The other teenage guys—and girls, I discovered—had either left to study in the nearest town or gone to the U.S. or Mexico City to work.

Ángel was an amazing player. He whizzed effortlessly around the court. As long as someone passed him the ball, he could pop it into the basket from anywhere on the court. The other team had three players guard him, but even so, he jumped above their heads to catch the ball, then stayed suspended in the air as though gravity didn't exist, and shot.

Mr. Lorenzo stopped to rest often. He sat next to me, breathing hard, wiping sweat with his handkerchief.

"Why don't you take off that flannel shirt, Mr. Lorenzo?" I asked in Spanish. "No wonder you're hot."

"I have to keep it on. My organism has been through a lot. You know, if an *aire* hit me, it could make me sick."

"An *aire*?"

"Like a cold wind. A cold, evil wind."

"Oh."

"Before the *violencia* in my country, I could wear T-shirts. But now, you see, I always have to protect myself against the *aires*."

This didn't make much sense to me, but then again, neither did Dika's glass.

"*M'hijo es muy bueno.* My son is good, no?"

"Incredible," I said. "How come he's not on the basketball team at school?"

Mr. Lorenzo shook his head. "He can't go to the practices. Says he needs to work after school to save money."

"Money for what?" I asked.

"My son has many dreams." He sighed. "All secret."

He paused to watch Ángel weave the ball around his opponents, leap into the air, and with one hand, toss it expertly through the hoop.

Mr. Lorenzo smiled. "You know, he is smart, too, my son. *Muy inteligente.* His teachers say he will get a scholarship, no problem."

"I didn't know he was a good student."

"Good student? *¡Sí!* He works hard. Math, A. Science, A. History, A. English, B. Always!"

Mr. Lorenzo was beaming. His hands were folded in his lap, thick, short fingers interlaced in a way that seemed modest, delicate even. This close to him, I noticed a small tear at the hem of his flannel shirt, a tear that had been mended with perfect, tiny stitches.

I wanted to put my hand over his, but instead I just said, "You must be really proud of him."

What would Mr. Lorenzo do when Ángel refused to come back? Would he stay there in Guatemala? And what about his wife? What if she was alive after all? Dika hadn't mentioned a word about this possibility. Had Mr. Lorenzo later assured her it wasn't true? Or was she in denial?

I thought about the glass, the flannel shirt, the sunglasses, my limes. . . . Was all this enough to keep us safe? Suddenly, I felt protective of Dika. True, I had my whole sack of imagined fears, but she had real fears, real traumas.

I was used to being depressed. I'd accepted it as part of being Sophie. But Dika . . . what would happen if Dika lost that crazy spark?

Nights were when Ángel could sneak into the kitchen with us and drink coffee and eat pink sugarcoated rolls and talk. Still, we were usually surrounded by people, so he secretly let his arms brush mine as he walked by or let his leg rest against mine at the table. Small, almost imperceptible things. Things I might have been imagining.

Just before bed, we brushed our teeth by the cistern—a huge concrete basin of water—and washed our faces. Ángel and I lingered and talked for an hour, alone, standing close enough for me to make out his dimple in the faint light. We talked, easily, about anything that came to mind. I told him about a showdown between a puppy and a turkey over a tortilla scrap; he told me about how he'd learned to talk to a burro. He showed me how you make a burro trot by pursing your lips and making rapid-fire kisses.

While our words were gently bobbing along on the surface, underneath, my feelings were darting like fish. Feelings of wanting to reach out my finger and touch his dimple. And more. When there were pauses in the conversation, I thought, Now, now we will kiss. In those moments, he looked as though he was going to say something important. A few times he took a breath and opened his mouth and then closed it again.

But just when the space between our bodies was shrinking, I felt awkward and nervous and my hands shook and I grew conscious of a zit on my cheek and wondered if my hair looked frizzy. And I heard myself saying, "Well, good night," and walked inside to the mattress that I shared with Ñola, and as she made strange little noises in her sleep, I lay awake, furious with myself.

I didn't mind sleeping with Ñola. She smelled like farm animals and musty chicken pens and tree bark and sweet urine. She smelled like oldness, but an outdoor oldness, not an oldness that came from sitting in front of a TV all day or playing bingo in a nursing home, but an oldness as natural as ancient trees and drying riverbeds and layers of sediment eroding on mountains. Ñola whispered things in her sleep that only I could hear. Not Spanish—was it the language of sleep or Mixteco? Did her murmurs offer wisdom gathered over the course of a century?

Dika and Abuelita shared a mattress, where they ate fruitcake and talked and giggled like two girls at summer camp who hadn't seen each other for ages. You'd think they were the oldest and best of friends. *Comadre,* they started calling each other, co-mother, the closest two women can be without being related by blood or marriage.

One night, I overheard Abuelita say to Dika, "Oh, how you and Sophie remind me of the *gitanos*!"

"*Gitanos*?" I asked. That was a word I'd never heard before.

"Gypsies!" Dika said.

I propped up on my elbow and looked over at Abuelita. "Why?"

"Your skin, and your accents," Abuelita said. "Like the *gitanos*! They were *buenas personas,* like you. Good people.

They came in painted wagons. In the very old days, they performed dances and songs for us, and later, they started setting up a big screen outside and showing movies. *María Santísima Purísima,* how I loved those movies! And the ladies went from house to house telling fortunes. We gave them tomatoes or eggs in exchange for a card reading. Oh, how I miss them. They no longer come."

"Why not?" Dika asked.

Abuelita shrugged. "*Quién sabe.*" Then she whispered, "You know, I have some *gitana* blood."

"Really?" I said.

Abuelita gestured to Ñola, asleep beside me. Abuelita smiled and began her story.

Long ago, when Ñola was seventeen, she fell in love with a young *gitano* man who traveled with his companions from town to town, staying for several weeks in each place. He met Ñola on his first day in town and over the next weeks, they spent every minute together. The man asked her to marry him and travel with his *gitano* family. She adored him, but her parents and neighbors disapproved. It was one thing to be entertained by *gitanos,* they said, but quite another to marry one. So her family advised her to find a man from her own village to marry.

After much agonizing, she told the man to leave without her, since she couldn't go against the wishes of her parents. But he begged her to come, and said he couldn't live without her. She finally lied, trying to make it easier on him, and claimed she was in love with a man from her village. Her relatives convinced her there were many other good men, that she would easily fall in love with another and forget all about this *gitano.*

The day after he left, she suddenly regretted her decision. She realized she would never meet another like him. She considered chasing after him, taking a horse and galloping to the next village where they were headed. But her parents told her, "Daughter, wait until next year when he comes back. Then, if he has been faithful to you, you can marry him." Secretly, they thought she would forget about him and find a local boy to marry. A month later, she still thought of nothing but him.

Then she discovered she was pregnant with his child. Eight months later she had the baby. She hoped and prayed he would come back. This time she would go with him, she promised herself. The baby was three months old when the *gitanos* returned. She watched for her lover and didn't see him. Finally, she asked the other *gitanos* about him. They shook their heads sorrowfully and said he was so heartbroken he had left for America to try to forget her.

Eighty years passed. She never married. Her son had children who gave her great-grandchildren and great-great-grandchildren. And not a day went by that she didn't think of her *gitano* lover and regret letting him go.

When Abuelita stopped speaking, Dika clucked, "Poor, poor Ñola."

I didn't say anything. The story seemed terribly sad to me. I let my hair fall over my eyes to hide my tears.

Was that what Ñola was whispering as she dreamed? Regret for a risk she didn't take?

Mr. Lorenzo and Ángel were planning to leave on Monday. Only three more evenings with Ángel. Three more chances to take a step toward him. One step, maybe that was all it would take.

13

The Box

The next morning, the village was crawling with teenagers. During the week they rented rooms in Huajuapan, where the nearest high school was. On weekends they traveled two hours to visit their families in the village. They came in the back of a pickup truck on Friday evening, and by Saturday morning the basketball court was full of them. Everyone stared at me and Ángel. Everyone wanted to talk to us, wanted to know where we were from, what we were doing here. I stayed quiet. Being the center of attention always made me blush and stumble over my words.

"Joo espeak Eenglish?" a girl asked, giggling. She was about my age. She wore a red tank top and her cheeks were rosy.

I nodded. I searched for something friendly to say, but my mind froze up.

"Joo like play basket?"

I shook my head, embarrassed, and looked over their heads at the mountains. Why did everyone but me instinctively know how to make meaningless small talk? And how much eye contact to make? And what to do with their hands?

Ángel talked with everyone, including the girls. He called to me a few times. "Lime-girl, shoot some hoops with us!"

"No thanks." I watched them play and envied the girls' coordination, how comfortable they felt with their legs exposed, pounding the pavement, unconcerned whether they were too fat or too skinny. During breaks, they bent over, hands on their knees, breathing hard. Then they threw their heads back and squirted water over their faces, their necks, their lips until they glistened. I sat on the sidelines with Pablo, eating guavas.

The girl in red was rooting wildly for Ángel. When he took a rest, she sprayed him with her water bottle, and then offered him some, giggling. As he gulped down the water, she patted his sweaty back. How could it be so easy for her to touch him after just a few hours?

"Looks like Ángel's got a new friend," I said to Pablo.

He nodded. "You're more prettier," he said loyally.

I kissed him on the nose. "Don't leave us, Pablito."

We ate lunch around four o'clock; then I helped strip corncobs, feed the chickens, and sort beans. When it got dark, Ángel said, "I'm going to the court. Everyone hangs out there on weekend nights. Want to come?"

I didn't want to go, but I didn't want to stay home either, so I shrugged. "I guess."

Pablo begged us to take him, too. I was glad to have his hand to hold. While we walked to the court, Pablo talked about how good Ángel was at basketball and how when he grew up he wanted to be just like Ángel.

A few times, Ángel let his arm touch mine, but I stepped away. This wasn't going to work. I knew it. Ángel was going to stay in Guatemala and make tons of friends there. How did I ever think I could make him stay?

The court was lit up. A crowd was gathered, including the girls who had been playing. They had miraculously transformed. They were showered, their hair shiny with gel and spray, comb lines visible, earrings dangling, thin gold chains nestled between their pushed-up breasts. Tight pants, high heels, shirts not quite reaching their waists, showing off a little mound of belly. Lips outlined in red and colored in pink beneath a thick coat of gloss.

Ángel was shaking hands with some guys standing in a clump under a tree. The girl who'd been squirting him now wore a sparkly red spaghetti-strap shirt and hoop earrings. She moved away from the group of girls and came over to me. "Goo' nigh'," she said in English, and then leaned closer. "Ángel. He joo boyfrien'?"

Inside, part of me shouted Yes! But a bigger part of me said—with scorn—Don't be stupid, Sophie. I shook my head. "No. *No hay nada.*" There is nothing. I'd had my time in his spotlight and now he was moving on.

The girl strutted over to Ángel and planted herself possessively at his side.

I stared at them, feeling the same sick feeling I'd had in Huajuapan after the parade stomped through the streets and left sad heaps of colored sawdust.

I walked quickly over to Pablo. "Okay, Pablito," I said. "Time for you to go to bed."

"*Pero,* Sophie, we just got here!"

I grabbed his arm. "Let's go."

"No, I'm staying." He squirmed out of my grasp and ran to Ángel.

I walked back to the house in the dark. I was Sophie the amoeba after all. Sophie the weak. A few streetlamps glowed and flickered and illuminated swarms of moths high in the air. Back at the house, Dika and Abuelita and the aunts and cousins sat inside the yellow glow of the smoky kitchen, sipping lemongrass tea and eating pastries.

I tried to sneak past them, but they saw me. Dika patted a wooden chair. "Sophie, come sit down."

"I'm tired. I'm going to bed," I said.

"Come, Sophie! Two minutes. We have plan."

I sat down, wary.

"Now, Sophie," she said. She spoke in Spanish so that Abuelita could understand. "My *comadre* and I, we were talking, and we have decided to do a *limpia*."

"A *limpia*?"

"To clean our spirits. You and me and Pablo. And what luck! My *comadre* knows how to do it!" She raised her teacup in the air, and Abuelita followed, and their cups clinked in a toast. Then Abuelita ladled a cup of lemony tea from the blackened pot over the coals, and placed the plastic bag of pastries in front of me. "Eat, *m'hija,*" she commanded. "Eat."

I took a dry bite. "*Gracias,* Abuelita. Why do we need our spirits cleaned?"

Dika rolled her eyes and muttered in English, "You are kidding, no, Sophie? You must to look at yourself. And you must to look at Pablo, this poor boy. He watches his parents die the last year. Do you not think he must to have *limpia*?"

Abuelita nodded and smiled at me, as if she knew something I didn't. "I think the *limpia* will be good for you, Sophie. At dawn we will do it."

Later, at the cistern, I splashed water on my face and thought about what Pablo had said about his grandmother curing me. Was this what he meant? Was it possible to clean up a spirit, to soap it up and wring it out and make it gleam? I dried my face on a rough towel, imagining washing away the gunk weighing down my spirit, scrubbing off the black stains from years of worries.

Inside the house, I settled on the mattress next to Ñola. Soon, with the corners of my lips turned up in a smile, I slid into dreams.

I was so excited about the *limpia,* I woke up before anyone else. At the sink outside, I splashed water on my face. The air was a magical shade of purple. I watched the sky, the shadows, the shapes of things slowly gathering light. Little by little, gaining color, losing their blue.

Soon Abuelita emerged in a dress and apron, followed by Dika in her pink quilted robe. Dika plodded over and kissed my cheek. Pablo trailed behind her, rubbing his eyes, looking around dazed. After trips to the outhouse and cistern, we gathered inside. Abuelita set up a small table with a white cloth and a clay pot with three feet and triangular holes in the side, filled with pieces of wood. She lit it and blew, fanning the flames, making smoke rise up and fill the room. Light snoring came from behind the sheet curtain, where Mr. Lorenzo and Ángel slept.

Abuelita arranged the chairs around the table. Pablo seemed to know what she was doing and helped her set things up. From a cabinet in the corner of the room, he took out a small tin that he carried carefully with both hands. He sat down, and Dika and I followed his lead. Abuelita settled into her chair by the clay dish. The fire had gone out now, leaving hot glowing coals. She opened the tin and took out a bag of what looked like little amber and white stones.

"What's that?" I whispered to Pablo.

"Copal. It smells good. It comes from inside a tree."

Abuelita picked out pieces and set them on the table in front of her. For a long time she chanted and prayed in Mixteco. I didn't understand her words, only the hypnotizing rhythms, rising and falling, wave after wave of words. I found myself watching things in the room, taking in their essences: the smoke, the hot coals, Dika, Abuelita.

Abuelita motioned for Pablo to sit down beside her. She moved a piece of copal over his legs, arms, stomach, chest, neck, head. Then she dropped the copal onto the coals and watched the pattern of the smoke. It swirled up, curving this way and that around the room. She spoke to Pablito in Spanish. "Look at those rays of light."

Sunlight was shining through the smoke, making the air look solid.

"Your *mamá* and *papá* are with us, in that light. Do you feel the sun on your face, Pablito?"

He nodded.

"That is your mother kissing you."

His pink birthmark did look like the soft imprint of lips.

Abuelita continued. "It is your father touching your cheek."

The light shone right in his eyes now, but he didn't blink. A smile spread over his face, a big, natural smile with neat white rows of teeth and two lopsided dimples. There was a small light around his thin body, a strength I'd never noticed. A hint of who he was before, maybe, who he would become. I saw not just Pablo the six-year-old boy, but Pablo the baby, the man, even the old man, all at once. I looked at my hands, folded in my lap, and saw a child's hands, shaping Play-Doh, and a woman's hands, touching her lover's waist, and a mother's hands, stroking a baby's head, and an old lady's hands, veined and wrinkled and calm.

Dika took Pablo's place in the chair. Abuelita moved the copal over her, which took a while since there was so much body to cover. We watched the smoke snaking upward in spirals.

"You get headaches sometimes, *comadre,* don't you?"

Dika nodded.

Abuelita held Dika's head between her hands, buried her fingers under the gray roots, and squeezed. Then she shook out her hands as though they were wet.

"That light you see through the glass, *comadre.* That

light is with you always. Remember this when your head aches."

She took Dika's arm, the one with the three scars. She squeezed it hard, then shook her hand out, and again, and again. "Now these scars are light."

Dika nodded.

It was my turn now. I sat in the chair and Abuelita moved the copal over me. "Oh, Sophie, *m'hija,* you are accustomed to hiding things. Don't keep everything inside for no one to see. Take a breath and let them flow into the light."

I took a breath and blew out. And another, another. Abuelita massaged my head, my shoulders, my neck, loosening up what was inside. She took off my sweater. I wore only a tank top underneath.

"Breathe," she said, massaging my arms. "Look at all this! Do you feel this?"

I did. Things were flying out of my mouth and drifting around the room like dandelion puffs: the smell of rain, colored sawdust, ribbons of music, tiny white sparks. Silky moss and curled petals and lime zest. I felt lighter and lighter, as though I could float right up with them all.

Later that morning, I helped the women get ready for a goodbye party in honor of Mr. Lorenzo and Ángel, who planned to leave the next day. We sat at a long wooden table outside the kitchen, with the ingredients for tamales spread out before us. My job was to scoop a spoonful of corn mush into a dried husk. Next, Abuelita dropped in a few chicken pieces, then Dika topped it with a dollop of green tomatillo salsa; then one aunt folded it up and the other put it in the steamer of a giant pot. We were each a link in the chain.

After the first dozen tamales, I started getting the hang of it, and my hands moved on automatic pilot. I chatted and laughed at the aunts' jokes about their lazy husbands drinking Coronas in the shade. Meanwhile, Mr. Lorenzo and Ángel wandered with Pablo and the cousins in the *monte,* chasing lizards and playing tag and splashing around in the stream.

After a hundred tamales, we cooked a giant vat of pozole thick with corn kernels, swirled with dried red chiles that we'd roasted and ground and fried in oil. The entire head of a bewildered-looking pig poked out the top of the soup. Next we boiled a cauldron of coffee and threw in a handful of cinnamon sticks and a gourdful of sugar. Earthy, rich smells of boiling corn and oregano and roasting chile and cinnamon filled the kitchen and seeped out the door.

Once the work was done, I went inside to change my clothes. My shirt was spotted with a mosaic of dried corn mush and salsa and coffee stains. I pulled out a silky black tank top, smoothed out the wrinkles, and reached for a cardigan to cover up my bony elbows. Then I stopped. I remembered the *limpia,* how the air, so crisp, had made my bare skin tingle. How new it made me feel. Quickly, I stuffed the sweater back into the bag and put on my coconut jewelry and took a deep breath and walked outside.

Over the thatched kitchen roof, the sun was dripping like beeswax into golden pools between the peaks. Ángel and Mr. Lorenzo and the cousins had gotten back. They were devouring oranges and setting things up for the party.

"Come help us, lime-girl!" Ángel called. Together, we set up wooden chairs in a circle between the kitchen and the bedrooms. He put the stereo speakers by the window and blasted music, *cumbia* and salsa and merengue.

Once everything was set up, the aunts brought us bowls of steaming pozole and tamales and sweet coffee and cinnamon rolls sprinkled with sesame seeds. As we ate, Dika hung on to Mr. Lorenzo, feeding him bits of her roll, pouting over his leaving. "Now when will you come back to me, *mi amor*?" she asked.

"In one week, *mi amor*," Mr. Lorenzo said, stroking her cheek. "In one week we'll return."

I glanced at Ángel. He had stopped chewing and was staring at an orange peel in the dirt.

"One week!" Dika moaned. "One week without *mi amor*! How I will survive?"

As we finished dessert, it grew dark, and Ángel turned up the music so loud it vibrated my bones. The uncles dragged the aunts—who raised their voices in fake protest—inside the circle of chairs and started dancing.

Dika plopped down next to me. "Now, Sophie"—she rubbed her hands together devilishly—"you must to tell Ángel."

"Tell him what?"

She winked and pinched my cheek. "You know! You see how I tell Mr. Lorenzo he is *mi amor*. You must to do the same." She adjusted the clasp of my necklace, and smoothed the coconut circles against my chest. "You cannot wait for the things to happen. You must to make them happen. And now I will not say more because I know you are angry with me when I say the things how they are."

I flushed. Dika was right. I felt as though I'd climbed up on the high diving board and was taking in the view. But the thought of stepping into the air still scared me.

After Ángel finished his pastry, he bowed to Dika, and ceremoniously asked her to dance. Watching Ángel dance was even better than watching him play basketball. He moved perfectly with the rhythm; he was a magical, flowing sculpture of music.

And Dika—who would have guessed she could move her body like that? She was in her element, like a sea cow in water, a graceful, beautiful thing, a strange mermaid. She followed Ángel's spins and dips without missing a beat. She added belly dance moves, snaking her arms above her head, gyrating her hips. Beads of sweat flew off her like tiny diamonds.

After a few songs, Mr. Lorenzo danced with her. He wasn't as amazing as Ángel—his movements were slow and deliberate and his eyes full of concentration, focused on which step came next. Still, Dika was glowing. She said to him loudly in Spanish, so that everyone could hear, "*Mi amor,* if you don't come back from Guatemala in exactly one week, I'll come get you and put you over my shoulder and carry you back!"

Ángel glanced at me and grinned. "Let's dance, lime-girl."

I shook my head. "I don't know how."

He pulled on my arm. "Come on. I'll show you."

But I shook my head and felt Dika frowning at me.

Ángel grabbed Abuelita instead, and after the song ended, he came back to me. I said no again, and then he grabbed an aunt, and for the next song I said no again, and then he danced with the other aunt, until he'd gone through every female but me and Ñola, who was lying beside the patio, watching the stars. I looked at Ñola and thought, That's me, that's who I'll be in eighty years, an old weird lady who hovers at the edges of life and watches the sky and hears a faint echo of laughing stars and lives on that memory.

The next song was my favorite, "Following the Moon." This time, when Ángel asked, I said yes.

Until very late we danced. I stepped on his feet and bumped into him on spins, but we laughed and I let the music move through me like water, and it was actually fun. Afterward, we all collapsed into wooden chairs, exhausted and sweating. Ángel sat next to me and let his arm rest on the back of my chair.

"So, lime-girl, why'd you run off last night?"

I shrugged, embarrassed. "I guess I was confused."

"I missed you," he said.

I looked at him. "Really?"

He leaned into me and lowered his voice, so low it crackled. "I dreamed about you last night, Sophie. You want to hear it?"

"Sure."

"You were inside a blue room, at night. The moon was shining through the window. You were lying on a bed inside a white mosquito net. There was a red glass necklace around your neck. That's all you had on."

I felt myself blush.

He continued. "I looked at your hips and I wanted to move my fingers over them. I wanted this more than anything."

A heat gathered in my center and ran down my thighs.

"But when I came closer I couldn't find the opening to the net, and I got tangled up, and you were inside, watching me, smiling. But you didn't help me."

I looked at him hard and tried to make out the pupils in the dark through his sunglasses. "I would have helped you." And then, quickly, before I could change my mind, I asked, "You want to go for a walk?"

He took my hand and pulled me up. I didn't look back to see Dika's reaction as we walked up the hill, past the outhouse, through the cornfield to an open meadow. Here we sat down and tilted our heads back, watching the moon, half full above us, small and clear in the sky.

Ángel took off his sunglasses. "Look," he said, pointing. "Our stars."

I nodded and stole a glance at his eyes. "I'll never know what's in your box, will I?"

He hesitated and then said, "Seventy-three hundred dollars."

"That's it? Just money?"

"It's a lot of money." He seemed hurt.

"I mean, I thought it was something mysterious, like a treasure map or old letters. Something special."

The insect songs rose and fell and rose and finally he

said, "It is special. I've been saving it for three years. I'm going to set up a business in my town."

I tried to let the gravity of this settle in. He'd spent three years planning for this. And he'd probably been dreaming of it since he was a little kid. "Does anyone else know?"

He shook his head. "Don't tell anyone. My dad thinks it's too dangerous there."

My stomach clenched. "Is it?"

"The war's over, but my dad says the soldiers kept their weapons and their way of thinking."

Suddenly my chest ached. What if something happened to him there? "Why are you going?" I whispered.

He lay back and watched the sky and I watched his face. "I always felt out of place in Tucson," he said. "Like part of me was somewhere else."

"But I feel that way too!" I said. "And I'm not running away."

"I have to go, Sophie. You know how Pablo feels here, at home, with all these memories of his mother? I think that's how it'll be for me, too."

I wanted to touch the curves of his cheekbones. Instead, I stretched out on my back beside him. I thought of Dika's urgent voice: *You must to tell him, Sophie! You must!* I thought of Ñola, who let her one and only true love slip away. I took a deep breath. "Ángel, I want to tell you something. I want to tell you that . . ." I stopped because what I'd rehearsed was *I love you and I want you to come back,* but that suddenly seemed pointless and selfish. Isn't that what it means to love someone—to help him do what his heart is calling him to do?

I looked at the sky because I was scared I'd lose my nerve if I looked right at him. My words came out slowly, drop by drop. "Every time I look at the moon I'll think of you. And this night. And the night in the van with you following the moon. And that first night, remember, when you stepped off the bunk. Moonlight was coming through the window, and sparks were coming off you. Did you know that? Sparks like stars.

"And every time I see the stars I'll see those sparks again. At first it will be a sad feeling. But over the years, it might change to a happy feeling with only a little bit of sadness. And maybe one day when I'm old like Ñola and lying on the ground watching the sky, maybe it will fill me with complete happiness to watch the moon and the stars and remember you." I took a deep breath, held it, and waited. My eyes filled with tears. Crickets sang back and forth in waves. In the spaces between their songs, silence.

I felt him staring at me. I dared to turn my face toward his. Tears were spilling out of his eyes. I wiped the tears from his face, and then, very easily, our faces moved together and we tasted the salt on each other's cheeks, each other's lips.

14

Mi Amor Is Gone

We kissed in the meadow for a long time. I touched the curve of his cheekbones, the muscled ripples of his shoulders, the dip where his hips met his waist. I had the feeling that I'd landed in a lush forest, a miraculous place that I needed to explore, down to every tree hollow and flower petal, because tomorrow it would all be gone.

We stayed together until just before dawn, when it grew cold and damp. The chickens woke up and the birds started chirping, threads of the world weaving themselves into a new day. We walked back to the room, hand in hand, and kissed again.

After he went to his mattress, I slipped back under the covers, wide awake, still feeling his hand slide over my shoulder, as though he were sculpting it. The particular smell of him stayed in my hair. And the taste of his skin, salty and smooth, lingered in my mouth.

A short time later, Abuelita got up, then Dika, and then there was motion behind the sheet, and Mr. Lorenzo appeared, and then Ángel. I stayed on the mattress and watched him walk by. He wasn't wearing his sunglasses, a small gift to me. I smiled at him, and he smiled back, tired and happy and sad all at once.

Within an hour, we were in the kitchen, sipping coffee, hovering over a tattered map spread out on the table. Mexico was a giant white funnel that curved to the east and narrowed at Oaxaca, then widened again into Chiapas. After Chiapas came Guatemala, the pale yellow of summer squash.

Mr. Lorenzo moved his thick, soil-covered finger from Huajuapan along a black line down to Oaxaca City, then farther south, toward the blue Pacific Ocean, and along the coast to Tapachula, the border town. "We'll catch a pickup truck to Huajuapan later this morning," he said. "Then we'll have lunch and buy food for the ride, and then take the evening bus. That way we'll get there the next morning so we can cross the border in daylight."

I glanced up from the map. "Why does that matter?"

Mr. Lorenzo cleared his throat and kept staring at the map. "Well, just a precaution. It's safer in the day. Not as many bus-jackings."

"Bus-jackings?" Dika cried.

"We'll be fine, *mi amor.* During the daylight it's safe, more or less."

Dika did not look convinced.

Mr. Lorenzo patted her knee, then moved his finger from Tapachula farther down across the beige borderline. "Next we cross into Guatemala and take a few local buses to here." He pointed to a space empty of marked roads, not far from the border, near a place called Tecún Umán. "Here is San Juan," he said. "Our town."

I saw nothing but yellow space, and for some reason, this made my stomach tighten. I looked at Ángel. He was sitting with Pablo on his lap, whispering to him and staring at me, but I couldn't make out what he was saying. "I don't see any town there," I said.

Mr. Lorenzo shrugged. "Our town is not big enough for this map."

"But how will you know where to go?" My voice sounded suddenly shrill, as though Dika had possessed me. "I mean, what if the roads have changed?"

"We'll ask people," he said. "No problem." He took Dika's pudgy hand in his. Her nails were candy purple, like grape-flavored bubble gum. She must have brought along a collection of nail polish. I was sure that yesterday her nails had been sparkly pink.

"And then, a week later," Mr. Lorenzo continued with a grin, "I will come back to my girlfriend." He gazed at Dika and she clung to him like a heroine on the cover of a cheesy romance novel.

None of us ate much of breakfast—the beans and tortillas and salsa felt stuck in my throat. And next thing I knew, the pickup truck was rumbling up the road and we were running out with Ángel and Mr. Lorenzo and their bags, flagging it down. The truck idled in a cloud of dust while Mr. Lorenzo kissed Dika goodbye and climbed on with his suitcase. Then Ángel pulled me to him and planted a long kiss on my lips, right in front of everyone. For a moment he looked hard into my eyes and I looked back. Then he gave Pablo a hug and hopped into the back of the truck with his backpack and duffel bag.

The truck pulled away in a puff of exhaust. Dika patted me on the cheek. "Ha! Finally! You take my advice!"

I didn't tell her it was too late. Instead I said I was taking a walk to the stream, and I managed to hold back the tears until I was out of sight. I headed into the patch of woods, where Pablo had said the spirit people live. The *duendes.* I was glad the *duendes* wouldn't let anyone cut down these trees. The light filtered through the leaves, making wavy patterns on the ground. Out of the corner of my eye, I caught flashes of light dancing like spirits. At the stream, reflections bounced off the water onto the undersides of fallen trees and branches, leaves and water and light moving, never the same from one moment to the next.

I took off my shoes and stepped from rock to rock. They were solid and cool beneath my feet, and the rhythm comforted me somehow, the focus on taking one step after another.

Then Pablo appeared. He must have followed me. I wiped the tears off my face and hoped it wasn't too blotchy.

"*Estás triste,* Sophie?" Pablo asked. Are you sad?

"*Sí, principito.* I'm sad."

"But you shouldn't be sad."

"Why?"

"Because Ángel told me to take care of you and make sure you're not sad."

"Big responsibility for a little boy."

"He said if I take care of you, he'll bring me a slingshot

and show me how to shoot lizards and we can make lizard tacos."

I felt angry that Ángel would get Pablo's hopes up, making a promise he didn't plan to fulfill. But then, a flicker of hope. "When did he say he'd be back?"

"One week."

"When did he tell you about the present?"

"Right before he left on the bus. When he hugged me."

Maybe he'd changed his mind. Maybe he was coming back. I would have a long week ahead.

"Sophie?"

"Yeah?"

"Will you read me a poem?"

Dika was melodramatic about Mr. Lorenzo's being gone. Still, she had no doubt he would come back. She knew he was hopeless and helpless as a devoted puppy without her. "Oh!" she cried every few minutes, placing her hand theatrically over her great bosom. "Oh! *Mi amor* is gone! Oh, I feel lonely! Oh, I miss him!"

I stayed at a quiet distance from everyone else. I stripped the corncobs, fed chickens, made tortillas, all with barely a word. Whenever "Following the Moon" came on, my eyes got watery, and I walked up the path past the outhouse to a clump of white bell-shaped flowers that Abuelita called *Reina de la Noche*—Queen of the Night—and looked over the valley.

Once, on the trail above the outhouse, I nearly tripped over Ñola. Her eyes were open. Usually she laughed when I almost stepped on her, but this time she looked at me with her clouded eyes and said something in Mixteco. She repeated it. Over and over. *Cuaá nanducuvé*. She flicked her wrist as though she were brushing something away. Then she started to get up, and I helped her. She plucked a large white flower from the Queen of the Night plant and handed it to me. *"Cuaá nanducuvé,"* she said, and then inched her way down the path.

I spread open the petals and found, inside, another flower forming, a smaller flower, tender still, and curled up in itself. I pressed my nose into the flower, and inhaled its sweet, musky scent.

15

Heavy Things, Sharp Things, Blood

At sunset, Pablo and I walked through the empty streets toward the village chapel. It was perched on the top of a hill, a forty-five-degree incline that left me breathless. Pablo darted back and forth between me and the turkeys pecking at the roadside. He had a special bond with all fowl, it turned out. Somehow he could distinguish one turkey from another, even though they all looked alike to me.

"Do you know how lucky you were to end up with a family in downtown Tucson who has chickens?" I asked.

He nodded.

"It's a sign," I said. Mom had told me not to pressure him. So I just repeated, looking straight at him, "It's a sign, Pablito." We reached the top of the hill, paused to catch our breath. Abuelita used to come here every morning at dawn to pray for Pablo. Now Pablo had asked me to come with him to pray for Mr. Lorenzo and Ángel. Pablo wanted to pray to the Virgin, too—talk to his mother and father through her. I liked the idea. *Closure,* wasn't that what it was called? To say goodbye and move on with life.

We stepped into the church's cool shadows and let our eyes adjust to the darkness. In an alcove near the altar was *la Virgen de Nieves*—the Virgin of Snows—which was a strange name because it never snowed here. She wore a white lacy dress shaped like an upside-down cone, and a sky blue veil with silver glitter in flower patterns. The aunts said that this church was built on top of a sacred Mixtec site for Cociyo, the god of the waters. I imagined people trekking up the hill to thank him for rain and ask for more rain, until sometime after the Spaniards came, when the god was forgotten, his water freezing into tiny crystals of snow. Now the Virgin of Snows had replaced him, and maybe someday she would transform and become water again. The substance was the same, the form different.

The church was empty except for one woman praying in the third pew. Pablo and I tried to walk quietly, but our footsteps echoed off the stone walls. The eyes of the statues of saints seemed to follow us. Each had its collection of candles, firelight flickering over their faces, animating their eyes.

Pablo held a little paper bag of candles we'd bought.

"Go ahead," I whispered. "Light one, Pablito."

"This one's for Mamá and this one's for Papá," Pablo said solemnly in Spanish. "Now, this one's for Ángel and this one for Mr. Lorenzo." With the flames of other candles, he lit his candles, melted their bases, and placed them in the pools of wax, his mouth half open in concentration. Then he knelt again and folded his hands in front of his chest.

I said a vague, silent prayer for Ángel to be safe and come back to me. I had never prayed to a Virgin before. But Virgins and spirits were important to Pablo and Ángel. The midwife who delivered Ángel had told him that if you need something done fast, the best strategy is to pray to the Virgin. She tells her Son what to do, and Jesus does it. That's the chain of command; mothers have the real power. I imagined the Holy Mother hearing my prayer and nagging Jesus about it over dinner in heaven: *Have you been protecting Ángel? You'd better get on that, Son.*

I sat on a bench two rows behind the woman. Pablo was still kneeling in front of the Virgin, his lips moving, his hands crossing his forehead, his chest, his mouth. When he finished, we left the darkness of the church through huge wooden doors.

The sky had gone from pale golden to the hues of blackberry and cherry and mango, all melting into one another. Pablo had stored-up energy to burn after being quiet in a church for fifteen minutes. He ran into the weedy graveyard and raced around the gravestones decorated with plastic soda bottles cut in half and filled with red carnations. Turkeys meandered around the wooden crosses, pecking at offerings of food that had been left there. He wove in and out of their paths while they eyed him cautiously at first, then went about their business. Finally, he circled back to me.

"Sophie, guess what?"

"What?"

"I telled my mother the poem."

"What poem?"

"I tell her, Mamá, I'm carry you heart in my heart." Then he switched to Spanish. "*¡Mira!* Watch how fast I can run, Sophie." He ran down the hill, his little legs moving impossibly fast, his arms flailing over his head, his mouth in a wide-open smile, calling out, "Yaaaaaaaaaaaaaaaaaah!" until his voice faded and he was a faraway splotch of red.

They were supposed to be back Monday morning. One week, that's what they'd said. On Sunday, I washed all my clothes in the cement basin outside. On Monday, I put on the white cotton sundress and the coconut necklace and bracelet. I brushed my hair and braided it carefully in two braids.

By sunset, they still hadn't come. Dirt smudges and salsa stains flecked my dress. I'd been preparing for the idea that Ángel wouldn't come back. But I thought at least Mr. Lorenzo would.

Unless they'd found Ángel's mother.

"Oh, *mi amor*! How I miss him! How worried I am!" Dika moaned in Spanish over coffee and sweet rolls Monday night.

"Something probably held them up," I said, unconvinced. "I'm sure they'll be here tomorrow."

Dika nodded. "Perhaps they missed the bus."

Before bed, I washed the white dress. As I hung it on the clothesline to dry for the next day, Pablo came out with his toothbrush and toothpaste. He neatly squeezed out the toothpaste—the all-natural stuff that Mom always got—and began brushing.

His mouth overflowing with foam, he asked, "Are you sad again, Sophie?" He spoke in Spanish.

"Yup." I tried to ruffle his hair, but he squirmed away. Lately, he seemed to be getting vain about his hair. Some of his cousins wore hair gel already, and they weren't much older than Pablo. "You know, *principito*, you should be speaking English to keep in practice for school."

He shrugged and asked me in Spanish, "Why are you sad?"

"Because I miss Ángel. And I don't know if he's coming back."

"Why don't you go get him?"

Toothpaste was dribbling from his chin onto his shirt, but he looked so serious I didn't mention it. "I can't."

He spit out his toothpaste and scooped a cupful of water from the cistern. I'd tried to make him use purified water, but he'd insisted this was how he'd always done it. He swished it in his mouth and spit onto the mud, then wiped his sleeve over his face. "Why not?"

"I don't know. Maybe he doesn't want to see me. And it's far away. And I've never gone somewhere like that alone." I twisted my ring around my finger. The moonstone in silver that Mom and Juan had given me for my fifteenth birthday, along with my e. e. cummings book of poetry. That night I'd underlined "and it's you are whatever a moon has always meant," and I thought, Someday I'll discover the one to tell this to.

Pablo looked thoughtful, as though he was considering

all angles of my answer. Finally he said, "But you're a big person."

"Well, sort of."

"So you can do anything."

Tuesday morning and afternoon passed, without even a phone call. Dika was fretting. She was sure something must have happened. That a thief had hijacked their bus and killed them. That they'd gotten in an accident or been kidnapped.

That night, I climbed up the trail in my dirty dress, past the outhouse, and stood next to the Queen of the Night. It smelled strong; something about the darkness released a mysterious, sweet scent. I let myself cry for a while.

When I was little and felt sad, Juan would put his arm around me and tell me one of his tales. It always made me feel better hearing how the scrawny heroine gets swallowed by some creature—like an elephant or wolf or whale—and then, right when she thinks all is lost, she discovers that the creature's gut is actually a passage to another world. Instead of dying in the belly of the whale, she's reborn. And this time there's nothing scrawny about her.

I took another whiff of the flower, then walked down the path to wash my dress again in the dark.

Wednesday morning I still clung to some hope. I put on the sundress, now clean and white again, and braided my hair.

Embarrassingly, Dika was primping herself, too. She had grown louder in her panic as I had grown quieter. "*¿Donde están?*" she screeched at breakfast on Wednesday Where are they? She threw her spoon on the table. "I have had it! I am going to Guatemala to find them."

"Tranquila, comadre," Abuelita murmured.

But Dika did not get tranquil. You could almost see smoke shooting out of her ears. "I am going to get them!"

"But, Dika," I said. "They said it was dangerous, remember?"

"Danger! Don't talk to me about danger. I have been in danger. And now I am scared of nothing!" She ripped into a roll with her teeth.

"Dika, listen." There was no easy way to say this. "Maybe they don't want to see us. Maybe they want to stay."

"Ha!" she snorted. "You know very little of men."

But she was quiet after that. Only the crackle of the hearth fire in the corner, the muffled squawking of chickens outside. There was an insecurity in her eyes. And she didn't start packing.

Wednesday night I couldn't sleep. Dika couldn't either. Neither could Abuelita, probably because of all our turning over, sighing, adjusting the covers. Even Ñola was murmuring more than usual in her sleep.

I whispered across the room to Dika, "Maybe you're right. I mean, they at least would have called us. Maybe something happened."

"I ask to my *comadre,*" she said, propping up on her elbow. "Psst, *comadre,*" she called, her face a few inches from Abuelita's.

Abuelita opened her eyes. She didn't seem startled to see Dika's face looming so close. "*¿Qué pasa, comadre?*"

“We are worried about *mi amor* and his son.”

Abuelita heaved herself off the mattress and turned on the bare lightbulb. She buried her head in a crate of fabric scraps and clothes and came up with a small box, smaller than Ángel’s, and made of old dented tin. She cleared the wooden table and spread out a white cloth, just as she had done for the *limpia.*

“Bring the chairs around,” she said.

She lit candles inside glasses and put them on the table and turned off the light. She opened the box and poured out a tiny heap of dried corn kernels. She looked at them with reverence. “The corn will tell me why the men aren’t back yet.”

She scattered the kernels, praying, moving her lips in the flickering candlelight. She studied the corn as though it were a book.

Dika whispered to me, “See how smart is this lady. My *comadre*.”

“Shhh!” I told her.

“Hmph!”

Abuelita was silent now, watching the kernels. Finally, she spoke in a grave voice. “Glass, there is green glass, brown glass.”

“The jewels,” Dika said. “Maybe they found them.”

“There is wood. And metal, too. Heavy things, sharp things, blood.”

PART 5

PATH TO THE MOON

"Here is my secret. It's quite simple: One sees clearly only with the heart. Anything essential is invisible to the eyes."

"Anything essential is invisible to the eyes," the little prince repeated, in order to remember.

—THE LITTLE PRINCE

16

Unforeseen Journey

Three more times, Abuelita threw the corn, and each time, it said the same. Always blood, sharp things, heavy things.

Dika pushed it. "But what kind of things, *comadre*? Is it Mr. Lorenzo or Ángel? Was it an accident? Are they coming back?"

Abuelita said the corn gave her no more details. Only the glass, the wood, the metal, the blood.

"Abuelita," I said. I hugged my knees and shivered in my cotton nightgown. "Can you ask the corn another question? Can you ask if Ángel found his mother?" I tried not to look at Dika, but I felt her eyes on me.

Dika said to me in English, in a low, hurt voice, "You think this is reason they don't come?"

"I don't know, Dika. Maybe. I mean, they never found her body."

Dika put her hand over her heaving chest, took a deep

breath, and said to Abuelita, "*Comadre,* please throw the corn again."

Abuelita chanted a few minutes with her eyes closed and finally tossed the corn onto the table. She examined it, moving her fingers over it lightly, and then looked at us, her face solemn. "Ángel has not found his mother yet. But he will."

A moment of shock. Dika pressed her lips together. In Spanish, she whispered, "If his wife is alive, he should be with his wife." Then she lay down on her mattress and stared at the ceiling. After Abuelita put away her tin of corn and copal, she settled next to Dika and stroked her forehead. I wished someone were stroking my forehead.

Just before sunrise, Abuelita and Dika had finally fallen asleep. Next to Ñola, I was trying to breathe deeply so that sleep would come.

Suddenly, Ñola said my name. "Sophie."

Maybe I'd imagined it. Did she know my name? I stared at her small, wrinkled face on the pillow, her white braids spread out like wings. Her mouth moved. "Sophie."

Then she said the same phrase she'd said while handing me the Queen of the Night flower. "*Cuaá nanducuvé.*"

"I don't understand Mixteco, Ñola."

"*Cuaá nanducuvé,*" she said again.

"*Cuaá nanducuvé,*" I repeated.

She nodded and laughed—"*heeheeheeheehee*"—and then, just as suddenly, fell back asleep. I repeated the phrase like a mantra in my head until finally, I slept.

. . .

I woke up to Pablo bouncing on the mattress. "Sophie, wake up!"

I opened my eyes. Light streamed through the flowered curtains. Ñola was gone, probably lying outside somewhere. Abuelita and Dika's mattress was empty.

"What, Pablo?" I groaned.

"Wake up!"

"Why?" A rush of excitement. "Is Ángel here?"

"No. But it's breakfast time. You slept late!"

I propped myself onto my elbows and held his hands, which were already grimy from playing outside.

"Hey, *principito.* What does this mean? *Cuaá nanducuvé.*"

"I don't know Mixteco."

"You understand it. Abuelita and Ñola speak Mixteco to you sometimes. Come on, what does *Cuaá nanducuvé* mean?"

"*Bueno. Cuaá nanducuvé.* It's like when my dad was in the field and it was time for lunch and Abuelita says *Cuaá nanducuvé,* then I have to go tell him to come back."

"So what does it mean, Pablo?"

"Go. Go find him."

All morning long, the words echoed in my head. *Cuaá nanducuvé. Go find him.*

The phone call came that evening, when the sun had nearly sunk from sight.

Dika and I were washing dishes outside, and my hands were red and raw from the harsh soap, cold in the evening air. *Go find him,* I heard in the lyrics of every song. Over the loudspeaker, the music stopped and a voice came on: phone call for *Señora* Dika and *Señorita* Sofía. We dropped the dishes and without even rinsing the soap off our hands, we ran. Dika could run only about five paces before gasping for breath and doubling over, clutching her belly. I ran ahead, taking long strides in my sandals, my feet pounding the ground.

When I was nearly there, a scream rose over the music. "Sophie!" It was Dika. Something was wrong. I sprinted back along the path, and found her struggling to stand.

I knelt beside her. "Are you okay?"

"My leg," she muttered. "I trip this damn tree root."

"Is it broken?" The skin on her ankle was scraped pink and bleeding. It was the same ankle she'd hurt climbing out of the pool the day she seduced Mr. Lorenzo.

"We see," she said. "Now help me to stand. We must to talk with my boyfriend."

I held my arms around her waist as she limped down the path. A few minutes later, breathless, we reached the shop with the phone.

"He'll call back in ten minutes," the lady said.

Dika plopped onto the bench, huffing and rubbing her ankle, while I paced the wooden floor, watching the phone.

When it rang, I snatched it up. "*¿Bueno?*"

"Sophie," Mr. Lorenzo said.

"Where are you?"

"*Buenas tardes,* Sophie," Mr. Lorenzo said. "Ah, can I speak with your aunt?"

"What's going on? Are you coming back?" I tried to make my voice calm. "Please, just tell me."

"*M'hija,* something happened to Ángel."

My legs grew weak. I waited. *Heavy things, sharp things, blood.*

Mr. Lorenzo's voice shook. "You know that there is much anger in our *tierra* since the war. People saw terrible things and the anger stayed in their hearts, and some of them—"

"Mr. Lorenzo, please. What happened to Ángel?" Out of the corner of my eye I saw Dika, tears in her eyes.

"*Bueno,* he is alive." He cleared his throat and still his voice shook. "That is the important thing."

My knees were about to collapse. I sat down on the bench beside Dika. She put her hand on my shoulder.

"He has been in the hospital for three days, Sophie," Mr. Lorenzo said. "I couldn't call you sooner because he was unconscious and I wanted to be there when he woke up." He was quiet for a moment, making little sniffling noises.

I clutched the phone. "What happened?"

"A gang attacked him one night, stole everything from him. They took his mother's jewels. They beat him and cut him badly. Knives, they had. Broken bottles. Beams of wood. They had too much anger in their hearts."

"But what—"

"I'm sorry, *m'hija,* but I only have enough money to talk for a minute. Listen, the gang stole our money and passports. We can't cross back into Mexico without them. We need you to get our visas and the photocopies of our passports—they're in my bag. Can you send them here?"

"Is that safe? To send that through the mail?"

"We have no choice, Sophie. Do you have a pen?"

My hands were shaking so badly I could barely hold the pen the shopkeeper had given me. I wrote the address of the hospital, and then the bank where I was supposed to wire them money. "Mr. Lorenzo," I said. "Will Ángel—"

"*M'hija*, listen, the time's nearly up—"

"Mr. Lorenzo?"

No answer. The line was dead.

We waited two hours for Mr. Lorenzo to call back, then shuffled home in the dark, very slowly, Dika limping at my side. She talked nonstop, moaning and asking me questions. *How long they will be there, Sophie? Where he is hurt? They will to catch the bad guys, no? Mr. Lorenzo's wife, she lives?*

My answer was a numb shrug. Nothing mattered except Ángel.

Back at the house, Abuelita sliced open some fresh aloe leaves, revealing clear slime that she rubbed over Dika's wounds. After examining the ankle, now purple and swollen, Abuelita announced it was only a bad bruise and deep scrape. She said it should heal fine if Dika stayed off it for the next few days. Pablo moved his chair next to Dika during our evening coffee and traced the blue veins of her thighs with his fingers. Sugar from his jam-filled pastry coated his chin like an old man's beard.

He must have sensed something was wrong, because he asked in a small, hesitant voice, "Where's Ángel and Mr. Lorenzo?"

"Oh, they'll just be back later than expected," I said, forcing a smile.

"Will Ángel bring me the slingshot?"

"Yes." My voice cracked. "He will. I just need to send them some papers is all." Dika and I had decided that the next day I'd go to Huajuapan with one of the aunts, and stop by the post office and the bank. But the aunts seemed doubtful the mail would arrive safely, especially since the documents were worth a lot on the black market.

I left the flickering firelight of the kitchen and went into the bedroom to find the visa and photocopies and extra money to send to Mr. Lorenzo. The room was still and dark except for moonlight spilling through the window. For a long time, I sat on the mattress and stared at Ángel's visa photo. It was a good picture. He looked just on the verge of breaking into a smile, with that faint dimple on his left cheek.

How hurt was he? Was he still unconscious? How were they paying for food if they barely had enough to make a phone call? What if the documents got lost in the mail? They wouldn't be able to pick up the wired money without picture IDs. They'd be stuck in Guatemala without money.

I unfolded the map and traced the route with my finger. Could I bring the documents and money there myself? I'd have to travel alone—Dika wasn't in any shape to travel with her swollen ankle. I could leave the next morning and then have lunch and get food for the ride and take the overnight bus there. Just like Mr. Lorenzo's plan. He had said the trip was safe in the daylight. More or less. And once I got there, we could go to the embassy to get new passports or whatever we had to do, and then come back together. Hopefully all three of us.

I stared at the dimple on Ángel's left cheek. This wasn't just about getting the visas to them. At the heart of things, Ángel needed me, I could feel it. His dreams had taken a beating along with his body. And I was the only one who understood all that he'd lost. I closed Ángel's visa with my fingertips toughened by stripping corn and making tortillas. I wondered how strong I was, wondered what Sophie *la Fuerte* could do.

That night I slept little, listening to Dika's distinctive snore and Abuelita's gentle breath and Ñola's murmuring. Did I want to be an old lady like Ñola, never having followed the moon? I closed my eyes and slipped into memories, heard snatches of *cumbia* music, saw a full orange moon through the windshield, felt sparks in the van's darkness . . . things that touched the core of me . . . which was not rusted scrap metal after all, but something deep and mysterious as the ocean.

A rooster crowed. I got up quietly and slung my backpack over my shoulder. I tiptoed into the room where Pablo and the cousins slept. I bent down and touched my lips to Pablo's cheek, right on the kiss-shaped birthmark. On the way out, I stood over Dika and Abuelita for a moment. A thin line of glistening drool leaked from the corner of Dika's mouth. I felt like hugging her. Beside her, Abuelita looked as though she was in the middle of a wild dream, her eyes darting under their lids.

I might not see these odd women again. I let the gravity of this settle in. For the first time in my life, I was taking a real risk. And yes, I felt fear, but it wasn't the endless loop of worries I'd grown used to. My thoughts shone clear and sharp as cut crystal. *This is the path I am taking. This is what I need to do.* I wrote a short note and laid it between their heads. Then I whispered goodbye to Ñola.

Her eyes opened.

I jumped. She looked like a ghost, her white hair loose from her braids, feathery wisps fanned out on the pillow. *"Cuaá nanducuvé,"* she said.

I nodded. "I know," I whispered. "I'm going to find him."

She reached up and took my hands, which were no longer *manos tiernas.* She pressed them to her cheek. *"Hee-heeheehee,"* she laughed. She moved her fingers over me, making little crosses, blessing me. She took off one of her necklaces—a square piece of leather imprinted with the Virgin of Juquila, the same Virgin on Ángel's pendant, the very miraculous one. Ñola put it over my head, adjusted it on my chest, pressed it over my heart.

"*Gracias,* Ñola," I said. I walked outside into the cool night air, to the roadside. The scent of Queen of the Night was so strong it felt like a tangible presence. I shivered under my thin sweatshirt and waited for the truck. Supposedly it passed by every four hours, starting around five a.m. I had my passport in my pocket and an extra hundred dollars—the emergency cash Juan had given me—tucked in my bra. A few sleepy-eyed people carrying bundles on their backs walked over to wait for the truck. They looked too groggy to ask what I was up to.

Soon the pickup truck bounced up the road, and once it stopped, we climbed into the back. By the time we reached Huajuapan two hours later, it had grown light. The driver dropped me off in the bus station parking lot, a black stretch of oil-stained asphalt. "*¡Feliz viaje!*" he called after me. Happy travels.

When I got to the front of the line, I smiled bravely, trying to look as if I traveled around Central America on my own all the time. The ticket seller was a middle-aged man wearing an intimidating starched shirt and a blazing blue tie. He seemed in a hurry. "Yes, *señorita*?"

"I'd like a ticket to Tapachula. The evening bus, please."

He clicked on the keyboard with manicured nails and shook his head. "Sorry, *señorita,* but it's full."

My mouth dropped open. "Full?"

He nodded. "That overnight bus is popular."

After a moment of shock, I started forming plan B. Go all the way back to Pablo's village? Or buy a ticket for tomorrow night and stay in a cheap hotel?

The man clicked a few more keys. "You're in luck, *señorita.* There's a bus that leaves in twenty minutes. It's only second class, but there's plenty of space on that."

I tried to think fast. People were waiting behind me, looking restless and rushed. "Um, what time does that bus get to the border?" I asked.

He glanced at the plastic map on the wall. "Oh, I'd say about six o'clock tonight. But second-class buses make more stops, so you never know for sure."

I chewed on my cuticle. "So, um, before dark?"

"I'd say so." He looked impatiently at the growing line of people. "Would you like to pick your seat?" He rotated the screen toward me, motioning to the available seats glowing green against the black background. The bus was mostly empty.

I swallowed hard. "Well, are you sure I'd get there before dark?"

"Nothing is sure, *señorita.*"

"But is it safe?"

He motioned to the TV, where the news blared. "Listen to the news, *señorita.* You only hear the bad things. If you worried about everything you heard, you'd never leave the house, would you?"

My teeth tore at my thumb's cuticle. "Well, I mean—"

"Look, *señorita,* we have many people waiting here." He smoothed his tie and looked at the next customer. "Please step aside."

"Okay, give me this seat, please." I pointed to a seat by a window.

Once I paid him and got the ticket, I realized there was no time to walk down the street to buy snacks. I'd have to get food at one of the stops. I took out my bottle of water from my backpack and waited on a hard, plastic seat, sipping self-conciously. The waiting area smelled like a mix of disinfectant, exhaust, and cheap cologne. On TV, a woman with bleached-blond hair gave the news—floods and murders and hijackings. I unfolded my map and saw that Ángel's town was not even a half inch from the border town, less than thirty miles as the crow flies. This reassured me. Even if the bus arrived a little late, I'd still have time to make it to Ángel's town before dark.

Soon I became aware of people staring, whispering, wondering what the foreign girl was doing alone at a bus station. A guy about my age was staring especially hard. He had a chubby face, kind of friendly-looking, kind of slimy. His hair was stiff and spiky, and its shadow on the wall looked like little sawteeth.

I touched the Virgin necklace that Ñola had given me. My eyes flicked to the clock, the white tiled floor, the buses idling outside the window, and back to the clock. Where had they cut Ángel? I pictured his face crisscrossed with gashes. I thought of Mr. Lorenzo's scars. The ones I had seen as a reflection in Dika's and Ángel's eyes.

The slimy-friendly guy moved next to me. Up close, I realized he was the source of the cheap cologne smell. "Excuse me, *señorita*, where are you going?"

"Guatemala."

"*¿Solita?*"

I nodded. "Yes, alone."

"You're brave!" He waited for me to ask about him, and when I didn't say anything, he just kept talking. "I'm going there, too. I study in the university here in Huajuapan, but I'll be visiting my aunt in Guatemala for a week."

I forced a smile. It was a good idea to know someone on this trip. That way, criminals might think we were together and not mess with me. This guy seemed pretty harmless. He could watch my back.

Once the bus arrived, he insisted on carrying my bag outside. "Excuse the bother, *señorita,*" he said. "But would it be possible for me to sit beside you?"

"Okay."

He sat down. "Do you have a boyfriend, *señorita*?"

I hesitated. He was looking right into my eyes, as the cop had done. I wasn't used to being flattered, and it made me feel cautious. "Yes," I said finally.

"Too bad," he said. "But we can be friends." He winked. "I'm Rodrigo."

"Sophie," I mumbled. "Nice to meet you."

Then he drilled me with questions—*Where are you from? What are you doing here? How old are you?*—until finally, I said I was tired, and closed my eyes and pretended to sleep.

To my surprise, I actually drifted off, and it did feel like drifting, floating through the air, as though gravity had been a figment of my imagination all along. Really, it was very easy to fly, if you could only hold on to that lightness. The feeling you got as a kid, running with joyful abandon, like Pablo flying down the hill, his arms outstretched like wings.

When I woke up, Rodrigo was staring at me. He must have been watching me sleep, waiting for my eyes to open. "Excuse me, *señorita.* Did you have a pleasant nap?"

I nodded and sipped water from my bottle and thought, A whole day next to this guy. The sun was shining through a filmy haze. Outside the window, flat fields stretched as far as I could see. Clusters of banana trees with giant green leaves spotted the roadside. I wished I could pluck a few bananas. My stomach was growling so loudly the whole bus could probably hear it.

"Can I offer you a cookie, *señorita*?" He held out a packet of cookies filled with red jam.

I took one. *"Gracias."*

"Excuse me, *señorita.* Your boyfriend, is he North American like you?"

"No. He's Guatemalan."

"He is? Well, he must be light-skinned then, because you white girls don't find us *morenos* attractive, do you?"

At first I looked out the window, chewing my cookie and ignoring what he'd said. But then I said, "Not that it matters, but his skin is darker than yours. His mother was Mayan. Is Mayan."

"Oh. And you're going to his town?"

I nodded. "To bring him something. In a town near Tecún Umán."

"*¡Señorita!* Are you crazy? Why don't you meet him in a tourist place like Antigua? There are many beautiful places in Guatemala. Ancient temple ruins, golden artifacts, handicraft markets, elegant hotels, colonial churches. You shouldn't travel around Tecún Umán. I have a cousin who lives near there, and she won't leave the house at night. There are bullet holes through her walls."

"Well, I'm not staying. Just going, giving my boyfriend something, and coming back here with his dad. And maybe him, too." My fingers wrapped around the old, worn leather of Ñola's Virgin.

"Aren't you scared, *señorita*?"

"I'm used to being scared," I said. It was true. I'd had plenty of practice. I could very easily imagine all the ways in which I might die on this trip—gunshot, knife wound, strangling—I used to envision these kinds of scenarios every time I walked down an alley in Tucson. But what was happening now felt different. This trip was something truly risky. The pure rationality of my fear felt good in a weird way. Maybe the way to let go of all my pointless, ridiculous worries was to delve into the real thing.

I dozed on and off, while on the bus's TVs, two cop movies exploded with screams and gunfire and ripped into my dreams. Twice we stopped in huge parking lots with gas stations and fast-food restaurants displaying piles of fly-covered empanadas on the counters. The bathrooms didn't have toilets, just open drains that you had to squat over. Those were covered in flies too. On the first stop, I took one look at all the flies and ran back to the bus as though they were chasing me. On the second stop, I had to go so badly I just held my breath, zoomed inside, closed my eyes, and peed for so long I had to take another breath. Afterward I wolfed down two empanadas before I could fret too much about whether the flies had first made a visit to the bathroom.

Around six in the evening, I was flipping through *The Little Prince* when the bus pulled into a parking lot. I shut the book and turned to Rodrigo. "We're here?"

"Oh, no. Two hours left. The bus usually gets there around sunset."

"But the ticket man told me six," I said.

"Those guys don't know what they're talking about."

I took a long breath. Okay, a minor setback. No big deal. At the border I'd just splurge on a taxi to take me right to Ángel's town. It was less than thirty miles. No problem.

Then, through the front windshield, I noticed the hood

propped up. I scrambled off the bus, and Rodrigo followed. The driver and his assistant were staring at the engine, looking puzzled, with a grease-stained toolbox open at their feet.

"What's the problem?" Rodrigo asked.

"Nothing major," the driver said quickly. "Just a ten-minute repair."

"This happens sometimes," Rodrigo assured me. "We'll be on the road again soon."

We stood under a tree at the edge of the parking lot, watching the men tinker around. The air pressed on me, steamy and thick, and soon sweat started trickling down my face. The ten minutes turned into forty minutes, which turned into two hours, and by then the sun was already dropping below the edges of the sugarcane fields beyond the parking lot.

Back on the bus again, I counted only seven other passengers, all of us sweaty, our clothes glued to our skin. We still had two hours left to drive, which meant we'd get to the border at ten at night. Trying to stay calm, I thought of my options: taking a bus back to Huajuapan? That would mean a wasted trip, but at least I'd be safe. In the rearview, I watched the driver mumble a prayer and rev the engine.

As he was turning out of the parking lot, I suddenly grabbed my bag and stumbled to the front. "Excuse me, *señor,* I—I need to get off. I need to catch a bus back to Huajuapan."

He shook his head. "No buses until tomorrow." And then he turned onto the road, nearly empty of cars. "Too late to turn back, *güera.*"

. . .

We reached the border town at 10:10 p.m. Even this late, the air was hot and dense. When I stepped out of the air-conditioned bus, my skin grew sticky, instantly coated with sweat. Outside, streetlights in the parking lot cast an eerie green glow in the mist. Stretched before us was a wide bridge with a low building at the entrance where three guards in uniforms paced, loaded down with machine guns and rounds of bullets strapped across their chests. It looked like the set of a cop movie.

"What now?" I asked Rodrigo. My mouth felt pasty.

"This is the bridge that takes you from Mexico to Guatemala, *señorita.*"

Four people from the bus were already crossing over the bridge. The others had mysteriously disappeared into the night. I headed toward the bridge with my backpack slung over my shoulder and my passport growing damp in my sweaty hand.

Rodrigo gestured to the building lined with clouded windows, dingy and nearly empty inside. "Go in here. I already have an ID to cross the border, but you'll have to show them your papers."

Papers? I needed papers?

Rodrigo saw my confusion. "*Señorita,*" he said hesitantly. "Your boyfriend will be waiting for you on the other side, right?"

For some reason, I didn't want Rodrigo to know quite how clueless I was. Pride, maybe, or maybe I was scared to admit it to myself. "Don't worry," I said. "I'll be all right." I would just stick to my plan of finding a taxi. It wouldn't be ideal traveling at night, but it was a short distance. I could handle this.

"Well, good luck, *señorita.*"

"Thanks." I watched him go. He flashed an ID to a guard who waved him through. The other people from the bus had IDs too, and walked quickly across the bridge, where cars waited for them. I was the lone tourist.

I took a deep breath, tried to smile, and walked into the room. It was mostly bare except for two metal folding chairs, an ancient computer, and some dented filing cabinets. Two men in uniform stood behind a counter, one barely older than me, the other middle-aged, his gut hanging over his belt. Looking amused, they watched me walk inside. The heavy man asked, "What's a *gringuita* like you doing out alone at night?"

I considered whether I should trust them. But in the end, I didn't have a choice. "I'd like to cross the border," I said in the most confident voice I could muster. I offered my passport to the older man and prayed he wouldn't ask me for anything else.

"You're all alone?" His eyes moved from the passport photo to my face.

"Well, uh, someone's meeting me, just on the other side," I lied.

"You are very brave, you know," the younger one said. He smoothed a finger over his wispy black mustache, a couple dozen sparse hairs, not enough to shave.

"Why are you coming to Guatemala?" the older man asked.

I bit my lip. "To visit my boyfriend. He's Guatemalan."

He raised his bushy eyebrows and stared at me. Then he shook his head. "Be careful, *señorita.* That's ten *quetzales.*"

"Are dollars okay?" I flashed a hopeful smile at him.

"Of course. One dollar fifty cents."

I dug some change out from my backpack and dropped it into his hand.

He stamped the passport and handed it to me. "Fortino, escort this *señorita* to the other side. Stay with her until her boyfriend arrives."

Fortino smiled. "With great pleasure," he said, and adjusted his machine gun. He didn't look old enough to be out of high school, much less wielding weapons. He made a movement to carry my backpack but I snatched it up first. "Thanks, I've got it."

He walked slowly, trying to stretch out the five-hundred-foot walk. Juan had told me not to trust anyone in a uniform. I wished Juan were here now, his snake tattoos rippling. He could make instant friends with anyone. By now, he'd be joking around with the guards like old buddies.

"Want to touch my gun?" the guard asked. His voice cracked. He hadn't even finished puberty yet.

I shook my head and tried to pick up the pace, but he dragged his feet.

"I could take you out sometime, *señorita,* show you around this area. There's a lake you'd like."

I tried to estimate how many more footsteps to the other side. We were utterly alone now, the building back in the distance and the parking lot on the other side, deserted. That was when I noticed someone standing beneath the streetlamp on the other side. Rodrigo. "Oh, see, that's my boyfriend now. Thanks." I jogged to the other side, my bag bouncing against my thigh.

Rodrigo looked nervous. "You all right?" he asked.

I nodded, breathing hard. I held Ñola's necklace in my hand, rubbing the leather between my fingers. And then, out of the blue, a voice inside me spoke. An old lady's voice, maybe what Ñola's would sound like if she could speak Spanish. *Sophie* la Fuerte, the voice said. Sophie the Strong.

I turned to Rodrigo. "Listen. Can you just tell me where I can find a taxi or a bus, please?"

"Your boyfriend's not picking you up?"

"No. He's—he's in the hospital."

"But there won't be any buses or taxis until tomorrow. The transportation companies don't let their drivers work here at night. Too many robberies on the road. The thieves make roadblocks so you have to stop and then they take your car and sometimes kill you."

Oddly enough, I didn't feel like crying. Things couldn't get any worse. There was a certain relief in this.

That was when a group of five guys came out of the shadows and swaggered toward us.

They wore baggy jeans and bright white tennis shoes, gold chains, and baseball caps. The same kind of clothes as Ángel's, only on Ángel they made me smile, because underneath was something very tender and good. These guys made the hairs on my arms stand up.

"*¡A la chingada!*" Rodrigo said under his breath. "Get ready to run."

They came close enough that I could see their zits and moles and scars. We were surrounded. "Good evening, *gringuita.* What's in your backpack?" "Hey man, what you got in your pockets?" They were moving in, closer and closer. "Show us what you got." "Why don't you walk over here with us and show us everything? Everything."

I tilted my head back, looked at the sky. The moon was a sliver of white. I closed my eyes and let the moment sink in.

It's strange, what you think about in the pinpoint of a moment when you might die. And I mean really die, not imagining poisonous gas seeping into the basement or toxins in your food or smallpox germs coating your alarm clock. I saw Mom's smooth face over me, felt her hair brushing against my cheeks. I heard Juan humming softly, the way he always did when he made green chile tamales. I felt the warmth of Pablo's body against mine while we slept with the chickens. And I thought, Even if I die now, I will know I've lived a good life.

I opened my eyes just in time to see a guy with a crooked nose reach his hand out for my upper arm. I took a deep breath and got ready. To scream, to run, to kick, anything.

But now he was looking over my shoulder toward the bridge.

Fortino, the guard, was heading toward us, his machine gun raised. He called out in his squeaky adolescent voice: "They bothering you, *señorita*?"

I tried to say yes, but my mouth wouldn't move.

Fortino yelled, "Okay, *cabrones,* hands up."

The guys cursed under their breath and held up their hands. "It's cool, it's cool, man. Just trying to help the *señorita.* It's cool."

"I'm going to count to ten. If you *cabrones* aren't gone by then I'll blow your heads off."

The guys backed up slowly toward the tree shadows at the edge of the parking lot.

I waved to Fortino. "Thanks."

"No problem, *señorita.* And don't forget about the lake offer."

"Okay," I called out as he walked away.

Just then, a seventies sedan with tinted windows zoomed into the parking lot and screeched to a stop, rubber burning, smoke pouring from the tailpipe, hip-hop salsa beats vibrating the car. Rodrigo grabbed my arm. "Get in," he said, pulling me toward the car.

I strained to see inside the windows but they were too dark. Rodrigo opened the back door. "Get in the car," he said.

I hesitated. "But—"

He motioned to the edge of the parking lot, where the figures of five guys still hovered, watching us, waiting. "Sophie." He wasn't messing around with the *señorita* crap anymore. "Get in."

17

Following the Moon

I clutched my backpack on my lap while Rodrigo locked my door, slammed it shut, and hopped into the front seat. In the driver's seat sat what looked like an aging prostitute from a movie. She wore a sequined halter top that barely contained her massive breasts and stomach rolls. Her fingers, draped casually over the hot pink fur of the steering wheel, were bedecked in gold rings and two-inch-long sparkly fingernails. She eyed me in the rearview and raised one eyebrow, a hairless black sliver of eyeliner. Then she slammed her foot down on the gas and sped down the deserted street.

"So, Rodrigo," she bellowed. "Tell me, who is this? Your girlfriend?"

Rodrigo glanced back at me and grinned. "She's from the North. Her name's Sophie."

"Welcome to Guatemala, Sophie!" She made a screeching

hairpin turn around a corner. "I'm Marta, this crazy kid's aunt."

"Nice to meet you." I wondered where we were going, where I would sleep. We passed some small motels and I considered asking Marta to drop me off, but changed my mind once I noticed the gangs of guys slouched on the street corners and the women in tight leggings and four-inch heels leaning against the concrete walls.

Being inside this car with two almost-strangers seemed safer than being on the street. A pair of baby shoes and a cascade of gold crosses swung from the mirror. In their midst dangled an orange flower deodorizer, which made the air smell like a gas station bathroom. Barbie-doll pink fur carpeted everything—the dashboard and front seats and steering wheel.

Marta shouted over the pounding music and broken muffler: "You will stay with us tonight, Sophie! Here you have your house. It is humble and not what you're used to in your rich country, but all that we have to offer is yours."

"Thank you," I called back. Maybe she wasn't a prostitute after all. She seemed too motherly.

The brakes screamed again and more rubber burned and we lurched forward. And then stopped. "Here we are!" Marta announced.

Rodrigo hopped out and ran to open the tall metal gates. He unlocked a thick chain, clanked open the doors, and after the car was inside, locked them quickly behind us. Two dogs bounded up to me, growling and foaming at the mouth, until Rodrigo kicked them away. There would be no sneaking out of this house once I was inside, that was clear.

We walked through a weedy lot piled with concrete blocks and metal pipes, into a kitchen that felt like an unfinished basement. A single bare bulb lit the raw cement walls and floor. Marta whirled around the kitchen, fixing us tortillas with beans and cheese. When I asked for limes, she was very apologetic that she had none. I devoured the food anyway.

She asked me a million questions about my country, as though she'd been waiting a long time for an expert like me. "Now tell me something," every question began. "Now tell me something, why are there so many bald men there in the North? What will happen to your blond hair when you get old? What color will it turn? Is your hair really this color or do you dye it? Really, you don't dye it? Well, how did your eyes get this color? You didn't dye them either? Really? Do things look the same to you or is everything blue?"

After every answer I offered, her eyes widened for a moment, as if she was deeply impressed. Then she made a joke and slapped the table. Even though I didn't get half her jokes, I laughed anyway, because it was the middle of the night and it felt a little like a slumber party and I was giddy at the idea of still being alive. Her loud, bawdy sense of humor reminded me so much of Dika, I felt as though I already knew her.

Meanwhile, Rodrigo had given up on trying to get my attention and turned to the small black-and-white TV in the corner. First there was a rerun of *Los Seeeempsons,* with "Marrrrge" 's voice extra-raspy and "Barrrt" 's voice extra-high-pitched. Next, a talk show about cheating husbands, where wives and lovers onstage were screaming and punching the men.

An hour passed, and another, and I started wondering when Marta would get tired. Earlier, I'd asked her what she did for a living and she'd said, "You know, a little of everything. I sew. Made this shirt. Took me forever to sew on these tiny sequins." Then she changed the subject to her good-for-nothing boyfriend, who stayed out with a different woman every night and staggered home drunk in the afternoons for naps. Until she got the dogs, that is. After that, he only sometimes stumbled to the gate, begging and pleading and swearing he'd give up his evil ways. Once in a while, if she was in the mood, she held back the snarling dogs and let him in.

Every time I blinked, my eyes wanted to stay shut, but I didn't have the heart to interrupt her. Eventually, she started yawning. "Oh, look at the time, Sophie. Wait here while I get your bed ready."

On the talk show, a large woman was bashing a skinny man on the head with her purse and the security guards were making a halfhearted attempt to hold her back. It looked staged, but still made me chuckle sleepily. Rodrigo stared at me. "My aunt was right. Your eyes are amazing. Your dad must be a thief."

"What?"

"Is your father a thief?"

That was what I thought he'd said. Why was he asking me that? Juan would never steal anything. Then I wondered if he meant my real father, who could be a thief for all I knew. A thief wasn't too far from a drug dealer and child abandoner. But I decided he wasn't my real father anyway. Juan was.

"No," I said finally.

He lowered his voice to a whisper. "Then who stole the stars out of the sky and put them in your eyes?"

I wished I knew how to say *cheese-ball* in Spanish. I fake-laughed. "Ha ha ha." I remembered Ángel's hand on the blue tablecloth that night in the restaurant. *I know exactly what color your eyes are, Sophie.*

"If you get cold tonight," Rodrigo whispered, "my room is right across from yours."

"Don't count on it, *amigo.*"

"Here's your room, Sophie," Marta said, fluffing a limp pillow. She'd put fresh sheets on my bed, and a fuzzy brown blanket with a picture of a tiger on it. I doubted I'd need it. The air, even at this time of night, was like a sauna.

She showed me how to unknot the mosquito net that hung from a hook on the ceiling, and placed a glass of water beside me. "Good night. Dream with angels."

I got under the covers and even though there didn't seem to be any mosquitoes, I let the net fall around me. The fabric was wispy thin, like fairy wings or spiderwebs. I remembered Ángel's dream about me.

Even though I was tired, I couldn't stop thinking about Ángel. In the corner of the room, an altar glowed with three candles flickering in red glasses. Light reflected off the framed saints and Virgins. I got up to go to the bathroom and nearly stepped on Marta, who was lying on a palm mat on the kitchen floor.

I'd taken her bed, I realized guiltily. She opened her eyes as I passed. She looked homely without her makeup—completely eyebrow-less, but nice. "Everything all right, Sophie? You warm enough?"

"Why don't you sleep with me, Marta? There's room in the bed."

We argued back and forth a bit, but I insisted, and finally she got into bed. Once the mosquito net had settled around us, she giggled. "Who's going to believe I slept with a *gringa*?"

I focused on the tiny woven squares of netting, rubbed the gauze between my fingers. "You know, Marta," I whispered. "Rodrigo isn't my boyfriend."

"Of course he's not. I was just kidding. Of course you must already have a boyfriend."

"His name is Ángel. But he's not exactly my boyfriend. I want him to be, though."

She patted my hand. "Well, I'm sure he will be. Now dream with angels, Sophie. With your Ángel." Her laugh was soft and kind and soon turned into light snoring.

I watched red light flutter on the pearly rosary beads, on the Virgin standing on the sliver of moon, wrapped safely in her sequined halo. The same iridescent sequins as Marta's halter top. I pictured Marta with her eyebrow lines furrowed, holding a needle and thread, sewing the sequins one by one onto the shirt, and one by one onto the Virgin's halo. Then I slept. I dreamed I was floating inside a golden oval that dangled from thousands of threads held by angels. And all of us were heading to Ángel.

. . .

The next morning, I woke up with the song "Following the Moon" in my head, and then I realized it was on the radio, blaring from the kitchen. I changed into my white dress and coconut jewelry, and wondered what Ángel was doing at this precise moment.

Marta was in the kitchen, making breakfast and dancing around in a patch of sunlight. She'd already painted on chile red lipstick and thick lavender eye shadow. Her eyebrows had turned back into distinct black lines. Her feet were squeezed into spiky high heels with straps wrapped far up the ankles, digging into fleshy calves. A few blue veins webbed her thighs below her skirt's hem. They made me think of Pablo sitting on Dika's lap, tracing his finger over her comfortable map of veins.

"*Buenos días,* Sophie!" She set a chipped mug of chamomile tea in front of me. And then a plate of steaming scrambled eggs and beans and a pile of tortillas. "Eat, Sophie, eat!" She presented me with a small plate of quartered limes. "I got up early and bought them for you at the market on the corner." She looked so pleased.

I drenched the food in lime juice. Then I slipped the moonstone ring off my finger. "For you," I told her, "to thank you."

She shook her head. "Absolutely not. You are our guest."

Before I left, I sneaked into the bedroom while she wasn't looking and set the ring on the altar between the still-flickering candles. I hoped it would at least fit onto her pinkie finger.

"Stay with us more time, Sophie," she cajoled when

we stood in the doorway saying goodbye. "You haven't met my sisters yet. They won't believe me unless they see you."

It was tempting to stay here, this place that already felt like home after one night. "Thanks, Marta, but I have to find Ángel."

"*Bueno,* Sophie, but remember, here you have your house. Always." She gave me a final hug, so tight my bones crunched together, so saturated in perfume I sneezed all the way down the block to the bus station—a big dirt lot filled with old school buses painted crazy colors. Rodrigo instructed me where to change buses at the next big town.

"Too bad you have a boyfriend," he said.

"Yup."

"A kiss?" he asked me, tilting his head and puckering his lips.

I kissed his cheek quickly and got on the bus.

Nearly everyone held bundles or children or babies in their laps. A few held chickens. People squeezed inside the bus, four and five people to seats that were made to hold two or three schoolchildren. This bus was not as luxurious as the one I'd taken here, not by a long shot. This one had torn plastic green seats, ragged curtains, no AC, and no action movies. The bags were strapped onto the top of the bus. I hadn't wanted to part with my backpack, but there wasn't enough room inside. It was still early morning and I was already sweating. I ate one of the bananas Marta had packed for me. Outside, mist rose off trees and green hills, like steam over a cup of tea.

After a half hour, I got off at the town where I'd have to transfer buses. It wasn't much of a town as far as I could tell—just a mosaic of mud and dust and colored tarps strung over wooden market stands heaped with fruit and vegetables. Vendors fanned flies away from raw meat and wet cheeses and bowls of bubbling soups. Through air thick with odors of overripe fruit, people called out to one another, kids screeched and laughed, *cumbia* music pulsed. Sweat poured down my cheeks and plastered my clothes to my skin.

I realized, suddenly, I'd forgotten to get my bag off the bus. But now I couldn't remember which bus was mine—there were seven or eight buses parked in a stretch of dirt, all old and painted crazy colors and packed with bags on top. What did I have in my backpack anyway? I mentally rummaged through the bag. There were clothes, but at least not my white dress—I was wearing that. Soap and shampoo and moisturizer and sunscreen, which I could replace, although it wouldn't be hypoallergenic. *The Little Prince* book—dog-eared and underlined and worn—a little piece of Pablo I'd brought with me. Still, I could buy a new one back home. What was in the outside pocket? My passport! My stomach jumped. How would I get back into Mexico? And Mr. Lorenzo's and Ángel's papers. How would they get back?

I started aimlessly weaving through the exhaust and yellow buses, scanning their roofs. That was when a young guy in a threadbare T-shirt and flip-flops worn down to the paper-thin soles jogged toward me. He held out my red backpack. "*Gringa,* is this yours?"

I felt like hugging him. "Thank you!"

"No problem," he said, and before I could say anything else, he disappeared into the chaos of smells and sounds and colors.

I wondered what it would be like to live here. It seemed very random that I ended up born in Tucson instead of here, instead of anywhere for that matter. And very random that my clothes were brand-new while the guy's shirt had looked about fifteen years old. If I lived here, he could be my friend. Marta could easily be my aunt. Dika could be Rodrigo's great-aunt. Anyone could be anyone else.

"Ahorita, gringuita." Any minute now, little *gringa*. That was the answer all the vendors gave me when I asked what time the next bus to San Juan would leave.

I waited a few minutes and ate another banana and watched two little kids chasing each other around the market stands, squealing and slipping on mango peels. They wore filthy clothes about three sizes too big for them. WORLD'S GREATEST GRANDMA, one of the T-shirts said. The other had dancing pigs on it and said I LIVE 4 AEROBICS.

Ten minutes passed, but no bus. I had to pee badly.

I asked another vendor, "When will the bus to San Juan leave?"

"Ahorita, gringuita," the woman answered.

"Do you know when exactly? Five minutes? Forty-five minutes?"

"Yes, *señorita*." She smiled reassuringly.

"But which one—five or forty-five?"

"Ahorita viene." Any minute now.

A half hour later, still no bus.

I peeked over into a ditch to see about peeing there, but there was a drunk guy passed out by a tree.

I returned to the woman's fruit stand. "Is there a bathroom here?" I asked her. With an apologetic shrug, she pointed to a cement building with BAÑOS spray-painted on the side.

I opened the door and walked inside. In seconds, my eyes adjusted to the darkness. Mounds of crap were piled up inside the toilets, on the toilet seats, on the floor next to the toilets. Thick clouds of flies buzzed everywhere. The stench was horrible. For a germ freak like me, this was straight out of a nightmare. I froze, afraid to breathe. I looked down and saw, on the floor, brown liquid that could have been mud or worse. And it was all over the soles of my sandals.

I couldn't move. My heart stopped.

I opened my mouth, but instead of a scream, a laugh sputtered out. And another. Uncontrollable belly laughter overtook me. I was doubled over, laughing and laughing until tears streamed down my cheeks. I'd spent my whole life worrying about germs, and here I was in the mother lode. And, well, I wasn't dead. I tiptoed out, careful not to splatter the puddles.

Still laughing, out in the sunshine, I gasped the sweet air and ran down to the ditch past the drunk guy. I hoped he wouldn't regain consciousness any time soon. I peed in the midst of dirty diapers and plastic bottles and cans faded from the sun. I peed, then laughed some more while I examined the brown stuff on my shoes. I thought of Dika with her head thrown back, shrieking with laughter, because what else could she do? Because she was alive.

"No, no, of course the bus is fine," the driver reassured passengers while sipping his beer. The hood was up and two guys were peering into the engine. People streamed onto the bus—women clutching the tiny hands of their children, some children with babies strapped to their backs, guys in baggy jeans and T-shirts and baseball caps, older men in once-white oxford shirts with graying collars and woven palm hats.

Once we were all settled in our seats, a man in grease-stained clothes told us to get off again. We watched the men tinker underneath the hood for a while until they shrugged and declared it okay. I wondered if it really was okay. Then I smiled because of course if a crash was going to happen, it would happen in an ancient secondhand school bus speeding along dirt roads with a beer-drinking driver. No, it was not an ideal situation, but the best option at the moment.

A boy on a ladder tossed my bag up top, and then I got on the bus. This time, more passengers rushed onto the bus, packing the seats. I had to stand in the aisle, my feet apart, bracing my hands on the seat-back and the bar overhead. A few men offered me their seats, but I said no thanks. Plenty of other people were standing, and if they could do it, so could I.

I felt glad I was standing, because I felt taller, as if my whole life, I'd let fear cram me into a small box, a space so tiny I was always curled over, my shoulders hunched, my back bent. That box had seemed too strong to break through, so I hadn't tried before. But maybe, all along, the box was just flimsy cardboard, and all I had to do was stand up, punch through the top, and climb out.

18

Kindness of Strangers

It rained on and off during the bus ride. The flat landscape wrinkled itself into hills, with mountains poking up in the distance. We bumped along valleys as showers pattered the windows, then around a curve, up into brilliant sunshine. I needed to figure out where exactly to get off the bus, so I looked around, trying to pick out the most trustworthy face. Most people were staring right at me. A woman in a matching flowered skirt and top at the back of the bus waved. "*Gringuita!* I'm getting off the bus at the next stop. Take my seat." I scooted into her place, next to a woman with two girls.

The woman was an explosion of color, draped in a thick, boxy cotton blouse with thin rainbow stripes, tucked into a wraparound skirt. Two little girls, about six and eight years old, were dressed like her, their hair braided with ribbons. The sour scent of woodsmoke clung to them, an ancient, warm smell that made me think of Ñola and Abuelita. The girls were eyeing me, their hands cupped over their mouths, giggling and whispering together in another language—a Mayan dialect, I guessed. Mr. Lorenzo had told me there were lots of Mayan groups, each with their own way of speaking and dressing.

The mother lowered her eyes and gave me a timid smile. Here was someone even shyer than me, someone I could trust. I gushed to her about how cute the girls were, and asked where they were going. The mother spoke softly in accented Spanish—short, choppy syllables. She said they were headed home, to San Juan.

"That's where I'm going too!"

She looked at me with surprise and seemed about to say something, but then closed her mouth. We chatted about the food and weather and plants in Tucson, and soon the girls warmed up to me. Each girl took one of my hands and sang an English song they'd learned in school: "*Pollito* chicken, *ventana* window." And on and on, rhythmically translating a strange collection of words.

Finally the mother, whose name was Juliana, looked at me and lowered her voice. "What are you doing all the way out here, *señorita*?"

"Visiting a friend."

"What time is he expecting you?" Juliana asked.

"He's not."

She gave me a strange look. "How will you know where to go?"

"I have the address."

Her voice lowered to a whisper. "Our town is not safe.

People with money are kidnapped and held for ransom. There are gangs, bandits. If they see a *gringa* alone, they will see a victim. Do you understand me?"

"Well, I'm just bringing something to my boyfriend and then coming right back with his father. And maybe with him, too." I looked closely at her face. Her lips were full, with a beauty mark hanging above the corner of her mouth, just like a model's. Her eyebrows were wrinkled in concern. "It's all right," I said. "People have been nice to me, helping me out."

"True, but it only takes a few bad people." Juliana moved closer. "The gangs recruit boys, and the boys can't say no. You're with them or against them." She had a lot to say, once she got started. But her voice dropped even lower now. She didn't want anyone else to hear, that was obvious. "That's how it was, too, when I was a girl, only then it was the army and the guerrillas."

"Who were they?" I moved my head closer, trying to hear her whispers over the rumble of the bus.

"The guerrillas were revolutionaries who fought for rights of poor people. At first poor people were happy about this. Then came the army. They tried to stop the guerrilla movement. In the end it was the people—like my family and neighbors—who suffered. Guerrillas forced us to give them food, and then the army came and punished us for helping the guerrillas. They killed people. They burned our houses and our crops and stole our animals. And even though the government tells us the fighting is over, *la violencia* has stayed in the hearts of some people."

Had Ángel seen *la violencia*? Was that why Ángel's mom disappeared?

"*Señorita*," Juliana said. "It is dangerous for you to be here alone."

But it was too late to go back. I was so close to seeing Ángel, only an hour away. "*Señora,* I need to see my friend."

"Well, if you must go, we will take you to him," she said.

When the bus let us off at the roadside, we walked along a road littered with plastic bottles and broken glass. Under branches of flowering trees, the girls found small mangoes scattered on the ground, inspected them for bruises, and handed the best ones to me until my backpack overflowed.

"Our town is not beautiful," Juliana laughed, "but it does have a lot of mangoes."

Ángel had fed me a mango early in the trip. I'd been asleep and felt the van pull over at the roadside. I heard Dika say something about buying sodas. A short time later, still half asleep, I felt Ángel's hands, warm and sticky over my eyes. "Smell what I found on the roadside," he said, and I breathed in the scent of paradise—flowers, tropical beaches, hidden islands, the ocean, palm trees, pure pleasure. "Open your mouth." I did. "Take a bite." I sank my teeth in, let them slide off, and mango juice ran down my throat, my chin, my neck. All of this as I was still half asleep, this taste that felt like diving into a dream flower and coming out on the other side, into the startling sweetness of reality.

Soon we were walking past houses, low houses of cement or wood, some painted pastels, some left raw, capped with flat roofs of tin or cement. People walked along the street in small groups, most in regular clothes like mine, only more worn. Some women wore colorful woven blouses and long skirts like Juliana. Almost everyone stopped in their tracks to stare at me. I was very grateful not to be alone.

Juliana and the girls led me to the hospital, a one-story building painted a dull yellow and coated with dirt and graffiti. It was small for a hospital, more like a health clinic, about a quarter the size of my high school. A few dogs lay at the entrance, and people dozed on palm mats outside—women with shawls on their heads, girls with disheveled braids.

"If you can't find your friend, come to our house," Juliana said, pointing down the road to a shack with walls of blue plastic.

I took off my coconut bracelet and necklace and handed them to the girls. Their faces lit up.

"No," Juliana said. "You don't need to give us anything."

"I insist," I said. The girls flashed wide, toothy smiles at their mother, and in the end, she let them keep the presents.

"Come to our house if he's not there," she urged. "And be careful."

We shook hands lightly, and the girls kissed me on the cheek. Off they went. I was touched by this kindness from people who had little to give but kindness. I thought of the folktales Juan had told me when I was little. In my favorites, there was always a journey. And there was always a heroine (I made Juan change all heroes to heroines) who was either timid or poor or sickly or had something else wrong with her, just like me. And there were always guides that the heroine met along the way, animals or people or spirits who helped her overcome obstacles to find her treasure.

I stepped around the people and dogs, through the hospital doors. To the left was a counter with no one behind it. I walked down a short corridor and, when I turned the corner, stopped short at a big room with patients waiting in rows of orange plastic seats. The place had the feel of a dingy bus station that desperately needed renovating. At the far end of the room, a nurse was weighing a patient as everyone watched.

I plastered a smile on my face and walked to the front of the room as every pair of eyes followed me. When I opened my mouth to ask the nurse how I could find a patient's room, everyone's chattering stopped. I was onstage. I hated being the center of attention, but I forced myself to go on. "I'm looking for a patient."

"Which patient?" the nurse asked, trying to act casual. She wore a white skirt and blouse, and her hair was slicked back into a bun. She was stout, with stumpy legs and thick ankles, and on her chin, a mole with a long black hair sticking out, which I tried not to stare at.

"Ángel Reyes," I whispered. I prayed he was still here.

She looked at me blankly. "Ángel Reyes," she repeated, wrinkling her eyebrows. Then she looked at me with a stern expression and leaned in close. "Are you from the North, *gringuita*? Did you come here alone?"

I nodded.

"It's not safe—"

I cut her off. "Look, I need to see Ángel. A guy my age. He got beat up and . . ." I couldn't finish my sentence.

"Ah, yes, of course. Ángel. Down that hall, fourth door on the left."

I walked to the back of the room and felt heads turning to follow me, the murmur of whispers and speculations. I headed down a narrow corridor, dark except for shafts of light that poured from the half-open doors. My sandals' rubber soles squeaked on the tile floor. Nervous sweat trickled from my armpits to my waist. I hoped Ángel wouldn't notice the damp spots under the armholes of my dress.

In the first room, I glimpsed a hugely pregnant woman, her belly a steep hill under the sheets. The second and third rooms each held three beds with older people snoring softly or awake and looking bored.

I stopped outside the fourth door. It was closed. My heart was about to leap out of my chest. I took a deep breath and knocked lightly. No answer. I opened the door.

PART 6

THE JEWELS

"When you look up at the sky at night, since I'll be living on one of them, since I'll be laughing on one of them, for you it'll be as if all the stars are laughing. You'll have stars that can laugh!"

—THE LITTLE PRINCE

19

Stairway to Heaven

Something entered me like a wave. Tenderness, seeing his eyes closed, without sunglasses. His neck naked without piles of gold chains. His hair with no baseball cap. A simple blue T-shirt. Bruises speckling his face, a stitched-up gash across the forehead. His left eyelid swollen and purple. His arms under the thin white sheet, one folded over his chest, the outline of his body.

He slept. Or maybe he was in a coma. But there was no monitor screen with beeping heartbeats. Didn't they have to do that if he was in a coma? A single tube was taped to his hand and attached to a plastic bag of clear liquid hung from a pole. My chest tightened. What if he was in a coma? What if he never woke up? He hadn't heard my knock. But the knock had been soft.

"Ángel," I whispered. No answer.

Well, he *was* a sound sleeper.

But this was midday.

I took a step closer. His chest was moving; he was alive, breathing on his own.

I sat down and watched him, marveling at the slightest flutter of skin. I watched the pulse at his neck, felt grateful for its rhythm. Grateful for the little creases at the edges of his eyes, for the skin that curved over his cheekbone.

I noticed three more bandages on his neck. And thin, dark lines of scabbed blood. I pictured how this had happened and felt furious at the guys who had hurt him, and helpless that I couldn't undo it. But most of all, I felt amazed at how delicate life was, like a petal underneath a hovering fingernail. And at the same time, life was strong, almost stubborn in its insistence that a body could be so battered and still heal. For a long time, I watched his chest rising and falling, rising and falling, as though my eyes controlled its rhythm.

After a time, I took in the room. It was weird. Sculptures of large breasts hung from the cinder-block walls, perfect white half-spheres with pink nipples, and signs that said MOTHER'S MILK, THE GREATEST GIFT. And next to them hung pictures of bottles and cans of formula with a big slash, like the slash through a cigarette on a NO SMOKING sign. Other signs were piled in the corner. This seemed to be a kind of large storage closet, with metal folding chairs stacked in the corner and two stretchers pushed against the wall with sheets and towels piled up. A bandage with dried blood lay abandoned on one of the stretchers. A broom and mop leaned in a pail in the corner. Over a second bed, a small window looked out to a scrawny tree. Sunshine spilled through the window, lighting up a rectangle on the tile floor.

I pulled one of the mangoes out of my backpack. Peeled the skin back, and took a bite. Ángel moved slightly. His eyes opened.

"Hi," I said, suddenly shy.

He stared.

I didn't know what to say. After two days of bus rides, how could I have nothing planned to say? "Want some water?" I handed him the glass from the bedside table.

He drank three long gulps, still staring.

"Hungry?" I offered him my mango. Why was I so nervous?

"Lime-girl?" His words were slurred, his tongue thick in his mouth. He bit into the mango. "This is a dream, right?" He brought his hand up to my neck. He moved my face toward his and kissed me. It tasted like mangoes.

At that moment, the door swung open and the stout nurse poked her head in. "Good! You're awake. Who wouldn't be for a pretty girl?" She winked at me and said, "He just woke up yesterday. He was unconscious for days, you know. His father went out to get some food. Very nice man. Imagine—he doesn't like our food here." She chuckled. "Now, don't you worry, *gringa.* He's just groggy from the painkillers. He'll be fine." The door swung closed behind her.

Ángel turned to me. "This isn't a dream, is it?"

"No." I laughed. "I brought you the visas and money."

"How'd you get here?"

"By bus. People looked out for me. They gave me a place to sleep and food to eat. There are lots of nice people in your country, you know."

He pulled me down so that our faces were close on the pillow. "I didn't find my mom, Sophie."

I felt a mix of relief and disappointment. Maybe the corn had been wrong.

"I found the jewels," he said. "I dug them up but then the guys stole them. The guys who did this to me. They stole the money too. And my chains and glasses and even my shoes. They took my shoes."

"What happened?"

He spoke in a slow, hoarse voice, as though his mouth was out of practice. "I was going to come back to you, Sophie. When I dug up the jewels, the first thing I thought was, *I want Sophie to see these. I want her to wear them.*"

We kissed again and looked at each other, so close our faces were out of focus and we could see our miniature faces in each other's pupils.

"How did this happen, Ángel?"

He brushed a strand of hair behind my ear. "It was the night before me and my dad were gonna leave. My dad went to say goodbye to some old friends and I went out to buy some food for the trip. I didn't think my box would be safe in the motel, so I carried it with me in my backpack. I put our passports and money in my backpack, too. So I buy a bag of tamales, and on the way back, I hear noises behind me, and voices, loud and drunk. Six guys. One of them says to hand over my backpack, and I say no. That's when they start hitting me. I put up a good fight for a while, but there are too many of them. Once I can barely stand, the leader tells them to stop. Two guys are holding me now, one on each side. Up close I see tattoos on their cheeks. Cross tattoos. The leader says, 'Look, you're a good fighter. We could use someone like you. What do you say? Join us?'

"I shake my head. 'Never.'

" 'Wrong answer.' The leader grabs a board with nails and whacks me. The guys are holding me and he's whacking me with the board. Then another guy breaks his beer bottle on a rock and starts beating me. Then, I'm on the ground, all curled up like this, and the leader gets out a knife and moves it to my throat. This is it, I'm thinking. This is the end.

"Suddenly a guy in a black baseball cap calls out, '*¡Ya!* That's enough. Let's go. Someone's coming!' So the others rip off my backpack and sunglasses and chains and shoes. Then they take off. I'm thinking I'm gonna die. I can't see anything. And just before I black out, I see the guy in the baseball cap look back at me, and behind him, a woman in a white dress, and I think, She's an angel and I am going to heaven. Then I think about you and I see the moon and you watching the moon and waiting for me, and then everything goes dark."

He closed his eyes, worn out from so much talking. I stroked his forehead and watched him sleep. As he drifted off, his muscles tensed for a moment and he called out my name.

"I'm here, Ángel," I said. "I'm with you."

. . .

When Mr. Lorenzo walked into the room with a plastic bag full of steaming tamales and saw me sitting at the edge of Ángel's bed, he nearly dropped the food. Once he got over the shock, he gave me the same tune as everyone else. "Oh, how dangerous for you to come here, Sophie. *Gracias a Dios* you arrived safely."

He took my hand in his, staring at me in disbelief. I wondered if he and Ángel noticed anything different about me, because I did. I noticed that the layer of heavy, thick stuff that used to separate me from the world was disappearing, like mist rising and floating away.

On my way to the bathroom to wash my hands, I heard moaning from behind a door. The pregnant woman's room. A nurse swished into the room, and I caught a glimpse inside before the door closed. The woman was straining, her face so red it was almost purple. Was she giving birth or dying? I stood for a few moments outside the room, waiting to hear the cry of a new baby, but all I heard were groans and grunts and the nurse commanding, *"Empuje, empuje."* Push, push.

Back in the room, we ate tamales and Ángel shared his soda with me. Even though the food was mushy, Ángel took a long time to eat because of his sore jaw. The nurse who had taken out his IV said that my company was the best medicine now. Mr. Lorenzo finished first and gave a satisfied smile, patting his flanneled gut. "Thanks to you, Sophie, we have our visas," he said. "And once Ángel is better, we will go to the embassy and get new passports. Then we will go back to Pablo's village and then to Tucson." Mr. Lorenzo missed his work. He worried that the pool wasn't being cleaned and the appliances not fixed and the flowers not watered. He missed going food shopping at Albertsons, missed his small kitchen and plaid sofa and favorite soap opera.

He looked at Ángel. "See, you're already healing, *hijo*. Your body is smart like your mind. In a couple days I bet you will be healed enough for us to leave."

Ángel stopped chewing. "I still need to find out what happened to my mother."

Mr. Lorenzo breathed out a heavy sigh. "*Hijo*, I'm telling you—"

"And I still need to get the jewels."

"Forget about that, *hijo*. You are alive. That is the important thing."

Ángel wiped his mouth with a napkin and folded it. He always folded his used napkins at perfect right angles. "I'm gonna get those guys."

It took a few seconds for this to sink in. "Don't, Ángel," I said. "Let the police deal with it."

"The cops are corrupt. They're friends with these *pendejos*."

I looked at Mr. Lorenzo. He was holding his head in his hands.

I kept talking. "Ángel. They won't just hand over the jewels."

"Then I'll kill them."

"What?"

"I'll kill them and find my mother and if she's alive I'll take her back with us."

Mr. Lorenzo looked up at Ángel. He took a breath, full

of effort, as if something very heavy were pressing on his chest. "*Hijo,* people did bad things to me. To the woman I loved. And the anger wanted to fill my heart. But I decided that my heart would be filled with light. So much light there would be no room for anger. That's what you must do. That's what your mother would want you to do."

Ángel closed his eyes. I wondered if he was wishing for his sunglasses so that he wouldn't have to look at us, so that we couldn't see his eyes. For the rest of the day, he didn't say anything about the jewels or the gang or his mother. He didn't say much of anything.

Mr. Lorenzo went back to the hotel to sleep, and I stayed with Ángel. I'd forgotten to bring pajamas, so I wore my white dress, which was as comfortable as a nightgown. Even so, I tossed and turned in the spare bed, thinking about how strange Ángel had acted all evening. He'd hardly spoken to me, and when he had, he'd stared at a spot on the floor. It was as though his face had turned to stone, his eyes hardened, like a statue. The nurse figured he was in pain, so she gave him a sleeping pill and pain medication.

I couldn't sleep. I got up and wandered into the hallway, down the corridor, which was now lit by flickering fluorescent lights. I stood outside the pregnant woman's room and listened. No more moaning, but no baby sounds either. Only silence and a strip of light under the door. I headed farther down the hallway, past a few offices, past the darkened cafeteria, quiet in my socks. I stopped in front of the bathroom; I didn't have to go, but I needed some destination.

Just when my hand was on the doorknob, I noticed music playing, American music. Classic rock. A scratchy Led Zeppelin song.

I padded farther down the hallway, and the music grew louder. Around a corner, I discovered a room lit yellow by a small lamp, filled with incubators and a sink and plastic basins. It was an unexpected sight, this secret room glowing in the middle of the night, while everyone else slept. The chubby nurse with the mole was pacing back and forth, holding a little white bundle. Ángel had told me she was the head nurse, Reina. *Queen* in Spanish. And she did seem to be the queen of the hospital. Always there, giving gruff orders with a smile and a wink afterward. I got the feeling she was the hub of the wheel that kept this little hospital going.

She rocked the bundle and swayed her hips, singing along: *"And we'rrre cli-i-mbing da estai-airrr-way to heaven."* In the shadows, her face looked soft, and I couldn't see the hair sticking out of her mole. She glanced up and jumped. "*¡Dios mío, gringuita!* I thought you were a ghost!" Her hand flew to her chest.

"Sorry," I said. "I couldn't sleep and I heard music and— Is that the new baby?"

She nodded. "One hour old."

"Can I see?"

She pulled back the blanket and there was a scrunched-up brown face and a shock of black hair and a tiny fist under the chin. The baby was wrinkled and funny-looking, with a kind of lopsided cone-head topped with a purple bruise. Its lips were white and cracked, and pink bumps covered its right cheek. This baby was definitely not cute, but something about it fascinated me anyway.

"Let's bring him back to his mother," Reina said. "Now that he's all weighed and measured and cleaned up." She clicked off the little boom box. "Want to carry him back?"

I couldn't believe she would trust me with this brand-new tiny life, but I held out my arms and she put him in. He weighed less than a bottle of detergent. On the way to the mother's room I took slow steps, careful not to slip in my socks.

"Will his head get more . . . normal?" I asked hesitantly.

"*¡Sí, claro!*" she said. "Just give it a few days."

"You know, I was a really ugly baby," I told her. "Even uglier than this one." I studied its smushed forehead. "Not that this one's ugly," I added quickly.

She laughed. "And look at you now. Nothing ugly about you!" She opened the door and I walked into the room. The mother was propped up on pillows, her hair fallen out of her braid, dark circles under her bloodshot eyes. Surprise flashed over her face at seeing me hold the baby. Then her face broke into a smile, revealing a thin line of silver around her front left tooth. She reached out her arms and I handed her the bundle.

She stared at him and pressed her lips to his misshapen head. Tears spilled out of her eyes. Tears of horror or happiness? I wasn't sure which, until she looked up and asked, "Isn't he beautiful?"

Now he was awake, waving his little arms in the air like

an upside-down bug. "Beautiful," I said. And once I heard myself say it, I realized I meant it.

Later, back in the bed across from Ángel, I drifted to sleep, thinking how strange that pain and birth—fear and joy—were so close, separated by just moments, by a thin wall, by slivers of chance.

I woke up with a start, this time to shrill voices shouting orders. I heard a panicked flurry of activity, footsteps racing down the hall, metal equipment clanking, voices rising, a woman sobbing.

"*¡Accidente, accidente!* Six guys! *¡Muy grave!* Very serious!"

In the fuzzy blue light of dawn, I saw Ángel in bed lying on his side, breathing deeply, the sleeping pills making him oblivious to the racket. I jumped out of bed and ran to the door, skidding across the floor in my socks. Outside the room, people filled the hallway. The men held their hats anxiously in their hands, and the women buried their faces in their shawls. And then I saw what they were looking at: two unconscious teenagers being half-carried, half-dragged down the hall. Their limbs were bent at odd angles; their heads drooped onto their chests; their mouths hung open, slack. A moment later, two stretchers squeaked by carrying two more boys, both motionless with wide-open stares and gray skin and blue lips.

A nurse rushed into our room and wheeled out the stretcher. I pressed myself against the wall, unnoticed. Blood covered everyone, everything. I'd never seen so much blood. The blood kept dripping and gushing, splattering the nurses' uniforms, spotting the floor.

I wrapped my hand around the warm leather of Ñola's Virgin necklace. For a moment, blackness started eating up my vision. I sank down to the cold tiled floor and let my head hang between my knees. I was about to throw up.

"Stand up, *gringa.*" The command was brisk and no-nonsense.

I looked up. Nurse Reina. The blackness faded, but I still felt nauseated. She grasped my hand and pulled me up.

"We need your help," she said.

She hurried out and a moment later returned with another nurse, who wheeled one of the guys into Ángel's room. "Come here, *gringa.*"

I followed them into the room and put my arms under the boy's shoulders while the nurses lifted his hips and legs. Together, we heaved him onto the bed. He was weak but conscious, able to help us adjust him on the mattress. His face was bleeding, his eyes half open, dazed.

The second nurse hung a fresh bag on the metal holder and stuck a needle into the back of his hand for the IV drip. She taped the tube to his hand, took his pulse, then moved a stethoscope over his chest. She cleaned and bandaged his wounds with quick, efficient movements, while Nurse Reina pressed her hands all over his body, asking him what hurt. She took off his black baseball cap and his tennis shoes, which had somehow stayed bright white, and stashed them in a cabinet.

Finally Nurse Reina turned to me. "Nothing's broken.

Possible concussion. But breathing fine. Pulse is all right. We'll be back to check on him when we can. Keep an eye on him, *gringa.*"

"But I think I'm going to throw up."

"Then move the trash can over here."

"I don't know what to do if—"

"Call for us."

"But—"

She lowered her voice so that the boy couldn't hear. "Look, *gringa,* this one will live. Two are dead already. The other three might make it with surgery."

"Okay," I said quietly. "I understand."

They left, and I was alone with him. I sat on the plastic chair beside the bed and stared at his face, clear of blood now.

That's when I noticed it: on his cheek, peeking beneath a bandage, a small tattoo. I couldn't tell whether it was a cross, but it looked like a homemade job, with blurry blue ink leaking outside the uneven lines.

My pulse quickened. I glanced at Ángel. He was still asleep on his side, facing the wall. Was this one of his attackers? Maybe. Maybe not. Maybe lots of guys here had tattoos on their cheeks. For the moment, he was just a confused, banged-up kid.

I studied his face. It was clenched, his eyebrows knitted. Tentatively, I touched his hand. He squeezed hard for a moment, and then his muscles relaxed. Still, he held on to my hand.

A shiny pink scar slashed across his forearm, a mark of

some old injury, maybe a knife fight. His fingers were elegant, the nails filed into ovals, the tiniest slivers of dirt underneath.

"What's your name?" I whispered.

"Mercurio." He tilted his head and eyed me sideways. His lashes were long and curled upward like a doll's. If his face hadn't been black and blue and spotted with bandages, he might have been good-looking in a gangly sort of way. "Where's Raúl?" he asked, his eyes scanning the room. "He's all right?"

"Who's Raúl?"

"My buddy. In the truck with us."

"I don't know," I said. "What happened?"

"Stupid truck."

"Did you crash?"

"Beto ran it into a tree. The truck was cursed."

"Cursed?"

"Cursed. And Beto had too many beers." He searched my eyes. "Where's Raúl? Is he all right?"

"I don't know, Mercurio."

"He's just a kid."

"Shhh, just rest." I tried to make my voice soothing. "It's okay."

He drifted in and out of sleep. At times he squeezed my hand and his breath grew quick and choppy. "Mamá? Mamá?"

My gaze rested on his tattoo. With my other hand, very softly, I pulled the bandage down.

A cross. I snatched my hand away. I tried to pull my other hand from his, but he hung on stubbornly. This hand might have beaten Ángel. Punched him and cut him with glass and held a knife to his neck.

Still, I wasn't sure. Maybe lots of people here had tattoos on their cheeks.

Time passed and it grew lighter outside and the streetlamp flicked off. Outside, there was a misty drizzle. From time to time, I glanced at Ángel, but he stayed asleep, in the same position. Mostly, I watched Mercurio's face. He looked about my age. His face still had the soft curves of a boy's—a delicate chin and the faint beginnings of a mustache. He didn't look like someone who would attack a random stranger. After a while, his eyes opened and focused on me. "Who are you?" he asked. "An angel?"

I gave a halfhearted smile. "Maybe," I said.

His eyelids floated closed again and he turned to face the other way. In that movement, the neck of his T-shirt opened, just enough to reveal a flash of gold. I couldn't resist. I reached over and pulled out the chains. One was a heart with wings, which I hadn't seen before. Another was *La Virgen de Juquila*—the Virgin of Oaxaca, the very miraculous one.

Ángel's Virgin.

My heart pounded. But maybe lots of guys had that necklace. For some reason, I wanted Mercurio to be good. Steadying my hand, I pulled out the third chain.

The third chain I could not argue with. The third held an old-fashioned silver key.

Ángel's key.

I ripped my hand from his, jerked my chair back. A sick

feeling sprouted in my stomach and spread outward. It was worse than the nausea from seeing all that blood.

Mercurio flopped his head back toward me. "Raúl's not hurt bad, is he? He'll live, right?"

I said nothing.

"What about me?" he asked. "Will I live?"

I looked away, stared at the silvery sunrise out the window. What would Dika do?

I drilled my eyes into his. "Can you live with yourself, Mercurio?"

He looked confused. "What?"

"Where's the money you stole?"

"What money?" He tried to lift himself out of bed, but my hand was already at his neck, my fingers still interlaced with the chains. I pushed him back down.

"The seventy-three hundred dollars. And don't lie to me."

"I didn't steal any money."

"Maybe if you're honest, you'll live." I was thinking of karma, when you do a good deed and the universe gives you something good back.

His eyes widened. I noticed my hand had tightened a little around his neck. He must have believed my karma comment was a threat.

"We spent it on the truck." His eyes flickered anxiously around the room and then rested on me again. "Who *are* you?"

"Where are the jewels?" I asked, my voice even.

"What jewels?"

"The jewels from the box."

"They weren't worth *mierda*. They were just glass."

Glass? No emeralds or sapphires or rubies? Was he lying? I moved my face closer to his, keeping my hand at his neck. "Where are the jewels, Mercurio?"

"Who *are* you?" he croaked.

"Where are they?"

"Beto threw them in the river."

From my pocket, I took a napkin—emergency toilet paper—and turned it over and handed it to Mercurio, along with a pen. I propped him onto the pillows. "Draw me a map."

He sketched a network of shaky lines and three puffball trees and tiny square houses and a bridge over a wavy river. "Go down this road," he said. "The one the bus comes in on. Turn left here at the purple house next to the plantain stand. Go to the bridge at the edge of the forest. Look to your right. They're at the bottom of the river."

He had drawn an *X* over the spot, like a treasure map.

"Thanks," I said.

He swallowed hard. "That woman I saw, while my *cuates* were beating up the guy, was that you?"

"A woman?"

"A woman in white. So pale you could almost see through her. It looked like she was floating off the ground. That's why I called off my *cuates*."

I let this sink in. Ángel's magical woman.

After a pause, I said, "You can rest now, Mercurio." At least he was the one who had called off the others. Maybe he'd saved Ángel's life.

Raindrops dotted the windowpane, like tiny diamonds,

like clear beads of glass. I tried to imagine Ángel's mother's jewels underwater. For a moment, I saw them as rubies and emeralds and sapphires. Then they became red and green and blue glass, and then I saw Dika staring at the sky through her pieces of glass.

"Please," Mercurio said in a thin voice. "Tell me how Raúl is."

I spoke without a hint of softness. "Two of your friends died and three might make it with surgery. That's all I know."

He swallowed hard and turned his face away. For a while, all I could hear were faint sniffles.

At midmorning, Ángel coughed and turned over in bed. He rubbed his eyes and gave me a groggy smile. "Morning, lime-girl."

"Morning." I willed my heartbeat to calm. "Listen, Ángel," I whispered. "There was an accident last night. Six guys got into a bad crash. Some of them died, but this one made it." I was trying to keep my voice quiet, but Mercurio must have heard me. He rolled over and looked at me and then at Ángel. Mercurio's long doll lashes were wet, his eyes rimmed with red.

Ángel sat up slowly, like a stiff old man. Between his gashes and cuts, pillowcase lines crisscrossed his face. "Who's this?" he asked, stretching and rubbing his neck. "A roommate?" He stood up slowly, steadying himself with his hands on the table. He shuffled toward Mercurio, his hand extended. "Welcome—" And abruptly, he stopped.

"Ángel," I said. "Let me explain."

He surveyed Mercurio's chains, the tattoo on his cheek. "You?" His voice was cold, sharp as a blade.

A flash of recognition in Mercurio's eyes. And then panic. "Wh-what are you doing here?" He tried to sit up but I pressed his chest back to the pillow.

Ángel took another shaky step toward him, narrowing his eyes.

Mercurio struggled to sit up in bed and fumbled frantically with the IV tube.

Ángel took a step closer.

In one desperate movement, Mercurio ripped out his IV and stood up, backing against the wall. Ángel walked toward him. It was obvious that every step was an effort.

"Ángel, let him go," I said.

He glanced at me, then at Mercurio, then he put his hand to his head and closed his eyes. He took a few steps backward and sunk onto his bed.

I touched his arm. "I have a map, Ángel. Of where they threw the—the jewels. We can get them together."

He jerked away, clenched his fists until the knuckles turned white.

"Please, Ángel."

He lay facing the wall. I sat next to him, but he scooted farther away, his muscles rigid. "Get him away from me." He pounded the cement wall with his fist. "Get him away or I might kill him."

"He has to be here," I said quietly. "There's no more space in the building."

"I'll smash his face in."

Mercurio had found his tennis shoes and was heading for the door when it swung open and Nurse Reina appeared, looking haggard. Spots of dried blood speckled her uniform, and hair fell loose from her bun. Her eyes swept the room, taking in the scene. "What's going on here?"

No one said anything, so I spoke. "Mercurio's part of the gang that beat up Ángel."

Understanding flashed across her face. She grabbed Mercurio's arm. "Now you, back in bed," she said in a voice so firm he didn't dare protest. Her expert hands stuck his IV back in place. "I am sick of you boys killing each other. Killing yourselves. You hear me?"

"Is Raúl all right?" Mercurio asked weakly.

Nurse Reina moved the stethoscope over his chest, her head tilted in concentration. "Raúl," she said. "The youngest one? Only thirteen?"

He nodded.

"Dead," she said. She picked up Mercurio's limp wrist, checking his pulse and watching the clock. "And you'll be with him soon enough if you keep this up." Nurse Reina gave him a long, hard look, then moved over to Ángel. He had turned away from the wall, and was watching Mercurio sob into his pillow.

Nurse Reina ignored his crying. "Now you," she said to Ángel. "Justice has been served. Let this be and move on." Silence as she moved the stethoscope over his chest and back, as he breathed in and out deeply, as she held his wrist and watched the clock and counted. "Perfect heartbeat," she said. "Perfect pulse."

And then, like a leaking balloon, she deflated, leaning against the wall and pressing her face into her hands.

I tried to think of something nice to say. Something hopeful. "There's that new baby," I whispered. "The beautiful one."

"Yes." She lifted her head. *"La muerte y la vida,"* she said. Death and life. "You know, my mother used to tell me, 'Death is at your side from the time you're born, *m'hija.* You need to be friends with Death. That's what makes you love Life. And when it's your time to die, you won't be scared. Because, *m'hija,* Death is your friend.' "

20

Remedios

Nurse Reina left and came back an hour later with two plastic booklets. The passports. She tossed them onto the bed beside Ángel. He flipped through the pages, ran his fingers over the brown specks of dried blood.

"Found them in one of the dead boy's pockets," Nurse Reina said. "Evidence." She looked hard at Ángel. "Want me to call the cops?"

Ángel glanced at Mercurio, whose sobs had turned into quiet gasps and sighs. "No. We have what we need."

Nurse Reina nodded brusquely and disappeared into the hallway.

A minute or two passed, and then Ángel scooted behind me and smoothed my hair between his fingers, from the roots to the tips. He parted it and divided each part into three sections. Gingerly, he braided, his hands moving rhythmically, over, under, over, under. Finally he spoke, in a hoarse whisper at my ear. "I'm glad you're here, lime-girl."

"Me too."

He finished the first braid and moved on to the second. "How did you find out where they threw the jewels?"

I smiled secretively. "I have my ways."

"I can see your *chispa* now," he said. "Your spark."

After the second braid, he let his arms fall around me and laid his hand over my chest, on the left side, in the space between my neck and shoulder and breast. His hand spread heat through my chest, and I melted back into him.

Out of the corner of my eye, I noticed Mercurio staring at us with the dazed, naked expression of someone stepping out of a dark place into brilliant sunlight.

While Ángel was taking a shower and changing his clothes in the bathroom, Mercurio told me, "I didn't think he was a real person. When we jumped him."

"He's as real as your friend Raúl." I smoothed my fingers over my braids. They felt strong, like two thick, silk ropes.

Mercurio pushed himself up in bed. "I mean, I thought he was just some *pendejo* showing off his money, you know?"

"He worked hard for what he has. He spent a long time saving that money."

Mercurio squeezed his eyes shut. "Why am I alive and Raúl's dead? I'm the one who got him in the gang. I should be dead."

"Maybe sometimes we get a second chance." I thought

of the flower Ñola had given me, its new, tender bud inside, waiting to open. "Maybe we can choose a different path."

Ángel came back into the room, his bare feet leaving wet tracks on the tiles, his hair dripping and his skin still moist. Pale, wet light shone through the window, giving him a hint of iridescence, like an opened-up mussel shell.

Mercurio started unhooking the chains from his neck, which looked hard with the IV tube taped to his hand. "I'm sorry, man. Here." He held out the chains, dangling from his long fingers. "Take them back. The money's gone, but here."

Ángel shook his head. "Keep them," he said. "And remember."

Remember that it is possible to let your heart fill with light.

Later that morning, Mr. Lorenzo bounced in, looking cheery until we told him about Mercurio and the accident. For a long moment, Mr. Lorenzo studied Mercurio's wounded face, his eyes still swollen from crying. "You are very lucky, son," he said finally.

Mercurio hung his head, stared at a crack in the wall. "I know, *señor.*"

Soon Mercurio's family arrived. His mother was a short, pudgy woman in a flowered dress who talked nonstop. First she smothered him with a hug, and then she started scolding him. "You see, *hijo,* I always told you these friends would lead to trouble. Didn't I always tell you?"

"Yes, Mamá."

"Didn't I?"

"Yes, Mamá."

When she found out that Raúl had died, she cried, "Oh, little Raúl!" and turned to me and Ángel and Mr. Lorenzo. "Raúl always called my son his big brother. His real big brother was shot five years ago." She turned back to Mercurio. "Remember? Remember how he always called you his big brother, *hijo*?"

Mercurio nodded, pressing his lips together.

His mother went on and on, and the more she talked about her son, the more tenderness crept up on me. It's hard not to feel tenderness toward someone seen through his mother's eyes. Mercurio had spent his early childhood in a Mayan village near Ángel's grandmother's village. Violence came there, too: Three of Mercurio's uncles were killed by soldiers. His family moved to San Juan, where it was safer. When he was thirteen, the gang recruited him. His mother lamented that her son hadn't wanted to be in a gang, but they'd said he was either with them or against them. He joined to survive.

More of Mercurio's family trickled in throughout the day. It was breaking hospital rules to squeeze twelve people into one room, but the nurses were too exhausted to care. We ate chicken tacos that an uncle had brought, while Mercurio's little nephew rolled a tiny yellow truck around people's feet. Mercurio's father and mother and aunt stayed at his bedside, fussing over him. Mr. Lorenzo talked to the uncle about politics while I played hand games with Mercurio's little sister. She looked about the same age as Pablo, and even had dimples like him, but she wasn't nearly as cute. I taught her Miss Mary Mac-Mac-Mac, and clap-clap-clapped my hands against hers. Every time we finished, she squealed, "*¡Otra vez!*" Again! Propped on his pillows, Ángel watched everything with an unreadable expression.

By afternoon, the rain had stopped, and the room was filled with smells of greasy chicken and fried plantains and fresh coffee. A radio blasted staticky salsa tunes. Mercurio's grandmother had built a little fire by the tree outside the window. She boiled a big blackened pot of water and sprinkled in ground coffee, just picked from their fields and roasted. She stirred in sugar with a long wooden spoon, and then, once the grounds had sunk to the bottom, she dipped out gourdfuls of coffee and handed them through the open window. We passed around the steaming, chipped ceramic cups and sipped and talked.

Mercurio was recovering fast. After a nurse removed the IV drip, he got out of bed and limped over to Ángel. You could tell he was trying to strut his lanky legs and swing his arms coolly, but he couldn't quite pull it off.

He wore his black baseball cap, the bill pulled low over his eyes. A pair of tennis shoes dangled from his hand, the bright white pair the nurse had taken off his feet. They weren't the shoes stolen from Ángel; another guy had been wearing those, and now he was dead, and who knew where the shoes had gone. But these shoes looked similar to Ángel's big clomping Nikes with silver trim.

"Here, man." In a quick, awkward gesture, Mercurio handed Ángel the shoes. "See if these fit."

Ángel slipped on the shoes, wiggled his feet inside. He nodded.

Tentatively, Mercurio asked, "You got gangs where you live?"

"Yeah. I don't mess with them."

"They don't recruit?"

"They do, but you can say no."

And I thought, suddenly, how easy it would have been for Ángel to join a gang. A gang was like a family, and all he had was his dad. Violence had touched his life too, and taken his mother from him. That must have injected a giant dose of anger into his heart.

"I don't go out much," Ángel said. "After school I just work. That's how I saved the seventy-three hundred dollars."

Mercurio looked at the tile floor. "I'm sorry, man."

Mercurio's mother waddled over with a plate of plantains. She was such a chipper, chatty woman, it was hard not to like her, in small doses at least. She had rosy cheeks and plump arms and fried, permed hair. Fake gold earrings with chips of red glass hung from her ears. The red glass and the bad hair made me think about Dika. Mr. Lorenzo had called and assured her everything was fine, but I could imagine her shrill voice commanding us to return the moment Ángel recovered. She would have been proud of how I handled Mercurio. If she were here now, she'd be passing around plates of fruitcake to celebrate.

Mercurio's mother smoothed his hair. "Son, after you're well enough to leave the hospital," she said, "we'll take you to Doña Remedios. She'll give you herbs to make these scars fade."

Ángel's head snapped up. He stopped chewing his plantain. "Doña Remedios? The healer from the village of Magdalena?"

The woman nodded. "You know her, then. She's an incredible healer, isn't she? She still lives in her village, even though most everyone else moved after the houses were burned. She rebuilt her house better than before."

Ángel turned to me. "Doña Remedios is the healer who helped at my birth. Remember I told you about her?"

I smiled. "Of course." The midwife who said he'd travel far and do great things.

"I went to her village my second day here," Ángel said. "To dig up the jewels and look for my mother. The place felt deserted, creepy, just a few old people around, and they only spoke *dialecto.* I asked them about Doña Remedios, but they shook their heads. I figured she'd died or moved or something, so I just got the jewels and left."

Mercurio's mother said, "Oh, but she was probably out gathering herbs or firewood. You should visit her. She is wise. Before the *violencia,* she had dreams of blood and machetes raining down. So when she heard the army was coming, she hid in the forest and didn't come out until the army trucks left with the bodies. Go visit her. She lives in the blue house with all the flowers."

"I'll go with you, Ángel," I said.

"But—"

"Don't tell me it's too dangerous."

"Okay, lime-girl." Ángel's face softened. "Know what?"

"What?"

"I think tomorrow's the day. The day I find out the truth."

. . .

Late in the afternoon, Mercurio and his family moved into the room next door. Nurse Reina let them borrow her boom box and mix tape. They played it three times in a row, singing with thick accents. Their voices floated through the wall. *"Wel-comb to da Otel Cah-lee-forrr-nia . . ."*

The doctor rolled her eyes at the music. She was a thin woman with chapped lips and hair glossed back in a tight, painful-looking ponytail. She examined Ángel and announced he was healing well and could leave the next day if he took it easy. She probably wouldn't consider a hike in the mountains taking it easy, but we didn't mention that. The swelling in Ángel's face had gone down, and now only a few bruises and pink scars lingered. He still had to walk carefully, like an old man, but the doctor said he should be back to normal soon.

Mr. Lorenzo insisted we go together to the village and then, as soon as possible, return to Mexico. He missed Dika desperately, talked about her constantly: the delicious beef balls she made, the little pastries she bought at Albertsons and served with thick, muddy-bottomed coffee, the toast and apricot jam she ate every day for breakfast.

At the bus stop, we piled our bags on the roof of the yellow bus. The village was a few hours away, in the mountains. I felt like an old pro at taking these ancient school buses now. I didn't even blink when a man sat next to me with a baby goat *baaah*ing in his lap. The bus rattled around curves of a dirt road, barreling through spots of drizzle and sunshine and fog. In the distance, mist shrouded the tips of volcanoes.

Ángel had made this trip to his mother's village many times as a boy. When his mother was twelve, she'd moved from her village to the town of San Juan, where she worked as a maid and learned to speak Spanish. Six years later, she married Mr. Lorenzo. She loved her village and insisted that her son be born there, and often took him to visit her family on weekends.

As the bus crawled higher up the mountains, it grew so cool I put on my sweater. The bus swerved around people with bundles of firewood on their backs, strapped to their foreheads. Chickens and dogs skittered out of the way at the last second. Burros trudged along the roadside, loaded with stuffed burlap sacks. We passed cornfields and tall pines and other trees I didn't recognize. Mr. Lorenzo pointed out the steep slopes of coffee plantations, which looked like forests but supposedly hid shiny green bushes with red coffee berries. He turned to Ángel. "We harvested coffee there, *hijo*."

Ángel nodded. "That's where my mother found me when I fell." He paused. "I have to know for sure if she's alive or not. Either way, I have to know."

We got off the bus in what looked like the middle of nowhere, a place thick with trees and sunshine reflecting off a hundred different shades of green. In the valley below us, mist gathered in pools.

Somehow, Mr. Lorenzo located a trail that we had to follow through the woods. It was just wide enough for the three of us to walk shoulder to shoulder. Beneath our feet, mossy rocks and gnarled tree roots jutted up. On either side of us, layers of green stretched as far as I could see. Every once in a while, Ángel pointed to a big tree, or a lichen-coated boulder, and said, "I think I remember that."

Light poured through the leaves, dancing and flashing over the mud. Through the branches, flowers dangled like bright bells. I veered off the path to have a closer look at an orange flower, its stamens and pistils spraying out like a fountain.

A hand clamped over my arm and pulled me back onto the path. It was Mr. Lorenzo, his eyes wide. He wiped his forehead with a handkerchief. "*Mire*, Sophie, you cannot leave the path."

"Why not?"

He rubbed his hand over his face.

I looked at Ángel and back at Mr. Lorenzo. Ángel stared at his feet.

"Sophie," Mr. Lorenzo said hesitantly. "I don't mean to worry you, but—"

"But what?"

"There could be land mines buried beneath those flowers."

"Land mines?"

"Left over from *la violencia.* Many people, many children, over the years have stepped on them. Lost arms or legs in the explosion. Some have died."

I continued walking, tiptoeing now, down the center of the path, as though balancing on a tightrope. As we walked, a strange thing happened: white flowers fell, tiny white blossoms dropping from trees.

After a while, my heartbeat calmed and my shaking stopped. "Ángel," I said. "When was the last time you saw your mother? In the flesh."

"These are heavy things, Sophie," he said after a pause. *"Cosas pesadas."*

"I know."

Mr. Lorenzo studied Ángel's face. "I thought you didn't remember that day. You were so little—only four or five."

"I remember," Ángel said. "It's jumbled in my head, but I remember. Me and my mother went to my grandmother's village to help harvest corn."

Mr. Lorenzo shook his head. "I never should have let you two go alone. Not with the rumors about what the army was doing to villages in the mountains." His face looked raw, exposed. "I've never forgiven myself for that."

Ángel stared straight ahead. "So that night, we're in her house, and word comes that the army is on their way. My grandmother wants us to go back to San Juan, but the last bus already left. She says we should walk back, but my mother's afraid we'll run into soldiers. Next thing I remember, we're in the woods, next to a giant tree with a secret hollow that I like to play in. My mother's burying a little bag of money my grandmother's been saving. For a new washbasin. It's all she has. By now it's almost dark and I can barely see my mother digging.

"She's about to shovel the dirt back on top, and I ask her, 'What about your jewels? Are you going to bury them, too?' She ruffles my hair and laughs. Her laugh sounds like a stream over rocks. The last time I heard her laugh. She takes the jewels from her neck and tucks them into the money bag, and drops it into the hole.

"Next thing I remember, we're back at the house, in bed. I'm snuggled against my mother. I feel her awake, and she's so warm and sturdy I know she'll protect me from anything. Suddenly I hear machine-gun fire. And smell smoke. And hear the soldiers yelling and people screaming. My mother wraps me in a blanket, hugs my grandmother, and runs into the forest with me, to the tree hollow. She tucks me inside, and tries to crawl in after me, but she's too big. 'Don't look outside,' she says. 'Don't make noise. I'll be hiding nearby.'

"She kisses me and I hang on to her braid. She unclenches my fingers and pulls away. Then she covers up the hole with branches. I put my hands over my ears and through my hands I hear screams. For a long time. I try not to make noise while I cry. I smell smoke, terrible smoke that makes me gag. Then there's the roar of trucks, loud at first, then fading. I wait for my mother to come. And wait and wait. All night I wait. I wait for the roosters to crow like they do every morning. But the light comes and they never crow.

"I remember wandering around the forest, calling for my mother. Then I see it: what's left of our village. At first, I can't make sense of it. Nothing is where it used to be. My grandmother's house is burned to the ground. So are the neighbors' houses and the animal pens. Just ashes and charred wood and stone. Dead chickens and goats and dogs. Things start spinning. All the broken pieces of the world. Someone picks me up. Doña Remedios. She presses my face into her shoulder. I close my eyes and see my mother.

"For the next year, until we leave for America, I see my mother everywhere. I see her through the window of a bus. I see her carrying a bundle of firewood at the roadside. I see her in a crowd at the market. She's always there, in the corner of my eye, and always, she slips away."

At the edge of the forest, we saw a cluster of houses pieced together with wood and mud and topped with thatched roofs, each house linked to the others by a maze of paths. Beneath a blue sky, chickens pecked at weeds sprouting from crumbling house foundations; nearby, a fat pig rested in the shade of a tree. The place had an empty, abandoned feel. There was something in the air, an odor of sadness. No hint of breeze. The air held impossibly still, like a dream.

We walked toward a violet-blue house at the end of the clearing. The house was strangely cheerful; bright red flowers in old tin cans cluttered the patio, and a spray of bougainvillea climbed the wall. In the shadows of a tree, an old woman was picking bananas and dropping them into a basket at her side. She wore a colorful blouse, loose and thick, embroidered with elaborate zigzags and flowers, and tucked into a long wraparound skirt that made me think of festive things, like rainbow sprinkles and jelly beans. Her hair was braided in two thin silvery ropes and pinned to her head. The moment we spotted her, she tilted her head and turned to us. Then she waved and motioned for us to come.

When we came closer, her face broke into a smile. "Don Lorenzo! Husband of Flor Blanca! Is that you?" She looked at Ángel. "And you, all grown up. *Mi querido* Ángel!" Before he could say a word, she hugged him and then examined the wounds on his face. "Looks like you got a bit beat up, but you're healing fine." She patted his face with her rough hands. "Ángel. The child who would do great things, go far in life. And you have. And you will do even more." She spoke Spanish slowly, in the same choppy tones as the Mayan woman I'd met on the bus.

Mr. Lorenzo shook her hand lightly. "Here to serve you."

"You see?" she said. "I may be old, but I never forget my friends."

She looked at me. "And you, *señorita*?"

"I'm Sophie."

"Oh, how good you came all the way here for your *novio*."

I blushed at the word *boyfriend*.

She held my hand in hers for a moment, then turned to Ángel. "Now, Ángel, you are here for your mother?"

He nodded.

"I will bring you to her."

My heart leaped. Ángel stared at her, speechless. Mr. Lorenzo stood frozen beside him. Afraid to speak, afraid to break the spell, we followed the old woman down a narrow path through the forest.

21

Your Heart in My Heart

We wove in between tree trunks and birdsongs and cricket chirps. Mr. Lorenzo and Ángel walked in a daze, one foot plunked in front of the other. Doña Remedios's steps were slow and sure, as though she knew every bump in the trail. Thick calluses protected her bare feet, and she stepped on twigs and stones without flinching. Once in a while, she pointed out a plant and told us what it was good for. She paused beside a bush with tiny leaves and rubbed them between her fingers. "Now, my daughter, smell this. This is what I use to cure people of *susto*."

"*¿Susto?*" Fright didn't seem like the kind of thing you could take medicine for.

"*Sí, susto,*" she said. "When the army came, we saw the soldiers do terrible things. The fear stayed with us. The fear made us sick."

She handed me some crushed leaves and I breathed in

the sharp, strong odor. I passed them to Mr. Lorenzo. He sniffed, and said, "I haven't smelled this in ten years."

Ángel said nothing, but I knew he was listening because he broke off a leafy branch and tucked it under his arm.

After walking for a few more minutes, Doña Remedios stopped by a plant with wide, light green leaves. She stroked them with expert fingers. "This root saved many people after the army burned their homes and chased them into the mountains. The people were dying of thirst because soldiers guarded the streams." With a stick, she dug around the base of the plant and extracted a brown root, thick and clawlike. Then she pulled a knife from a sack at her waist and peeled off the brown skin, revealing white flesh. "Here, daughter, drink the water."

I chewed and sucked the moisture out. It was juicy all right, but gave me only about a spoonful of water. How many of these would you need for a whole glassful? "Why did the soldiers do this?" I asked.

Mr. Lorenzo answered, his voice solemn. "They wanted to get the guerrillas. The army said the guerrillas were like fish. Fish that they wanted to kill. And the Mayan lands were their pond. The army decided to drain the pond so the fish would have no place to swim. So they burned villages and crops and killed people and stole their animals."

Doña Remedios nodded. "What he says is true." She picked a fuzzy leaf from a low-growing plant. "Now, look, daughter. This I use to cure people's aching heads and aching bones. Their heads hurt because they are filled with bad memories. There is no room for good thoughts. And their bones hurt because sadness weighs them down."

I glanced at Ángel. He was walking with the same glassy stare. I wondered what he was thinking about. Maybe he was feeling as if he were in the middle of his favorite dream, the one where he found his mother. Maybe he didn't want to say anything that might wake himself up.

"Almost there," Doña Remedios said.

We turned a bend, and there, ahead, was the light and space of another clearing. An expanse of grass and wildflowers rose into a hill. And scattered over the hillside, dozens of small crosses, some the color of the ocean, some the color of the sky. Tin cans of flowers encircled the base of each cross. A swallow flew across the graves, dipped, landed on the arm of a cross. It was too beautiful, the sunshine lighting up the petals and tips of grass, a butterfly floating from flower to flower. It did not match what was buried underneath.

Ángel spoke, his words heavy. "My mother isn't alive, is she?"

"Of course she's alive." Doña Remedios tapped at his chest with her thick finger. "In your heart."

Ángel pressed his lips together and stared at the graves. Mr. Lorenzo put his arm around Ángel's shoulders.

Doña Remedios took his hand. "Remember what I told you that morning when I found you?"

Ángel's voice was a whisper. "That she turned into flowers." He sounded unconvinced.

Doña Remedios nodded. She led us to a lopsided cross painted blue-green. Three cups of white calla lilies leaned against the base, secured with smooth stones. FLOR BLANCA TOJIL YOC read a wooden plaque, scratched in uneven letters.

We stood, motionless, under a tree with mottled copper and green bark, its leaf shadows moving over our faces. A musky sweet smell filled the air, maybe coming from the tree's fruit, which hung like golden ornaments. Mr. Lorenzo dropped to his knees and closed his eyes and whispered something under his breath, a prayer, maybe. Eventually, he stood up and put his arm back around Ángel, who hadn't budged. "She loved guavas, remember, son?" He plucked some fruit from the tree and handed one to each of us. "Remember how she blended them with sugar and water? How she passed cups around during coffee harvest?"

I bit in. It was impossibly sweet. Like the coffee berries Ángel had tasted after he fell down the mountain. How can there be so much sweetness when you know what's buried underneath?

Ángel held the guava in his hand, running his fingers over the smooth skin. Without his shades, his eyes seemed so exposed I could barely stand to look. "Are you sure it's her?" he asked.

She nodded. "Yes, love. With my own hands I reburied her. You see, a few years ago, they found a big grave. A place where the army dumped the people they'd killed. As the healer, I could name the bodies. I knew who had a tooth missing here. An arm broken there. A cracked rib. A smashed nose. Old wounds, from childhood. Your mother, she broke her right arm once."

Mr. Lorenzo spoke in a brittle voice. "She fell from a tree when she was eight."

Doña Remedios continued. "And her left finger was crushed."

"A heavy grindstone fell on it," Mr. Lorenzo said. "Just a year after our marriage."

Doña Remedios nodded. "And she was missing two teeth."

"An infection." Mr. Lorenzo looked at Ángel. "While she was pregnant with you, son."

"All of these things I remember clearly." Doña Remedios knelt down, sitting on her heels. "The little misfortunes of life. All of these things have stayed in my head. I saw the remains of your mother, son. I saw the old wounds that had healed long before her death. The scars on her finger bones, her arm bones, the spaces in her mouth. And the new wounds. Bullet scars on her skull, her thigh, her shoulder blade."

Mr. Lorenzo lowered his head and put his hand on Ángel's back.

Doña Remedios waved her arms toward the graves. "Look. Now our neighbors are back where they belong, in peace. Every week I put flowers on their graves. Their spirits are happy."

Strange that being around death can make you feel so alive. So quiveringly, tinglingly *not* dead. And yes, there were bones beneath our feet. Land mines and ashes of homes. But around us were crickets and fruit trees and flowers and sunshine and warmth.

I turned to Doña Remedios. "Those plants you showed us, can they really get rid of the bad memories?"

Doña Remedios plucked another guava. "They help with the pain, but something else helps more."

“What?” I asked.

Ángel was watching her expectantly.

“When people know the truth. When people come to the grave and say goodbye. That is what finally makes their hearts feel good.”

I looked at Ángel. A tiny white flower rested on his shoulder, one that had clung there since our walk. I picked it up and offered it to him. Flor Blanca. White flower. On his shoulder, silently, this whole time.

And with that gesture, something inside him changed. His frozen face melted. He leaned over his father, pressed his face against the flannel shirt, and together, they cried.

The next day, in crisp morning sunlight, Ángel and I stood on a rickety bridge, surveying the map that Mercurio had drawn. Mr. Lorenzo was spending the day taking care of loose ends: wiring money from his bank in Tucson, paying the hospital bill, buying food for our trip back. Ángel and I planned to spend the day looking for the jewels.

I looked at the *X* on the map. I felt like a heroine in one of Juan's tales, on the brink of finding the treasure. I used to feel it wasn't fair we didn't live in a kingdom riddled with pots of gold and fairies and heroines on quests. I'd ask Juan why we got ripped off, stuck in a boring world without magical treasures. He had said, “Maybe the real treasure is something more important than gold.” I'd pouted and said, “But I want a real treasure.” He'd kissed the top of my head. “You're my real treasure, Sophie.”

Ángel and I peered over the rail at the stream. It was

about thirty feet wide, but hard to tell how deep—probably at least six feet in the middle. Ángel pointed below. "That's where the *X* is," he said. "See anything?"

Little moving blobs of light opened and closed over the water. Tree leaves and branches and sky slid over the surface. I squinted, but all I saw were shadowy forms of stones at the bottom. No jewels. "I don't see them," I said finally.

"Let's go down and look from the shore," Ángel suggested. He was trying to stay hopeful. We shuffled down the steep embankment from the road to the water's edge.

The night before, in the hotel room, Ángel and Mr. Lorenzo had shared one narrow bed, and I'd taken the other. In the dark, over the fan's rushing and clicking, we'd talked about our plans. Mr. Lorenzo wanted to go back to Dika and Pablo as soon as possible, but Ángel refused to leave without the jewels. I suggested we look for them the next day. "We'll find them," I said confidently. "Don't worry."

Now, as Ángel clung to my hand, I hoped I could deliver my promise. We walked along the pebbled bank, scanning the water, peering beneath the leaf reflections.

"Rest here, Ángel," I said, motioning to a flat boulder. "I'll go in."

"I can go in, lime-girl."

"You'll get your bandages wet. Let me do it."

So he perched on the rock, bending his legs up and folding his arms over his knees.

Like bits of an old dream, I remembered my fears of pesticide runoff, leeches, amoebas, poisonous fish, sharp rocks, rusted metal. I looked at the sparkles on the water, the shades of green and blue mixing on the surface, and then focused my eyes underneath, on the hidden things.

I hadn't packed a swimsuit. A little playfully, a little nervously, I said, "Close your eyes, Ángel."

He put his hands over his eyes, making a show of pressing tightly. I glanced up at the road. No one had passed in the last fifteen minutes. I pulled the white dress over my head. I folded the emergency money inside the dress. Then, quickly, I stripped off my bra and underwear, and dropped them in a heap on the white fabric.

Despite the sunshine, the air felt cool. The breeze moved over my skin, light, like fingertips. Goose bumps popped up, my nipples contracted. I couldn't believe I was doing this. Back in Tucson, I'd been too embarrassed to even roll up my sleeves and expose my pointy, wrinkled elbows.

I waded into the water and gasped at the coldness. Once it was up to my shoulders, I called out, "Okay, you can look." But Ángel's hands had already lowered. He smiled shyly.

I didn't give myself a chance to blush. In one quick movement, I undid my ponytail, shook out my hair, and dove under. Tentatively, my eyes opened. Stones, green leafy things, darting schools of fish, tiny creatures moving around me. I rose to the surface, breathed in deep, then dove again, searching the bottom. It felt like a different world, this underwater place, the muffled sounds, pulsing blood, bubbles of breath, the tinkle of sand and pebbles, the light, hazy and filtered.

Again and again, I dove down, until I finally saw it, a gleam of red light over a rock. I moved toward it, saw my hair floating, my magnified hand reaching out, the fingers like someone else's, clasping the beads. I splashed through the surface, and held the necklace triumphantly in the air for Ángel. The red spheres were bursting with light. There was something magical about this, finding jewels in the darkness.

Suddenly I understood what Juan meant about the treasure. It didn't matter that these were not rubies. The glass held the final laugh of Ángel's mother. It held Dika's hopefulness. It held the promise of light.

Ángel stood up on the rock, beaming.

"How many more, Ángel?" I called out.

"Three."

I draped the strand of beads over my head, and dove under again. Nearby, I found three others, waiting in their red halos. I looped them around my wrists.

Once I emerged, I checked the bridge and road for people. Deserted. I waded out of the river, dripping with water and glass. I squeezed out my hair and put on my clothes and climbed onto the rock beside Ángel. I started to take off the necklaces, and he said, in a low, quaking voice, "Keep them on." We sat on the warm rock and he touched my arm. His hand on my skin, and then mine on his. Gingerly we touched, moving around his healing wounds, in a sunlit, underwater world.

We spent all day by the river, snacking on quesadillas, napping, eating guavas, and napping some more. A day outside of time. Ángel said he used to play in this very spot as a child while his mother washed clothes in the river. He rediscovered a path that he remembered leading back to the *centro* of town. So at sunset, when it was time to go, we decided to follow it. The trail was overgrown, covered by leaves so thick almost no sunlight peeked through.

A few minutes into the trail, it started to snow.

Not snowflakes, but flowers, those tiny white flowers. We stood perfectly still beneath the branches and let the white flowers cover us. We felt the rhythm the forest breathed: trees growing, leaves uncurling, petals forming, sap flowing, roots spreading. The little worlds inside fallen trees, fungus and insects making soil. Giant ants slicing up leaves, carrying the pieces to their nests. Life, death, life. And on and on and on.

The flowers fell and fell and I thought, They have to run out, but they kept falling.

Night came, suddenly. One moment there was green light, the next minute, purple shadows melting into darkness. We walked hand in hand now, one foot tentatively in front of the other, stepping over tree roots whose outlines we traced with our feet. Our hands were outstretched, grazing branches and tree trunks. Did our journey last a minute? An hour? A lifetime? For parts he led, parts I led, until we reached the end, where a huge, brilliant moon was just rising over the hills.

PART 7

THE RETURN

The stars are beautiful, because of a flower that I can't see.

—THE LITTLE PRINCE

22

Proposals

On the bus ride back, Ángel sat next to me in the window seat, sleeping most of the time, and Mr. Lorenzo sat across the aisle. This time, the VCR played all G-rated movies. During *Babe*—Pablo's favorite movie, about an orphaned pig—I kept thinking about him, remembering which parts made him smile, which parts made him squeeze my hand.

Meanwhile, every so often, something would remind Mr. Lorenzo of Dika and he'd lean across the aisle. "Psst. *Oiga,* Sophie, don't you love how Dika yells at characters in movies?" A few minutes later: "Isn't it *maravilloso* that Dika knows every cashier at Albertsons by name?" And then: "Did you know she knows even their children's names?" Then: "And she gives them advice!" He mimicked Dika's shrill voice. "Oh, Mr. Perkins, you tell to your daughter this ex-husband is bad news!" He laughed. "You must to talk with this crazy uncle, Sheila. You must!" And on and on, Dika this, Dika that, until the credits were rolling.

Then he tapped my shoulder. "Sophie," he said. His voice had turned serious.

I looked at him. "*¿Sí?*"

"Sophie." He took a deep breath. "You are like a daughter to Dika. So you are like a daughter to me. You are almost family now. So may I tell you something?"

"Okay," I said hesitantly.

"This is something that used to weigh heavy in my heart." His face grew somber. "Many years ago, after my wife's death, I went to peace rallies to protest the army's massacres of Mayans. And the army came to punish me for that. They broke into my house one night. *Gracias a Dios,* they did not take my son. He was seven years old."

His voice dropped to a gravelly whisper. "They blindfolded me and threw me in a truck bed and brought me to a bare room. All night they beat me. Each time, just before I blacked out, I saw a picture of my son. As an orphan. The last round of beating was the worst. They told me they would kill my son if I denounced the army again. After the last blackout, I came to at the roadside, where they'd dumped me. It was just before dawn. I was too weak to stand. I rolled onto my back and watched the sun rise. And once the sun was up, I heard my wife's voice. '*Take our son to a safe place.*' I looked around, but she was nowhere. From her voice, I found the strength to stand. A month later, my son and I headed north."

I thought of the scars on Mr. Lorenzo's back, the cigarette burns, the knife cuts. I felt as if my chest had just been cracked open, the way surgeons break their patients' ribs before open-heart surgery, leaving everything exposed.

"Don't be sad, Sophie," he said. "Remember what Doña Remedios said? That people's hearts feel good after they say goodbye?"

I nodded.

"Well, my heart feels good now, Sophie."

"I'm glad," I said.

"*Mire,* Sophie," he said. "I heard my wife's voice again. For the second time since her death. She wishes me to marry Dika."

I blinked. Now that my chest had split wide open, it was as though hummingbirds were flying in and out, and dragonflies, and butterflies—thousands of shimmering, beating wings.

He cleared his throat. "Sophie, do you give me your permission to marry her?"

"My permission?" My heart fluttered the way her heart would flutter.

"Because you are like a daughter to her." He looked like a little boy, so eager and earnest. Dika would be ecstatic. I pictured her in a frilly white dress, low-cut, with necklaces nestled in her cleavage. Her hair freshly bleached and curled, topped with a glittering crown. The deep joy on her face matching Mr. Lorenzo's.

"Yes," I said. "You have my blessing."

He kissed my hand.

"Have you told Ángel?" I asked, glancing over at Ángel. He was still asleep, his head leaning against the window.

"Ángel feels good in his heart now, too. He wants Dika to be his second mother."

This would make Ángel some kind of distant stepcousin. I imagined us all eating Thanksgiving dinner together, a jumble of turkey and tamales and special beef balls, for years and years to come.

A day later, in the chill of early morning, Mr. Lorenzo and Ángel and I stood in the back of the truck as it bounced around the curve to Pablo's village. We passed the hill with the cross and the nursery school and everything that Pablo had excitedly pointed out on the way. It felt like years ago. A different Sophie had first turned that curve, a Sophie on the verge of transformation. Rounding the curve now, I felt strong. Sophie la Fuerte.

Almost there. The church steeple came into sight. The cluster of houses in the distance. I missed this place. I missed Ñola's *heeheehee* laughter and Dika's and Abuelita's crazy antics and the smell of Pablo's hair.

We were on a straight stretch now, and the truck sped up. The stones and bumps in the dirt road sent us nearly flying into the air. Wind whipped our hair, billowed out our shirts. I hung on to the metal beam on the side of the truck.

Ángel smiled at me. "What are you thinking about, lime-girl?"

"About Pablo," I said. "You think he'll come back?"

Ángel brushed the wild strands of hair from my face. "You really want him to, don't you?"

I nodded and moved my hand to Ñola's necklace. The smooth leather between my fingers made me feel better.

The whole family was waiting as the truck pulled up;

they must have heard it coming. Pablo and his cousins raced to us, shouting and laughing. Abuelita raised her arms, praying and crying and thanking God we were back safely. Ñola stood by the house in the shadows, smiling her toothless grin.

And Dika. Dika jogged to the truck in her high heels, a little lopsided with her bruised ankle, her breasts nearly bouncing out of her blouse, a low-cut turquoise number with ruffles flapping in the breeze. She hurled herself into Mr. Lorenzo's arms. Unbelievably, he heaved her up into the air and spun her around. Then he set her down and bent over, gasping for breath and rubbing his back. Dika threw her head back and howled with laughter. "Look! Look how strong he is, my boyfriend!"

Slowly, Mr. Lorenzo lowered himself onto his knees until he was eye to eye with the varicose veins in her thighs. He looked up at her face, towering over him, and spoke in a deep, romantic voice. "Dika, *mi amor*, with the permission of your great-niece, Sophie"—and here they both glanced at me while I tried not to giggle—"I ask for your hand in marriage."

Dika shrieked. An impossibly high-pitched sound that echoed through the village. Maybe even as far as neighboring villages. Then she pulled him up and planted a long kiss on his mouth, leaving a smear of magenta. "Yes, yes, a thousand times, yes. I will marry you, Mr. Lorenzo."

The aunts applauded; the kids jumped up and down, squealing and clapping; Ñola nodded, knowingly; Ángel hugged Dika and let her turn his cheek pink with a shower of kisses. Abuelita clasped her hands together in delight, then pressed my hands between hers. *"Manos fuertes,"* she said. Strong hands.

Pablo ran over and wrapped his arms around my waist. I bent down and nuzzled my nose to his hair and breathed deeply, trying, very hard, to hold on to the smell.

That night we had an engagement party for Dika and Mr. Lorenzo. Dika spent hours primping. She insisted we spread avocado on our faces to make our skin smooth and soft. We sat on the mattress together, and she rubbed green mush on my face. Then I scooped up more green mush and rubbed it on her face. She laughed and twitched. "Oh, that tickles me!"

Once I finished, she said, "Now we must to wait five minutes." We wiped our hands on a towel and waited.

Dika reached into the pocket of her shorts and pulled out her shard of red glass. "You know, Sophie, when the soldiers take me to the prison camp, I am angry. I hate these guards. I want to kill them. Then I want to kill me. I take my glass." She held out her left arm and turned up her palm. With the other hand, she held the shard of glass over her inner arm, over the three scars. "I cut my arm. One. Two. Three times. I think, for sure I will to die. But no. I cannot! My heart is too strong." She held the glass up to the square of light at the window. "And then, I look the glass and you know what I see?"

"What?" I asked. Her eyes were wide and looked extra-white, framed in her green mask.

"The happy life. With a man I will to marry. A man I do

not know yet. And a new family. In a place that is never cold." She patted my knee. "And now I am here. In the happy life."

I smiled and wiped the avocado off her face with a towel. The skin underneath was soft and coated with a layer of grease.

"How my face looks?" she asked, excited.

"You look sixteen, Dika," I said.

She beamed, and then, with surprisingly tender hands, wiped away my mask.

For the party, we dug into the seventh fruitcake. The night was festive, with laughing and singing and dancing. I even danced with Mr. Lorenzo and Pablo and his cousins. After a while, we collapsed in our chairs, hearts pounding and blood flowing and sweat dripping. Ángel sat on one side of me, and on the other, Pablo, who was holding his new prized possession—the lizard slingshot that Ángel had brought back for him, as promised. I pulled Pablo onto my lap, expecting him to squirm away because, after all, his cousins were around and they might think he was a baby. But he stayed in my lap and settled his arms around my neck. I held him and felt the rhythm of his chest against mine.

Abuelita sat down and asked Pablo the question that had been stuck in my throat all day. "*Mi amor*, you must decide soon. They are leaving tomorrow. Will you stay or go, my child?"

I wrapped my arms around him tightly. Ángel smoothed his hands over my braid.

Pablo frowned. "*Pero*, Sophie, can't you all stay here?"

"No, *principito,*" I said. "Ángel and I have to start school soon. And Dika and Mr. Lorenzo need to get back to their jobs."

At the sound of their names, Dika and Mr. Lorenzo headed over with a pile of fruitcake slices balanced on cups of coffee. Little bits of sugar and crumbs sprayed out of Dika's mouth as she talked. "Oh, finally Pablo decides, poor boy."

"So what do you want to do, Pablo?" Abuelita asked, her voice gentle.

He stared at his lap. "I don't know."

Dika patted his head with her freshly manicured nails, hot pink and gleaming. She spoke in Spanish. "I have loved you from the minute you ate my Fig Newtons in the hospital." She took another bite of fruitcake. "I will love you always, little boy."

Mr. Lorenzo put his arm around Dika's great shoulders, and said, "Pablo, you are like a grandson to Dika and me. And whether you live here or in Tucson, we will spoil you like all grandparents spoil their grandchildren."

Ángel got on his knees so that he was eye to eye with Pablo. "Choose what will make you happiest. Either way, I'll visit you and tell you stories and play ball with you."

Now it was my turn, and I didn't know what to say. My mouth wasn't working. It flat-out refused to open. I was afraid if I opened it, I would cry and beg, trying to bribe him with videos and trips to the bowling alley.

I held Ñola's Virgin between my fingers. "*Principito,*" I said. I steadied my voice, pushed the tears down inside my chest. "You do what you need to do. You'll always have enough money to live well. I'll make sure of that. And you'll always have more love than you know what to do with. And no matter what, I am always your sister."

"Sophie." He buried his face in my shoulder. "I want to stay here."

A moment of pain, a deep stabbing sensation in my chest, and then, a watery feeling, the hurt rising to my eyes and dissolving into tears.

That night, I stashed my hundred dollars of emergency money in the eighth tin of fruitcake, which Dika had given to Abuelita. They would find the money after we were gone, when it would be too late to refuse. On my way back to the bedroom, I encountered Pablo, brushing his teeth at the cistern.

"Sophie," he said, toothpaste foam dripping from his chin. "Will you sleep with me and the chickens?"

"With pleasure, *principito.*" We carried blankets to the patch of dirt by the chicken coop. We lay together and watched the sky, and as he drifted off, I whispered, "Whenever I look at the stars, I will hear you laughing and it will be the best sound in the universe."

Early the next morning, when the sky was purple-blue, growing lighter pink in the east, my eyes opened. Only a few stars left. I was curled around Pablo, but suddenly I noticed another presence behind me. A steady breathing. I turned over.

It was Ñola. At some point in the night she must have settled down beside us. She patted my hand and said something in Mixteco.

At that moment, Abuelita emerged from the house and headed up the path to the outhouse. She glanced at us, surprised.

Ñola repeated her words in Mixteco.

Abuelita laughed and shook her head.

"What's she saying?" I asked.

"She says she's happy you went after your *amor.* She missed her chance, but you didn't. Now she can die in peace. And I told her she'll probably live another twenty years."

I smiled at Ñola. "You made me strong. Thank you."

Abuelita translated, and Ñola giggled.

"Heeheehee . . ."

EPILOGUE

I'm happy. And all the stars laugh sweetly.

—The Little Prince

23

Laughing Stars

The wedding was extravagant—Dika spent eight months planning it down to the last detail. It was in our backyard at eleven o'clock a.m. Dika looked just how I'd imagined: a dress covered with opalescent beads, a plunging sweetheart neckline, a strand of red glass beads dipping between her breasts, a ten-foot-long train, a veil to her ankles, a rhinestone crown, and transparent shoes straight from *Cinderella.* I was her maid of honor. She'd tried to convince me to wear a bright blue dress studded with fake sapphires the size of grapes, but in the end she let me wear my white sundress.

As we stood together at the altar—between the mesquite tree and the chicken coop—she whispered, "Sophie. I don't have daughter. But if one day, much years ago, I have daughter, I want her exactly like you. Beautiful and brave." She pinched my cheek.

Mr. Lorenzo winked at us. He wore a tux with electric

blue trimmings, Dika's choice. She'd put her foot down and made him ditch the flannel shirt for the wedding. He'd lovingly complied.

Ángel stood at his side, decked out in a tux too, and without sunglasses. He'd bought a new pair when we'd gotten back, but his eyes had already gotten used to bright light. These days, he only used shades when we went to the pool. He had replenished his supply of gold chains, though, and now they glinted in the sunlight. He smiled at me and I smiled back, plain old simple smiles that said, *Hey, life is good.*

After the ceremony and a big meal and a three-level fruitcake at the reception, Dika and Mr. Lorenzo left in a limo for their honeymoon in Vegas. Since there was still daylight left, Ángel and I drove to the desert to watch the sunset.

We parked the van and followed a dried streambed. It was April, the end of dry season, when the air is scorching and the earth parched, every last bit of moisture evaporated.

I felt a drop of water on my arm. And another. And another. "It's raining, Ángel!"

When it rains in the desert after months of nothing, when you can't even remember what rain smells like, a raindrop feels miraculous. Soon the wet season would begin, and the wildflowers would come out—brilliant orange poppies and yellow yarrow. Silvery sage and the mustard grass would fill the air with a bitter sweetness. It is in the harshest places where you appreciate beauty the most.

Unexpected beauty, tiny succulents pushing through dried, cracked earth, and spilling out tiny pink blooms.

The rain grew harder and lightning flashed in the sky. We ran under a rock overhang to wait out the storm. I wondered if somewhere in the desert a band of migrants were tilting their heads back and praising the raindrops.

Ángel touched the glass beads around my neck. He'd given me a strand, which I wore on special occasions. And when I did, he liked to roll the beads between his fingers, feel the warmth they absorbed from my skin, listen to them click against one another, trace the circle of red light around my neck.

The sun set through drops of water, a fiery crimson lighting up half the sky under an ocean of orange. Soon the rain stopped, and the sky cleared, and after a while, the first star came out, and then another, and another, and soon stars filled the whole sky, like scattered handfuls of tiny white flowers.

RED GLASS

LAURA RESAU

A READERS GUIDE

★ "Resau's memorable novel deftly blends Latin America's richness and mystery with the brutal realities its emigrants carry away. . . . A vibrant, large-hearted story."

—*Publishers Weekly*, Starred

QUESTIONS FOR DISCUSSION

1. How do you feel about the decision of Sophie's stepfather, Juan, to help Mexican immigrants as they illegally cross the border into the United States? How do you think he might have come to the decision to help them? Did your feelings about his actions change at all after you finished the story?

2. Why do you think Sophie forms such a strong connection with Pablo? Why do you think she's so open to him, while she's guarded with people her own age?

3. Do you think the relationship Sophie forms with Pablo makes her more open with Ángel? How does Pablo play into their budding romance?

4. Sophie describes herself on page 9 as "a free floating one celled amoeba, minding my own business." Do you think she would still describe herself this way at the end of the novel? What has changed in Sophie's personality?

5. On page 25, Sophie says that when she learned Dika was coming to live with her family, "I'd pictured a skeletal woman in a shawl, deep half-moon shadows beneath haunted eyes." Why do you think Sophie expects Dika to be this way, and why do you think her assumptions are proven wrong? How does Dika defy Sophie's expectations?

6. Throughout the trip to Pablo's village, Ángel is secretive about the contents of the box he carries. After Sophie reads to Ángel and Pablo a poem by e. e. cummings, which ends: "i carry your heart(i carry it in my heart)," Pablo asks Sophie, "You think his mom's heart's in the box?" Ángel suddenly turns serious and leaves the room. Why do you think Ángel reacts this way? Given the actual contents of the box, why do you think Pablo's comment hits home for Ángel?

7. Talk about the relationship between Dika and Mr. Lorenzo. What draws them together, and how does their bond deepen over time?

8. On pages 106 and 107, Sophie, Ángel, and Pablo watch a parade in the small Mexican town of Huajuapan. Earlier, Sophie admired colorful sawdust pictures the people of the town made on the ground with stencils. Now she says:

> *I realized something that gave me chills: The parade was destroying the artwork. . . .*
> *"I can't believe they're doing this!"*
> *Ángel spoke calmly. "But I think that's the point, Sophie."*
> *"What?" I felt faint. . . . "To make something incredibly beautiful, and then, before you even get to enjoy it, mess it up?"*
> *He gave me a puzzled look. "What about the memory? You'll have that."*

Why do you think Sophie and Ángel react so differently to the destruction of the pictures? What is different about their backgrounds? Do you think that by the end of the novel, Sophie might react differently?

9. On page 121, Sophie and Ángel discuss the pros and cons of Pablo's remaining in his home village. Do you think Sophie and her parents are right to let Pablo make the decision himself? Do you think he makes the right choice?

10. On page 144, Sophie has a *limpia*, or spiritual cleansing. She says:

> *Things were flying out of my mouth and floating around the room like dandelion puffs: the smell of rain, colored sawdust, ribbons of music, tiny white sparks. Silky moss and curled petals and lime zest. I felt lighter and lighter, as though I could float right up with them all.*

What do you think is happening to Sophie in this scene? Is she being permanently changed? If so, in what ways?

11. Sophie struggles with her feelings for Ángel, unable to tell him how she feels. In the end, she takes a perilous journey to reach him. Why do you think she decides to go to him in Guatemala? Is it purely for his sake, or is she trying to prove something to herself?

12. On page 201, Sophie encounters a nightmare of a public bathroom. But although she is afraid of germs, she notes:

> *I opened my mouth, but instead of a scream, a laugh sputtered out. And another . . . I thought of Dika with her head thrown back, shrieking with laughter, because what else could she do? Because she was alive.*

What do you think Sophie realizes at this moment? How does it change her outlook from this point on?

13. Even as he recovers in the hospital, Ángel dreams of risking his life again to recover his mother's jewels. He tells Sophie and his father on page 219, "I still need to get the jewels. . . . I'm gonna get those guys. . . . I'll kill them and find my mother and if she's alive I'll take her back with us." Why do you think Ángel is so obsessed with the jewels that he is willing to risk his life again? What do the jewels represent to him?

14. On page 223, after viewing a new baby in the hospital where Ángel is recovering from his attack, Sophie notes, "I drifted to sleep, thinking how strange that pain and birth—fear and joy—were so close, separated by just moments, by a thin wall, by slivers of chance." Can you think of examples from each of the characters' lives where fear and joy—or pain and joy—are separated by moments, or slivers of chance?

IN HER OWN WORDS

A Conversation with Laura Resau

Q: *Red Glass* deals strongly with the experiences of illegal immigrants, especially those of Mexican immigrants crossing the border into the United States to Arizona. What made you want to write a novel that dealt with this controversial issue?

A: I didn't set out to write on a controversial subject—it just happens to be something I feel passionate about. Over the past twelve years, my life has been deeply touched by the challenges faced by Mexican immigrants and their families on both sides of the border. During the years I taught English and did anthropological research in rural Oaxaca, nearly everyone I met had relatives working in the U.S. as undocumented immigrants. As I became close with several families, I witnessed how emotionally painful it was for kids and parents to be separated by national borders. Yet I also saw how vital emigration was in order to rise out of poverty and provide for children's basic needs—shelter, clothes, food, health care, and education.

Here in Colorado, I've found that having lived in Mexico helps me relate better to my ESL students. Since I speak Spanish fluently (and love dancing *salsa, cumbia, merengue, reguetón, bachata* . . .), I've formed friendships with Latino immigrants in my community, who have shared their often heart-wrenching stories—from illegal border crossings to anecdotes about their children back in their home country. I've also spent time helping them deal with immigrants' rights issues in their day-to-day lives.

A few years ago, I was visiting the family of an immigrant friend in their indigenous southern Mexican village. I strongly bonded with his adorable kids (whose birthdays and preschool graduations I'd already seen in home videos back in Colorado).

After the visit, when I was saying goodbye, the four-year-old boy looked up at me with these giant, sad eyes, and pleaded, "Laura, *no te vayas a Colorado.*" Don't go to Colorado. And I realized that for him, Colorado was this strange land that sucked in all the people he loved—his father and uncles and cousins, and now, me. In *Red Glass*, I wanted to bring light to the many different emotional facets of the immigration issue, and let readers feel this for themselves.

Many people don't have the opportunity to travel to immigrants' home countries, meet their families, or speak with them in their native language. But through literature, they can. I hope that after getting to know Dika and Ángel and Mr. Lorenzo and Pablo and Abuelita, readers bring greater compassion to the immigration debate. I hope they dare to reach across walls and borders—both real and imagined—to make human connections. And I hope that when immigrants and their children read *Red Glass*, it resonates with their experiences and inspires them to write their own stories.

Q: Sophie begins the novel as a very timid character, but as time goes on, she opens up and eventually does some seemingly risky things. Are you at all like Sophie?

A: Yes, even beyond the bony elbows and allergies and rash-prone skin! I drew on certain parts of my self and magnified them to create the character of Sophie. On and off throughout my life, I've struggled with anxiety, panic attacks, insecurities, and feelings of awkwardness and self-consciousness, although not quite to the extent that Sophie does.

When one member of my writing group read the scene where Sophie is trying to decide whether it would be safer to let her toothbrush air out (and risk having a cockroach crawl over it) or put it away (and risk germs multiplying on the moist bristles), this member marveled, "How did you come up with such weird, paranoid details?" Of course, the reason is that zillions of these kinds of thoughts have passed through my head over the years.

That's the beautiful thing about writing—you learn to embrace your flaws as things that make you human, as struggles you can let your characters experience. If everything had always been perfect and easy in my life, I suspect my characters would be pretty flat and boring. (At least, that's what I keep telling myself when I'm feeling extra-anxious about something!) The best part is that as a writer, I can learn from my characters and gather courage from their triumphs.

Q: Have you ever had an experience like Sophie's that changed your understanding of risk?

A: Going to live in Oaxaca was a huge risk for me. I didn't even speak Spanish at the time. After college, I just knew I wanted to live in a different culture, so I applied for jobs all over the world, and then waited for responses in my parents' house in a Maryland suburb. During those weeks, I spent lots of time reading Pablo Neruda's poetry and feeling very restless because the last thing I wanted to do after college was to be stuck back in my childhood home.

When a university in Huajuapan, Oaxaca, offered me a job—on the condition that I be there in a week—I said yes. I was terrified. I was about to jump off a cliff and I had to trust that I would fly. In the week before I left, I desperately listened to Spanish language tapes and read everything I could find about Huajuapan . . . which was one short paragraph in a guidebook that said the town was not worth visiting because an earthquake in the eighties had destroyed anything of tourist interest. So I worried about surviving earthquakes, in addition to germs and potential guerrilla violence and strange food. (At that time, I always ordered a hamburger when forced to go to a Mexican restaurant.)

But the fear that eclipsed all others was the idea of living a boring, closed-up, anxious life. So I took the leap.

And it worked out beautifully. I loved Huajuapan. I loved the people, the location, the food (homemade chocolate *mole, pozole,* sweet tamales, *memelitas, picaditas* . . .) Taking that leap was one of the best decisions of my life. During my adventures in Oaxaca, I realized that if I died, at least I'd die while I was *truly living*. My landlady, Doña Jose, told me the words of wisdom that Nurse Reina tells Sophie: "Death is your friend, Laurita." And as morbid as it sounds, these words helped me shrug off the panic and anxiety that had plagued me for so long. Of course, I did experience plenty of small catastrophes, including an amoebic infection, but as my microbiologist dad said, "What doesn't kill you makes you stronger."

Ultimately, like Sophie, I found that opening myself up to new people and places and ideas gave me a perspective on my own problems. And this gave me the power to change—to let myself live an adventurous, joyful life instead of a closed-up life of fear.

Q: Can you talk a bit about the inspiration for different characters in the novel? Were any of them based on real people?

A: Each of the characters is a kind of mosaic of different people I've known and imagined. Often, one person in particular sparks a character, yet each character eventually becomes his or her own unique creation.

The seed of Dika was a Bosnian woman I tutored in Tucson during grad school in cultural anthropology. Like Dika, she had a zest for life and defied any stereotype of a trauma-stricken refugee. We cried together as she told me her house in Bosnia was now "kaput"; we giggled together as she told me the *groserías* (bad words) she'd learned from her Mexican coworkers at the factory; we smiled together as we sipped delicious, thick coffee on her porch; we grumbled together as we waded through red tape for her daughter's visa; we laughed together as she recounted her escapades with her Mexican friend teaching her to drive. (Somewhere in there I taught her a little English, too.) Once, I came early to our session, and saw her lying on a lounge chair by the dazzling turquoise pool, her tan skin soaking up the sunshine, eyes closed, face to the bright blue sky, a faint Buddha smile lighting up her face. I stood there, deeply touched, and tried to feel how the world felt to her. I wondered how the sorrows and joys of her life could coexist.

The seed of Mr. Lorenzo was my Guatemalan refugee neighbor and friend. Like Mr. Lorenzo, he wore warm flannels even in the hottest weather because he felt that the traumas he'd lived through made him more vulnerable to cold winds (*aires*). One day, my Guatemalan friend told me, "After the *violencia,* Laurita, I decided to let my heart fill with love, so there would be no room for anger. The people from my country who let their hearts fill with anger became *sicopático.*" I'd never heard the word *sicopático* before, and I wondered about the definition. Later that day, alone in my house, I realized with a sudden chill what it meant: psychopathic. My friend had *chosen* to be a kind human being, not a psychopath. We all encounter traumas, some more devastating than others. I wondered if there comes a time when we have to make a choice: will we let our hearts fill with bitterness, anger, sadness, or will we fill our hearts with light and love?

Ángel's character was inspired by friends I've had who have immigrated from Central America and Mexico. At first glance, based on the way they dress and walk, you might assume they're involved in something shady like gang activity. Yet if you got to know them, you'd realize they are intelligent, sensitive young men who, despite hard lives, have a strong sense of honor and oceans of tenderness just below the surface. Several of these guys have brought me to tears when telling me stories of their childhood and illegal border crossings.

In addition to drawing on inspiration from friends and students, I also watched videos and read oral history books about the violence in Guatemala and the former Yugoslavia. People talked about prison camps and bombed-out homes in Bosnia, and massacres of entire Mayan villages and atrocities committed by paramilitary groups in Guatemala. This research was excruciatingly sad. I only hinted at the depth of these war horrors in *Red Glass* because I wanted to focus on the hope and wisdom and compassion that can also result from surviving a trauma. As Sophie comments, how can you comprehend the beauty that sits side by side with the horror in the world? I wanted to explore this beauty.

Q: How did you decide to weave the excerpts that you use into the novel—e. e. cummings and the selections from *The Little Prince?*

A: I've loved *The Little Prince* ever since I first read it in French class in high school. I strongly connected with the book, and underlined and starred my favorite quotes. I still have my original copy, and used many of these underlined quotes in *Red Glass.* I loved *The Little Prince*'s themes—the idea that what is essential is invisible; the need to look beyond the surface, deep into people; the process of creating a bond with another person despite the risk; the idea of reexperiencing the joy of a person you miss by hearing stars laugh or seeing flowers in the night sky. It seemed natural to weave these quotes into *Red Glass.* And of course, there's the little boy wandering alone in the desert—a kind of mythical image that contributes to *The Little Prince*'s mystical, almost surreal tone. I loved this parallel and wanted this magical feeling to permeate *Red Glass.*

Q: Tell us about the mystical elements in the novel: for example, Abuelita's *limpia* or the throwing of the corn. What inspired you to include these ceremonies in the novel? How do they affect Sophie's decisions?

A: While living in Oaxaca, I became friends with several *curanderas* who invited me to participate in indigenous healing practices like corn-throwing divination and *limpias.* These were enlightening and transformational experiences for me. I've noticed that big epiphanies often occur in the context of a ritual, or are affirmed by a ritual. For me, these healing practices have been intense sensory experiences that have made me drop to a very deep level of reflection. It seemed natural that a ritual like a *limpia* would be an essential element in Sophie's transformation to a more confident person.

The writer in me also loves the multisensory nature of these rituals. I've written dozens of pages about them in my notebooks, recording all the smells and textures and sounds. (Even years later, one notebook still smells of woodsmoke and copal incense.) *Limpias* and divinations make beautiful scenes, full of natural poetry and imagery that speak to readers on the level of dreams and symbols of the unconscious.

Q: Sophie is helped along the way by the kindness of strangers. What inspired the characters of Rodrigo and Marta?

A: I had a lot of fun writing these characters. In my travels by bus around Mexico and Central America, again and again, I encountered people who completely defied my preconceptions. And often, these people not only saved my butt, but made my life richer in many ways.

Once, after I'd only been in Oaxaca for a few months, I decided to go alone to a town called Tlaxiaco for their Saturday market. After hours of grueling bus rides, we arrived, and within minutes, I was pickpocketed and left with no money, stranded in this town. Did I mention I was starving and had to pee really badly? Long story short, a teenage guy I'd talked with on the bus (whose gelled hair and abundant cologne inspired Rodrigo) saw me looking distraught. When I explained my situation to him, he invited me to his house. After I peed (for about five minutes behind a ragged curtain that didn't quite cover the toilet nook just off the main courtyard) and flushed it down with a bucket of water, his mother asked me to eat lunch with them.

I was touched. They didn't have enough money for running water, yet they lent me—a strange *güera*—money for bus fare home, and invited me back the next weekend for lunch again. It turned out that this boy's mother was a *curandera.* She was the one who gave me my first herbal steam bath, told me my first stories about *naguales* (humans who change into animals), and taught me to speak basic Mixteco (all of which appear in my first novel, *What the Moon Saw*). In short, getting pickpocketed that day (and trusting a kind stranger on a bus) was one of the best things that have happened in my life.

The conversations between Sophie and Rodrigo were taken from conversations I had again and again with guys in Oaxaca. (At that time, I was in my early to mid-twenties, before the wrinkles sprouted up, and was often told I looked like a teenager.) There were plenty of amusing pickup lines, assumptions made about me as a *güera*, and protective warnings about traveling *solita*.

The questions that Marta asks Sophie are also questions that people asked me—about bald American men, about the color my hair would turn when I was older, about whether my eye color was real, etc. In some respects I was a novelty to people I first met, but once we got to know each other, we connected on a deeper level, which is what happens with Sophie and Marta.

Q: In Guatemala, Ángel is nearly killed when gangsters attack him and steal his money and his mother's jewels. Why did you decide to have the gangsters who almost kill Àngel end up in the same hospital he does?

A: I wanted to give Ángel a chance to face his anger and have the choice that his father had—to decide whether to fill his heart with bitterness or light. I also wanted to put a human face on the gangsters, who made self-destructive choices as they struggled to grow up in a community where political and gang violence have left a big mark.

I also liked the idea of the nighttime hospital as a setting for drama. After I was stung by a scorpion, I found myself in a small-town Oaxacan hospital in the middle of the night. It was a very surreal experience, complete with sculptures of breasts on the walls!

A CONVERSATION WITH LAURA RESAU

Q: What do you think the future holds for Pablo? Or for Sophie and Ángel?

A: I wanted to make it open-ended enough that readers can create their own stories for these characters' futures. Personally, I think that Sophie and Ángel and Dika and Mr. Lorenzo will make sure Pablo has money to not only have his basic needs met, but also get a good education, hopefully including college. This would allow him to get a good job and rise out of poverty. I see Pablo getting plenty of love and care from his *abuelita* and extended family in Oaxaca as well.

I envision Ángel and Sophie staying close throughout their lives, either as friends or as boyfriend-girlfriend (and eventually as husband and wife?). Before you accuse me of being overly optimistic and fairy tale–ish, I have to tell you that I am happily married to the guy I fell in love with when we were Sophie's and Ángel's ages. We did go our separate ways for a while—I traveled the world, and he moved out West. We each had relationships with other people—both good and bad—and then, after a decade apart, we got married. So I do believe it's possible to form a deep relationship with someone as a teenager and eventually, one way or another, make it last forever. This is what I like to imagine for Sophie and Ángel, but of course, you can create whatever future you'd like for them.

Q: What project of yours can we look forward to next?

A: I'm excited to be starting a series! It's about a teenage girl, Zeeta, who lives in a different country every year with her flighty mom. On her travels, she finds adventure, romance, magic, mystery, and bits of wisdom. The first book, scheduled for release in fall 2009, is called *The Indigo Notebook*, and it's set in the Ecuadorian Andes.

ALSO BY LAURA RESAU

What the Moon Saw

LAURA RESAU

978-0-440-23957-4

Fourteen-year-old Clara has never met her father's parents. She knows he snuck over the border from Mexico as a teenager, but beyond that, she knows almost nothing about his childhood. When she spends the summer with her grandparents in the small Mexican village of Yucuyoo, her grandmother's adventurous tales of growing up as a healer awaken Clara to the magic in Yucuyoo, and in her own soul. An enchanting story of discovering your true self in the most unexpected place.

Before We Were Free

JULIA ALVAREZ • 978-0-440-23784-6
Under a dictatorship in the Dominican Republic in 1960, young Anita lives through a fight for freedom that changes her world forever.

Finding Miracles

JULIA ALVAREZ • 978-0-553-49406-8
Fifteen-year old Milly has never told anyone in her small Vermont town that she's adopted. But when Pablo, a refugee from Milly's birth country, transfers to her school, she is forced to confront her true identity.

Falcondance

AMELIA ATWATER-RHODES • 978-0-440-23885-0
In this suspenseful novel, a falcon shapeshifter journeys back to the homeland his parents have tried their best to forget, and is forced to choose between his duty and his destiny.

A Great and Terrible Beauty

LIBBA BRAY • 978-0-385-73231-4
Sixteen-year-old Gemma Doyle is sent to the Spence Academy in London after tragedy strikes her family in India. Lonely, guilt-ridden, and prone to visions of the future that have an uncomfortable habit of coming true, Gemma finds her reception a chilly one. But at Spence, Gemma's power to attract the supernatural unfolds; she becomes entangled with the school's most powerful girls and discovers her mother's connection to a shadowy group called the Order. A curl-up-under-the-covers Victorian gothic.

Rebel Angels

LIBBA BRAY • 978-0-385-73341-0
Gemma Doyle is looking forward to a holiday from Spence Academy—spending time with her friends in the city, attending balls in fancy gowns with plunging necklines, and dallying with the handsome Simon Middleton. Yet amid these distractions, her visions intensify—visions of three girls in white, to whom something horrific has happened that only the realms can explain.

Walking Naked

ALYSSA BRUGMAN • 978-0-440-23832-4
Megan doesn't know a thing about Perdita, since she would never dream of talking to her. Only when the two girls are thrown together in detention does Megan begin to see Perdita as more than the school outcast. Slowly, Megan finds herself drawn into a challenging almost-friendship.

Colibrí

ANN CAMERON • 978-0-440-42052-1
At age four, Colibrí was kidnapped from her parents in Guatemala City, and ever since then she's traveled with Uncle, who believes Colibrí will lead him to treasure. Danger mounts as Uncle grows desperate for his fortune—and as Colibrí grows daring in seeking her freedom.

Code Orange

CAROLINE B. COONEY • 978-0-385-73260-4
Mitty Blake loves New York City, and even after 9/11, he's always felt safe. Mitty doesn't worry about terrorists or blackouts or grades or anything, which is why he's late getting started on his Advanced Bio report. He considers it good luck when he finds some old medical books in his family's weekend house. But when he discovers an envelope with two scabs in one of the books, his report is no longer about the grade—it's about life and death.

The Chocolate War

ROBERT CORMIER • 978-0-375-82987-1
Jerry Renault dares to disturb the universe in this groundbreaking and now classic novel, an unflinching portrait of corruption and cruelty in a boys' prep school.

I Am the Cheese

ROBERT CORMIER • 978-0-375-84039-5
A boy's search for his father becomes a desperate journey to unlock a secret past. But it is a past that must not be remembered if the boy is to survive. Since its publication in 1977, Robert Cormier's taut, suspenseful novel has become a celebrated classic—with chilling implications.

Bucking the Sarge

CHRISTOPHER PAUL CURTIS • 978-0-440-41331-8
Luther T. Farrell has got to get out of Flint, Michigan. His mother, aka the Sarge, has milked the system to build an empire of slum housing and group homes. Luther is just one of the many people trapped in the Sarge's Evil Empire—but he's about to bust out.

When Zachary Beaver Came to Town

KIMBERLY WILLIS HOLT • 978-0-440-23841-6
Toby's small, sleepy Texas town is about to get a jolt with the arrival of Zachary Beaver, billed as the fattest boy in the world. Toby is in for a summer unlike any other—a summer sure to change his life.

The Lightkeeper's Daughter

IAIN LAWRENCE • 978-0-385-73127-0
Imagine growing up on a tiny island with no one but your family. For Squid McCrae, returning to the island after three years away unleashes a storm of bittersweet memories, revelations, and accusations surrounding her brother's death.

Crushed

LAURA AND TOM McNEAL • 978-0-375-83121-8
Audrey Reed and her two best friends are a nerdy little trio, so everyone is shocked when the handsome, mysterious Wickham Hill asks her out. Soon Audrey is so smitten that she hardly pays attention to the vicious underground school newspaper, which threatens to crush teachers and students—and expose some dangerous secrets.

Zipped

LAURA AND TOM MCNEAL • 978-0-375-83098-3
In a suspenseful novel of betrayal, forgiveness, and first love, fifteen-year-old Mick Nichols opens an e-mail he was never meant to see—and learns a terrible secret.

A Brief Chapter in My Impossible Life

DANA REINHARDT • 978-0-375-84691-5
Simone's starting her junior year in high school. She's got a terrific family and amazing friends. And she's got a secret crush on a really smart and funny guy. Then her birth mother contacts her. Simone's always known she was adopted, but she never wanted to know anything about it. Who is this woman? Why has she contacted Simone now? The answers lead Simone to question everything she once took for granted.

Pool Boy

MICHAEL SIMMONS • 978-0-385-73196-6
Brett Gerson is the kind of guy you love to hate—until his father is thrown in prison and Brett has to give up the good life. That's when some swimming pools enter his world and change everything.

Stargirl

JERRY SPINELLI • 978-0-440-41677-7
Stargirl. From the day she arrives at quiet Mica High in a burst of color and sound, the hallways hum with the murmur of "Stargirl, Stargirl." The students are enchanted. Then they turn on her.

The Gospel According to Larry

JANET TASHJIAN • 978-0-440-23792-1
Josh Swensen's virtual alter ego, Larry, becomes a media sensation. While it seems as if the whole world is trying to figure out Larry's true identity, Josh feels trapped inside his own creation.